EXODUS 2069

BATTLE FOR A CLIMATE CHANGE PROMISED LAND

A NOVEL

JAMES ESH

Copyright © 2020 James Esh

ISBN: 978-1-64718-436-0

Published by BookLocker.com, Inc., St. Petersburg, Florida.

Printed on acid-free paper.

The characters and events in this book are fictitious. Any similarity to real persons, living or dead, is coincidental and not intended by the author.

BookLocker.com, Inc.
2020

First Edition

Library of Congress Cataloging in Publication Data
Esh, James
Exodus 2069 by James Esh
Library of Congress Control Number: 2020910348

When the ram's horn sounds
(When you hear the sound of the trumpet)
The entire people must utter a mighty war cry
And the city wall will collapse then and there

The Book of Joshua 6:5

For Kathy
Who taught me what I know of love

Contents

PROLOGUE

Mother Nature struck back in a preemptive sneak attack, a blitzkrieg in the blink of a geological eye. Over the span of a single decade, nearly one-third of the Greenland ice fields slid into the North Atlantic, raising sea levels six feet and changing everything.

Shifting air currents had cloaked naked white glaciers in a blanket of black soot from apocalyptic fires raging across the northern hemisphere. No longer able to reflect the sun's relentless assault amid rising temperatures, those ancient shimmering ice giants teetered on their primordial foundations. Twisting rivulets of melted snow flowing to the ocean, like so many water slides in a vast amusement park, cleaved crevasses to the bedrock and lubricated the slide of entire glaciers into the sea.

Two billion climate refugees were birthed in those rising waters, eighty million in the United States, overwhelming the social order and collapsing the world economy in the late 2030s. Emaciated dead bodies on the streets of American cities conjured images of medieval Europe during the black plague, while the Midwestern breadbasket was decimated by cycles of flood, drought, and superstorms. The already hyperpolarized federal government fractionated into feudal, tribal disunion.

A cabal of wealthy families stepped into the void along the eastern industrial heartland. With much of their industry in ruins, they sought to stabilize the social order into one amenable to new profits by opening food banks and basic medical facilities around cheap block housing and factories. An enormous pool of desperate workers flocked to fill jobs at subsistence wages and long hours for basic survival needs provided by this "Eastern Oligarchy," as it came to be known.

The west coast states of America, insulated to a degree by geography and climate, were spared the most extreme weather events in the rest of the country. Led by California, they had achieved the goal of 100 percent renewable energy by 2036, and breakthroughs in fluoride-ion batteries allowed more than ten times the energy storage of old lithium-based systems. As atmospheric rivers brought torrential rains at the expense of the Sierra snowpack, an artificial intelligence (AI) system designed and managed a network of progressive earthen dams extending from the high mountains to the great reservoirs of the Central Valley, mitigating the cycle of winter flooding and summer drought.

Faced with the great world depression, California in 2041 sued its federal parent, contending that since the federal government had abdicated its constitutional responsibility to "ensure domestic tranquility" and "promote the general welfare," then those rights and responsibilities may be assumed by the states, individually or in federated concert with other states. In the face of martial law, food riots, and economic collapse, the Supreme Court agreed. California, in federation with Oregon and Washington, became an effectively independent sovereign nation within the United States.

Disillusioned with a democracy paralyzed and corrupted by wealthy special interests, the California electorate took a page from their founding fathers and reinvented government. The People's Budget Constitution guaranteed every person a right to decent housing, nutrition, medical care, and a job in an economy directed by an AI entity. A wealth tax mobilized and distributed the resources of the rich over a period of five years; predictions of a mass exodus by the wealthy proved wrong in the absence of any other safe destination. The technology, transportation, and aerospace sectors, already concentrated on the west coast and gutted by the collapse of the world economy, were incorporated into the AI new order as public utilities.

By the late 2040s, climate change had slowed. Nearly a third of the world's population had died. Manufacturing and use of fossil fuels withered to a small fraction of its former peak. The most susceptible Greenland glaciers had already calved into the sea, and the remaining ice pack covered with new reflective snow. The human race had been given a stay of execution.

PART ONE

BEGINNINGS

1

JOSEPH

January 31, 2048—Nebraska, South Midwest Federation

Joseph Straily came into the world on a winter's morning that threatened to freeze your corneas and claim your digits if you dared venture forth into that cold. The polar vortex had once been held captive in its arctic circle prison by strong winds. But those prison bars were opened wide as the planet warmed, weakening the jet stream and setting the northern beast free to roam southward as it saw fit. The infant's mother, Jeannie, cradled her second child to her breast, bathed in oxytocin-fueled maternal joy, bonding with this new life that knew nothing of and cared nothing for harsh realities seeking to prey on him. For his part, Joseph was a blur of contented consciousness; life was as simple and inviting as a warm nipple.

The two-room shelter smelled of urine, feces, blood, and placenta-stained sheets piled in the corner. An exhausted midwife appeared much older than her thirty-five years as she gathered her supplies into a leather bag. She addressed the father in flat tones that could have been a recorded message. "Put the soiled linen outside in the snow until it melts enough to wash them. Be sure your wife takes the supplement pills on the dresser. Your food ration will be increased fifteen percent; the extra is only for the nursing mother. I will be back to check on you in about a week."

James Straily silently nodded without looking up from where he sat in a corner chair by the window, his attention focused on the storm outside. Every couple of minutes, he wiped away condensation on the glass with his sleeve to watch the falling snow be pulled in chaotic patterns by wind that howled its dominance. He bore an odd sense of detached calm, the calm of a soldier before the battle or a suicidal jumper standing on the precipice. James was not an unfeeling man. At the birth of his daughter five years earlier, he had felt the wonder of a miracle and the irrational burst of a father's hope that anything was possible. But five years ago, he had been a fifth-generation farmer, lord and caretaker of the Nebraskan ancestral lands first homesteaded by his great-great grandfather. He had defended his birthright against invading hordes of bean beetles and rust fungus expanding their tropical realms northward in the warming climate. But water is life, and crippling drought brought a final blow in the form of the great dust storms, ghosts risen from the grave of the Dust Bowl more than a hundred years past.

There were those who said the drought was caused by the California technology cabal when they began to control weather in the West. Others saw the hand of God delivering the end days, preparing the faithful for a Second Coming that would herald a new kingdom on earth. Some continued to place their faith in their own technology federation that promised redemption in an energy network of small nuclear reactors and water from the Great Lakes. But James could not lift his head far enough above the fog of his own failure to see or blame grand forces at play. In the fifteen months since losing his land, he had become just another mouth to feed, unable to provide anything of substance for his family. Public assistance for families with able-bodied heads of household was limited and would soon expire for the Strailys.

3

The unearthly howling outside called to him, urging him to do the right thing for his family. His eyes fixed upon little Linda pretending to nurse her doll at the foot of the bed. Words came in a gentle whisper.

"Goodbye, princess. I am so sorry. I love you more than you can imagine. You will be better off with Mommy and your brother when I am gone. Will you remember me? Please remember me and know that I did the best I could for you. Take good care of Joseph and be kind to your mother."

Tears fell upon a tender smile as he recalled all the blessings he had once known in what now seemed another world, a world where life had sprung from the earth and children had a future. And then, peace, as he accepted the sacrifice before him. James Straily rose from his chair, walked slowly to the door, lifted the rifle from its rack high on the wall, and stepped out into the beckoning storm.

2

REVEREND

Twenty-one years later—March 10, 2069, Topeka, Kansas

The Most Reverend Robert Jackson fidgeted with his tie in front of a full-length mirror in the dressing room adjacent to his office. He rarely wore a tie these days. It had been a staple in his youth when he'd felt the need to project a mature image. Self-conscious of his slender five-foot nine-inch stature and a face that seemed to shave years off his chronological age, he had sought to add gravitas through wardrobe. But now, in his late forties, the gray accents in his hair and ascendancy in the Christian Church belayed that concern, and the baby face lent an attractive youthfulness appreciated by his female parishioners. Today, the tie reflected his disquiet about the meeting he was about to take. After a long look in the mirror, he snatched the tie off and reprimanded himself for his insecurity. He stepped toward the office, paused, and then reached for a white clerical collar—the one with a solid-gold stud in front.

He closed the dressing room door behind him and crossed to where he stood looking out the floor-to-ceiling glass wall of his penthouse office above the choir loft. Reassured by seeing children at play outside the parish school, the two-story medical building, and the sprawling community outreach center, he was reminded of the good things he had accomplished and built for his parish family through meetings like the one he was about to join. Still, these people always left him feeling a little dirty.

At the sound of the door opening, he retreated to stand behind his marble-top desk and turned to greet his guest. Bill Thomas crossed the plush red carpet and offered a handshake that both men held a little longer than necessary. Mr. Thomas's designer silk suit, worth more than most parishioners made in a year, was intended to impress or intimidate as needed. It did neither in this situation. Pastor Jackson was the charismatic head of Christ Our Savior, the largest megachurch in the entire US Christian Alliance. He had met with more important Eastern Oligarch figures than this one; they all wore the same pretentious "uniform." Still, he nervously buttoned his coat before sitting down.

The pastor signaled toward a chair across from him. "Welcome back, Bill. And may I begin by saying thank you for your organization's generous donation. It allowed us to expand the children's center and remodel the church sanctuary."

Mr. Thomas sat down and leaned back, crossed his legs, and silently looked around the office. He fixed his eyes on a seven-foot crystalline statue of Mary looking up at Jesus from the foot of the cross. "I think you forgot to mention remodeling your office. New desk?"

So, an opening jab. Bob was indeed self-conscious about the contrast between the opulent setting of his office and the impoverished lives of most of his flock. But people needed to see their leader as someone blessed by God's favor. He deflected the comment.

"This is where we conduct the business of the Lord. All for the greater glory of God."

"Right. So, what say we conduct some glorious business? We appreciate your sermons and outreach condemning the

West Coast Allied States and their AI masters as idolaters and heretics. There's still enough people and politicians on our coast who are believers, or are unwilling to say they don't believe, to keep the AI Party in the minority. But they are getting stronger and more difficult to control. We need to do more to discredit those communist California bastards." Bill pulled a cigarette and lighter from his inner coat pocket and leaned over the desk to grab a drink coaster to use as an ash tray. He lit the cigarette without asking if Bob minded and took a leisurely puff before continuing. "They haven't been hit by climate change like the rest of us, and they're really good at taking credit for dodging that bullet. But the fact is, the East Coast would be anarchy without a strong hand keeping things in order. And we both know the Midwest is going to be a third-world shit show long before that Great Lakes pipeline ever gets finished. So, we have a proposal for you."

The reverend squinted and leaned back to register offense at both the crude caricature of his native region and the secondhand smoke in his face. He fixed his eyes not too subtly on the cigarette as he spoke. "Bill, I'm glad our interests have aligned these past years. But the Midwest is where God's people live. He won't abandon them. The hand of the Almighty will be our salvation from your shit-show scenario."

Bill leaned forward, and his tone took a harsh turn. "And maybe what I'm proposing is the Almighty offering you His hand. Maybe this is your salvation. How 'bout you listen to me."

Pastor Jackson stiffened but didn't flinch. Without giving any ground, he said, "I'm listening."

"Your people are losing hope, and you're losing numbers. They need something they can see and hear and touch. They need a promised land. And you're the Moses who can lead them there. What we propose is a new Exodus, one quietly financed by my people. You can lead a caravan of thousands, maybe hundreds of thousands of true believers to the closest thing there is today to a promised land, California. Now, they will try to stop you at the border, of course. Their whole population control crap won't allow it."

The eastern California border was infamously fortified, a Great Wall of electrified fencing, deadly drone patrols, and military checkpoints at major highways. It was a key element, along with restrictions on childbirth, in the program for maintaining a sustainable population as dictated by a governing artificial intelligence system. Although harsh, some would say ruthless, the AI was widely accepted within the state because it delivered stability and operated without favoritism or corruption, unlike the failed old political system.

Bill continued. "But if you're as good as we think you are, you will have too many people to be turned back or ignored. The whole country—hell, the world—will be watching to see what that inhuman AI overlord does with a real humanitarian crisis. The political divisions it will spark within the state and the images of callous disregard for human life just might bring down their whole system. And once you are there in numbers, you can spread the good word far and wide. Your people can take land for farms. The authorities will have to negotiate some kind of live-and-let-live with you. It might be something like the Quakers used to be in Pennsylvania, or maybe it will be you and your descendants calling the shots. We don't care. But with our support and your leadership, you can't fail." He smiled condescendingly. "God willing, of course."

The pastor realized his mouth was open and not saying anything. This crazy proposal threatened everything he had built and struggled to preserve. Abandon his home, his church? Moses? Who did they think they were dealing with? He barely controlled his disdain as he leaned in and locked eyes. "What makes you think I would uproot my people and put them in harm's way? And what's in it for you? If you think you can control me, control us, by your financial backing, you are mistaken. My allegiance is and always will be to my Lord, and only to my Lord."

"We know that; it's why I came to you and not some televangelist swindler closer to home. There's plenty of religious celebs who can be bought. But this has to be a legitimate grass roots movement. It has to be credible the way Gandhi and Martin Luther King were. You might have to face some people and pressure that make you wish I was all you had to deal with, but we think you have the courage and conviction to stay true to your beliefs. I hope it doesn't require you to be a martyr, but it might."

Bob recognized the attempt at flattery and evasion. "You didn't answer the question. What's in it for you?"

Mr. Thomas took a few seconds, then nodded his acquiescence. "Okay. Our people figure that, within three generations, the world's population will be only half of what it is now, maybe less. The planet is going to keep getting hotter. That's a fact. The question is, who's going to make it and what kind of world will they live in? Right now, those socialists on the West Coast have the upper hand because they got a head start on mitigating climate change. But they've turned the land of the free and home of the brave into a land of the fee and home of the AI slave. On our coast, we prefer good old Darwin; let those who have proven themselves superior and successful survive. That can only happen if a strong hand can maintain order."

Mr. Thomas tapped ashes into his makeshift ash tray and continued in a more somber, insistent tone, using the cigarette as a pointer aimed threateningly at the reverend. "This is a fucking war, and the winner gets to inherit the earth. Now, as you have so eloquently preached, those AI-worshipping socialists have abandoned their god. But the more they prosper, the more people, the more youth, ours and yours, get sucked into their twisted ideology. That makes them a threat to your survival as much as ours."

Bob had always concealed his contempt for the thuggish Oligarchy reps. He rationalized their mutual alliance as an innocent and rewarding acceptance of shared interests. Their financial support was life or death for those who turned to the Church in desperation. Now he was feeling cornered. He abandoned the pretense. "So how do I know you won't desert us as sacrificial lambs at the California border? Thousands of martyrs would serve you well."

Mr. Thomas relaxed and leaned back. His fish was on the hook; now just reel it in. "True enough, but we can do so much better. The religious community is the middle ground in this war. When California spurns you, we can openly bring humanitarian aid to our brothers and sisters in Christ for as long as it takes and in full view of the world media. And that is only the beginning. Your presence will stir civil unrest, and we can use that to strengthen the hand of dissident groups we know there. The threat of social chaos spreading from California will strengthen our hand on the East Coast."

Bob Jackson would not be so easily torn from his ministry, his life's work. "What about the church, the programs that are helping my people right now, right here?"

Bill answered with a shrug of his shoulders. "Not everyone will go with you. We can continue to support those efforts in your absence."

The charismatic preacher experienced something he had forgotten possible; he didn't know what to say. Bill's words stabbed at a private wound kept hidden from the world. His own faith had been weakened by the despair and suffering of those who trusted in him to deliver salvation but were destroyed, despite their faith in God and in him. He needed a tangible sign, a path to redemption, as much as anyone. But to abandon what resources and security he had been able to offer his flock—the church, the children's health center, the food banks, and community outreach—was this revelation or temptation?

Mr. Thomas stubbed out his cigarette, stood and brushed his hands over his sleeves. He spoke casually. "I don't expect an answer. You'll need time to think and pray. You have two weeks. We'll talk again then. While you deliberate, keep this in mind. This is going to happen, with you or with someone else. If you decline, you won't be receiving any more support from the people I represent or anyone who does business with them. If anything were to happen to your beautiful church, you and your people would be on your own while you wait for the hand of God to save you."

Reverend Jackson stared at the door after Bill closed it behind him. He had always considered money from the Oligarchy as divine providence. Now it appeared that a bill had come due.

3

PROPHET

Two Weeks Later—Christ Our Savior Church

The final notes of "When I Think about the Lord" wafted over congregants standing with arms and voices raised to heaven. The choir took their seats, and the congregation followed suit. Pastor Jackson looked out from his ornate high-back celebrant's chair on nearly ten thousand souls packed into Christ Our Savior megachurch. The weight of those souls pinned him to the chair. The congregation, in numbers usually reserved for Christmas and Easter celebrations, had been told to expect an announcement of profound import for their faith community. Rumors that their beloved pastor was ill or planning to leave them were rampant. For the many who depended on Church charities for their survival, for feeding and educating their children, Reverend Jackson was the face of God's providence. An anxious stillness fell over them. Children were hushed, crying babies carried away. Finally, as a nervous murmur began to stir, he rose and strode purposefully to the pulpit. The silence was again absolute. His modest stature standing behind the lectern was projected onto the Jumbotron, a 3-D figure of Jovian dimensions towering godlike over those assembled.

"My dear brothers and sisters in Christ, you know that I have been in seclusion these past two weeks, seeking God's will for us. This has been a time of trials for all God's people. We suffer drought and thirst while godless machines in the

12

west steal the rain God would send us. Our young are seduced and recruited by the power brokers and sin mongers to the east. We have called out to our God to deliver us as He did His people in Egypt, as He has promised to do in the second coming of our Lord Jesus Christ. Our prayers have been unceasing, and I was called to open myself, fasting and praying, to understand the answer to our petitioning."

The reverend hesitated and looked out on people whose lives he was about to throw into turmoil, people who had placed in him their hope for salvation, not only in the next world, but also very much in this one. If ever there was a time to be filled with the Spirit, this was it. With a silent prayer for grace, he walked to the center of the altar and transitioned from speaking to preaching, his voice louder and animated, rising and falling.

"The Spirit led me into a spiritual desert, and the devil tempted me, as he did our Lord. He tempted me to love what we have built, this beautiful building and its facilities and school. He showed me a vision of a grand cathedral and the power and influence I might wield from such a lofty pulpit." Then quietly, the reverend said, "He knew my weakness was my pride and ambition."

He fell silent, humbled and head down, walking slowly across the broad expanse of the altar. Shouts of blessings and encouragement filled the silence. He looked up with a smile that brought cheers and a chorus of "Amen!" The faithful, relieved that this didn't seem to be a farewell sermon, came alive, speaking words of encouragement to each other and spreading hope. A loud voice rang out from the congregation. "He ain't leaving us. He is leading us!"

He continued, his voice soaring above the spreading excitement. "But God does not need a cathedral to live amongst us. He needs only the temples of our souls where the

Spirit dwells and manifests among us. When I rejected Satan, I was led to scripture, to that very promise of deliverance in the end days when our Lord will indeed come, and I assure you: we have come to the end days. The signs are all around us as God's creation has turned against the sins of mankind, just as Jesus told us would happen. My spirit was drawn to the scripture of the end days, to the Book of Revelation, and God spoke to me in the words that glowed and lifted from the page, these words:" He turned and accepted an oversized, ornately bedecked Bible from a young altar server and read the scripture.

"'I saw four angels, standing at the four corners of the earth holding back the four winds of the world to keep them from blowing over the land or the sea or any tree. Then I saw another angel rising with the sun, carrying the seal of the living God; he called in a powerful voice to the four angels whose duty was to devastate land and sea. 'Wait before you do any damage on land or at sea or to any trees, until we have put the seal on the foreheads of the servants of our God. And I heard how many had been sealed: a hundred and forty-four thousand.' That is Revelations 7:1–8, thanks be to God." He punctuated the reading by loudly slapping the book closed and cradled it to his side with one hand as he fell silent again, walking forward and descending the top two stairs between him and his people. His tone softened and sought to explain, teaching now rather than preaching, his flock still trying to discern his meaning.

"The Lord has not rewarded the heathens in California for abandoning Him. He has withheld his anger to allow them to prepare the land where he will come again, to allow His people to gather and receive the seal on their foreheads. The four angels of fire, drought, flood, and famine have waited in that place. The fifth angel rising with the sun is surely the weather satellite that has allowed their land to be fertile and thrive. But it is all prepared for *us*, God's people, to inherit and welcome our Lord, coming as Paul tells us, on clouds to save those who are eagerly waiting for Him."

And now he came alive, his words fortifying his own faith as they sought to impart God's will into the hearts of His people. He built to a crescendo, extending his free hand in an arc of blessing across the assembled faithful, extending the Bible toward them with the other hand. "The time has come to leave our old world behind."

People rose, Bibles held high over their heads amid shouts of "Preach," "Amen," and "Praise the Lord," empowering their preacher to speak God's Word and opening themselves to hear it.

Then stretching his frame and pointing to the horizon, he brought them to the summit. "There is a promised land that God will lead us to, and He will protect us as we make this holy pilgrimage. Preparations have begun, and word is being sent to all the churches. In six months' time, we will set out from this place we have called home for our new home in California!" His words were nearly drowned out now by people standing and shouting God's praise.

"All who are called to the journey will receive the indelible mark of the lamb on their forehead. And the scripture says of those with the mark," he continued, reciting scripture from memory now, "'They will never hunger or thirst again; sun and scorching wind will never plague them, because the Lamb who is at the heart of the throne will be their Shepherd and will guide them to springs of living water; and God will wipe away all tears from their eyes.'" The sermon concluded with the reverend calling on the Holy Spirit to reassure and embolden his flock. After the final hymn was sung, people surrounded him, thanking him, some filled with the Spirit and wanting to touch their prophet; a few expressed concerns and were drowned out by the throngs whose long-suffering prayers had been answered. California! Exhausted from fasting and sleep deprivation and feeling devoured by the adoring throng pressing in on all sides, Bob eventually escaped to the safe haven of his office, only to find Bill Thomas patiently waiting there. Bill rose from his chair and extended his hand.

"Hell of a sermon, Reverend. I knew you were the man for this."

Bob didn't make eye contact or offer his hand as he walked by. His voice reflected a deep weariness. "Thank you, Bill. I just spoke the truth as the Spirit revealed it."

Bill adjusted his unrequited handshake to gesture toward the seat behind the desk. "I know you must be exhausted, and I won't keep you today. I just need one thing from you, a name."

The pastor sat and now made eye contact. "What name?"

"I know your outreach program has rescued a lot of tough kids from the street. I will need one of them for our special advance-guard program. We are looking for someone eighteen to twenty-eight years old who knows his way around the streets, a survivor, preferably a loner. He needs to be smart, physical, and very importantly, a true believer who will do whatever it takes to accomplish your mission."

Bob was attentive now, suspicious. "Why do we need to put one of my people at risk? I'm sure you have highly trained and reliable agents of your own."

"Yes, and AI knows who they are, or at least she will as soon as they try to enter the state. We need every aspect of this operation to be genuine grass roots and God fearing. If someone is caught and questioned, they can't be linked to the Oligarchy. We'll have your back behind the scenes, but this needs to be your Crusade. We want someone who has almost no past that can be traced."

Bob sat up straighter as he processed the choice of words. Crusades were holy wars. People died in misguided violence; it was not a part of Christian history that the reverend wished to revive. "What would these people you train be called upon to do?"

"Only what is absolutely necessary. We will handle that sort of thing. Again, it is best if you are unaware and can't be connected to activity that might discredit you. You need to trust us on this. We want the same things you do."

"I don't need to trust you, but I suppose I will have to trust God to guide you in deciding what is absolutely necessary. There is a name that comes to mind. One of our youth ministers, Joseph Straily, came to us five years ago after he was arrested for severely beating a man in an alleyway. He claimed the victim was abusing a prostitute he knew. He was only fifteen years old and had been on his own for a couple years, getting by with petty theft stuff. Since he had avoided any gang affiliations and had no priors, the court diverted him to us for a six-month rehabilitation program. Once he stopped trying to escape and came to trust us, he latched onto the Church and the Word like a drowning man reaching for a rope."

"Excellent. How do I find him?"

"He is in residence here at the rectory complex. I'll speak with him tonight. Come back tomorrow morning around nine."

4

LEAVING HOME

Fifteen days later—Outskirts of Topeka, Kansas

The church van came to a stop in a parking lot in an abandoned neighborhood. The pastor placed a hand on Joseph's shoulder. "This is the place. The people who are going to train you are allies, and I trust them to do what they promise. But remember: they aren't people of faith. You're here to become a soldier for the Lord, not for those who train you. Keep Him ever in your heart and pray daily for guidance."

Joseph looked into the eyes of the man who was as close to a father as he had known, and nodded a tight smile. His eyes shifted downward. Expressing emotions was not a skill learned in childhood, as it was for most people. He summoned the words and the courage with a grimace, speaking softly, gaze still at his feet.

"Reverend, you and the church are my only true family. I owe you my life. I won't fail you." Feeling awkward and unsure if he had spoken appropriately, Joseph reached for the door handle before the surprised pastor had a chance to respond. He clutched his duffel bag of clothes and a well-worn Bible and crossed the cracked, weed-strewn parking lot of an old National Guard armory.

The brick building was single story, about the size of a large home on an acre of land. To one side a rusting bulldozer sat with its front blade askew. The door was not locked.

Joseph knocked once and entered. Daylight streamed through a high horizontal window in the foyer where a large man in camouflage pants and a khaki T-shirt sat at a desk. Beyond the entry area, double doors opened to a spacious meeting room with high ceiling and a hardwood floor with exercise mats and gym equipment. The man rose and extended his hand.

Hank Willard, at the age of forty-three, no longer had the powerful ripped physique of his youthful days as a navy SEAL, but what he had foregone in physical prowess was more than offset by hard-won wisdom. The experience of two decades maneuvering through both war zones and the halls of military politics had taught him the art of judging what a person, enemy or ally, was capable of doing under duress. He took note of Joseph looking around to acquaint himself of his surroundings before meeting the handshake. *Good first impression. Always know your playing field.*

"Have a seat, Joseph. My name is Hank, and I'll be training you for the next few months. Each day here will entail training in weapons, explosives, coded communications, and undercover work as well what you need to know to fit in without drawing attention in California. I understand you've taught a class on praying with the Psalms in your youth outreach. Your cover will be as a theology graduate student working on a thesis about the Book of Psalms in the age of AI. I hope you won't need to use these skills, but you need to be ready for whatever action we direct you to do. Consider this an audition. If you are good enough, then you will be given the specifics of your mission. If not, you will never speak of this again to anyone. Are you ready to commit to all that and whatever you may be called upon to do to make the Exodus project succeed?"

Joseph's cold emotionless stare was as much an answer as his words. "Hank, my whole life has been about being ready for this. When do we start?"

"Let's start with your new identity. Your cover name is Joseph Stuckey. We've created a background file of Joseph Stuckey who grew up in Elwood, Nebraska, and moved to Oklahoma City at age fifteen where you entered school at Christ our Savior. That's for your cover. You need a numerical call sign for code communication; the pastor suggested 144 for the 144,000 with the seal on their forehead."

Joseph took a few seconds to respond as he silently recalled Psalm 144: *Blessed be Yahweh, my Rock, who trains my hands for war, and my fingers for battle.* He allowed a hint of smile and nodded. "Yeah, 144 works just fine for me."

"Good. We start right now with how to use a knife."

For just a moment, Hank detected hesitation as Joseph flinched and then blinked. "Do you have a problem with that?"

Joseph shook his head. "No, no problem at all." He quickly banished the specter of that memory back to the dark crypt where it belonged.

* * *

Joseph sat at the kitchen table, wearing headphones as he always did when mother and sister were entertaining guests. It had been like this as long as he could remember. As a child, he often slept on a foam pad in the kitchen corner, but at age thirteen, he was already approaching six feet in height and slept on an army-surplus cot. When there were no guests, he preferred the living room couch.

Music blared in the headphones, so Joseph didn't hear the kitchen door open or the approaching footsteps. The table skidded on the linoleum floor as the headphones were jerked away, and he was startled to his feet, spinning around. The stranger was shirtless and muscular, about Joseph's height but at least twice his age and half again his weight.

"Take it all off, boy. I want to look at you."

Joseph's heart was pounding too loudly and too fast for him to hear or understand. He stared and forgot to breathe.

"Can you hear, boy? I told you to get naked. Now do as you're told."

Understanding began to take hold, and Joseph's first reaction was denial. This had to be a mistake. "No, I'm not like that. You need to go see my sister. I don't do that." His voice betrayed either his fear or his puberty as it broke into a squeak midsentence.

The stranger chuckled. "I already saw your sister. She said you were a virgin, but I thought that was just hype to jack up the price. Looks like it's up to me to break you in and make a man of you." He stepped forward and roundhoused the back of his fist across Joseph's cheek, knocking him backward, sprawling across the table, then rolling onto the floor.

The iron taste of blood in his mouth woke Joseph from his stupor and transported him to a familiar place. This was not his first fight. He had been the object of ridicule and bullying from the time he was old enough to leave the house. At first, he hadn't known what the chants of "Whore baby! Whore baby" and "Who's your daddy?" meant or why no one wanted to be his friend. As he grew to understand that other families were not like his, he also learned that the surest way to stop the taunting was with his fists.

Joseph rose and charged his attacker, but this was no schoolyard bully. The bigger man delivered a blow to his midsection before Joseph could land a punch. The jab knocked the air out of him, and he could not get a breath. It doubled him over, and the stranger pulled his T-shirt over his head so he could not see. A wave of nausea rose as he felt his pants pulled down around his ankles, and he could not walk. The stranger spun him around, shoved him forward over the table, and held him down with a hand against his neck. Finally, he was able to gasp and pull in a breath of air.

"That's right kid. Just relax and enjoy it."

Joseph felt the painful penetration and heard the panting, then moaning as he was thrust harder and harder against the table edge. Nausea overwhelmed him, and vomitus was trapped against his face by his shirt. Choking and gagging on the stench, he panicked, trying to free his hands and pull the shirt away.

And then it was over. He slumped to the floor and managed to pull off his shirt, gasping, tears running through vomit on his face. He had always fought and survived all the taunts, the beatings, the shame and isolation, never giving in. But now it had mastered him, destroyed him like he had not imagined possible. He tried to get up but something in him was too broken. He turned to look at the demon who had claimed his soul, the image blurred by tears. He watched as the rapist, his back to Joseph, wiped off his penis with a kitchen towel and spoke. "Next time I'll teach you few new tricks, now that you know your place."

Next time. Next time? Next time!

And then a third person was impossibly present in the room, looking through Joseph's eyes, hearing through Joseph's ears the faint music still playing in the headphones. It was someone who had been living silently inside of him for many years, growing much faster, much stronger, much angrier, and birthed now in the violence of the rape. This Joseph rose silently and moved first to the sink, then approached from behind as the older man checked his wallet to be sure no one had pickpocketed him during his visit. The voice was steady now. "Hey, mister."

"What, you want money? I already paid for you." He turned back toward Joseph. "I'll be back—" but the words failed as Joseph drove a butcher knife upward from below the ribs, driving the man backward. He hadn't been trained that this was the best kill move; it seemed instinctual. The presence that had awakened in him left no room for doubt or hesitation, no remorse. The body began to slump down, but Joseph pinned shoulders against the door so he could pull the knife out and plunge it again. He looked into the bulging eyes and gaping mouth. "Yeah, I guess you were right, you son of a bitch. You made me a man after all. See you in hell."

Joseph watched the body fall. He walked to the sink, washed his face, and cleaned the knife before replacing it in the rack. Calmly throwing a towel over the spreading puddle of blood so as not to track it on his shoes, he plucked the wallet from a back pocket. Nearly $200 and a ring that looked like it would bring a good price would hold him for a while. He took the shirt and a leather jacket from the chair where the rapist had left them and put them on. Then Joseph walked out the back door, mounted his bicycle, and headed down the driveway.

He rode south on the Hwy 283 frontage road. Lexington to the north would be the nearest big city, but the house was on the south side of the village of Elwood, and Joseph didn't want to be seen riding back through town tonight. Kansas was only about thirty miles away; it would be best to get out of state.

Joseph seemed to be two people inside of one head. There was an undercurrent of shock and dismay. *You (We? I?) just killed a man! There was so much blood, someone will come for us.* But that voice was muted and far away. The other voice was elated, triumphant. *We are free! Victorious!* For the first time, Joseph understood that he had been caged all his life, a child born into a prison. But he had struck a blow and escaped as a man.

Both voices urged him to get far away as fast as possible. He stood bent over the handle bars, legs pumping at a furious pace until finally his thighs tightened painfully from the effort, as the adrenaline subsided. Joseph, feeling suddenly weary and light-headed, stopped in a grassy clearing. The pain in his pelvis flared as he swung a leg to dismount the bike, and he realized his hands were shaking as leaned the bike against a sycamore tree.

Feeling both overheated under the leather jacket and chilled by the sweat as evening came on, Joseph sank to his knees. He was aware his head hurt and touched the cheek where the stranger had struck him; pain ricocheted through his right temple and eye, triggering a mental replay of the attack. Joseph rocked back, clutching knees to chest as the face of his rapist filled his mind's eye and humiliation flooded his consciousness. But he also felt the presence of that other person who had taken charge of the life they shared. Joseph could still feel him inside now and was frightened by the rage and the power there. But he also took comfort and nestled himself in that womb of protection. It began to calm him, warm him, speak to him.

They will probably think mother and sister did this and robbed the asshole because he refused to pay. Nobody will think to blame the weird, skinny little brother. Sister usually handles the cops with a cut of her earnings or with her services when things are tight, but that won't work for a bloody corpse in the kitchen. Maybe they'll have the good sense to run before anyone misses him.

He answered the internal voice out loud. "I hope so. They took care of me all right until tonight." Tears again flooded his eyes at that last thought. "How could they sell me like that?"

Sister had changed since she started accepting payment in drugs. It was the drugs, not his sister. He sat up.

It doesn't matter now. Good luck and good riddance to both of them. I'll be in Kansas by daybreak.

5

A MISSION

Week one of training—March 29, outside the National Guard Armory

Hank watched Joseph struggling on the final leg of his ten-lap run around the grassy one-acre perimeter of the armory in the early light of dawn. He froze the stopwatch time as Joseph passed in front of him, doubled over, breaths coming in audible gasps. "Thirteen minutes, ten seconds. When you can do it in under ten minutes, we won't have to do this every morning."

That first week, Joseph learned how defend himself against a knife attack, with and without a knife of his own. He learned the advantages and techniques associated with every blade from common pointed household items to a machete. There were weight training and agility exercises, but the payoff for Joseph was the afternoon lessons about his destination, California. They sat outside on the grass on a warm spring day after lunch. Hank explained how California had avoided the long periods of drought that had shaped the tragic trajectory of Joseph's family and had reshaped his homeland.

"A massive pipeline extends from dams on the Columbia and Snake rivers in Oregon and Washington to the central valley of California. In exchange for water diversion, California provides its northern neighbors with power on demand from its massive solar, hydroelectric, wind, and satellite energy projects."

"How can they afford to do all of that? I've heard that Californians are mostly poor."

Hank explained how the state's economy had been turned over to an AI system in the days of the Great World Depression. "It provides citizens with jobs and all their basic needs as well as unlimited, free virtual entertainment generated by an AI. It's true that citizens don't have much cash, but they don't need it. The state governing system actually has considerable wealth, and after all the AI systems interconnected, the central AI now controls education, entertainment, reproductive rights, and nearly all aspects of life; so that's the trade-off."

"What about the Christians? Does the AI persecute them?"

Hank shrugged. "No, that would be counterproductive. AI simply renders them irrelevant. Only about 5 percent of their citizens self-describe as Christian. About 20 percent still claim some form of personal spirituality, but it's dying out. The AI pays lip service to freedom of religion, which is why we can get you into the state on a religious studies student visa."

"Will the Christians come to our aid at the border?"

Again, Hank shrugged. "If they do, we may not need you. If they don't, then you will be a one-man Christian wrecking crew."

***

Week four of training, the firing range.

Joseph slowly lowered the smoking muzzle of his AR-19 rifle, eyes fixed on the shredded upper torso and head of the silhouette target fifty yards down range.

Hank expressed his approval. "You have a good feel for the heavy artillery. Most people have to get over fear of the recoil on a repeating semiautomatic with bump stock. Do you have some experience with these weapons?"

Joseph answered without taking his eyes off the proof of his marksmanship in the distance. "No. But the more powerful the weapon, the more powerful I am as an instrument of God's will. Give me whatever you've got." A growing sense of his own strength and ability to impose his will on an enemy exhilarated Joseph. He found himself fantasizing about how he would tear down the walls and gates of California like Samson had done at Gaza. He would never again be a victim.

Hank studied his student. *The kid certainly has the moxie and determination; but there's something else. Something on the fine line between dedicated and fanatic.* It was not the first time Hank had sensed in Joseph an uncommon intensity, sometimes anger, that seemed easily aroused from just under the surface. He probed his student further. "A target is one thing. Aiming at a person will test you in a way you can't anticipate. I can teach you technique, but I want you to think about what it means to take a life, even if it is in combat for a good cause."

Joseph turned and coolly locked eyes with his instructor. "I don't need to imagine it. Trust me."

Hank watched Joseph shoulder his assault rifle and head back to the armory to disassemble, clean, and reassemble the weapon repeatedly, timing himself as he did so. Joseph was a hell of a cadet and often pushed himself harder than Hank pushed him. He was quick, fearless, and determined but rarely spoke. Something about him felt off, like he was hiding something. Hank was good at reading people, but he needed to break through Joseph's emotional armor to see what was driving him, get him to open up a little.

Hank entered the armory and put a hand on Joseph's shoulder. "Give it a rest, kid. Relax, shower and get some decent clothes on. You're halfway through training, and we're going out tonight to celebrate. There's a great little place a couple miles from here."

Joseph glanced nervously about the room as he entered Hops and Chops, following several steps behind Hank as they headed for a booth. Hank ordered two Pale Ales when the waiter brought the menus. Joseph pushed the beer mug away when it came. "I don't drink alcohol."

Hank affected shock and dismay. "Well, that's a serious defect in your training then. When you are operating in theater undercover, having a beer with a person of interest is a basic skill for gaining information and making valuable friends or allies. People don't trust someone who won't have a beer with them"

Joseph stiffened. "I'm not going to California to make friends."

Hank saw his opening. "OK, Joseph. Why *are* you going to California?"

Joseph stared at his beer mug and then, after a pause, looked up. "Reverend Jackson asked me to do this. I owe him my life, so here I am."

Hank smiled. "Here you are. Now drink your beer. I don't like to drink alone."

By the time the waiter returned, Joseph had finished most of his drink. It was a diversion from making conversation, and Hank was content to let him drink in silence. Hank ordered lamb chops with potatoes and gravy for both of them and signaled with his finger to refill the mugs. "I hope you like lamb chops, Joseph." He was pleasantly amused to see Joseph physically relaxing, leaning back and looking around at their fellow patrons.

Joseph was focused on a nearby table where lamb was being served. "I've never had lamb chops, but it looks and smells awful good. At the refectory, we get culture burgers sometimes."

Hank encouraged the lubricating effect of the ale on Joseph's tongue. He made small talk for a few minutes before pressing on. "So you've never had a beer and never had real meat. What do you like to do for fun? Do you play soccer? Baseball? Hike? Fish?

Joseph quaffed what remained of his second beer. He felt he was acquiring a taste for it and was feeling proud of himself. He was even starting to enjoy the conversation. He leaned in and spoke in a near whisper as though revealing a carefully guarded secret. "I read and pray the Psalms. Most Christians ignore them, but the Psalms speak to the soul, not the mind. They are the outpouring of grief and desperation from God's children in captivity, and the celebration of God's vengeance on those who persecuted them. They are the conversation between God's children and their loving Father."

The food arrived, and the conversation lagged while Joseph savored his first experience of real red meat. He was also finding that he enjoyed the way beer affected him. When the waiter noticed his empty pint glass and offered to refill it, Joseph hesitated at first. He had not experienced the effects of alcohol, but he had certainly witnessed people lose control when they drank. And yet, after two Pale Ales on an empty stomach, he was feeling more confident and in control than ever. He handed his glass over for the waiter to fill before Hank could suggest otherwise.

Hank processed what he had heard in response to asking about "fun." *Grief, desperation, captivity, vengeance, father.* There was a story here, but he elected not to press any further for it in this public place, given Joseph's inebriation. Joseph was starting to slur his words as he asked about the next stage of training.

Joseph finished his meal and realized he badly needed to relieve his bladder. Rising abruptly and awkwardly, he collided with a waiter, fell backward against another dining couple, and soiled himself. Overcome with humiliation, he mumbled slurred apologies and tried to help the waiter up, but nearly fell again. He steadied himself, saw the front door, and bolted for the exit with Hank in close pursuit.

"Joseph, wait here. I'll pay for the meal and be right back. It's OK. Everything is OK."

But Joseph could not wait. Humiliation was his greatest fear, his Achilles' heel. It had stalked and tormented him his entire childhood, deprived him of friendship, and driven him from his home. Now he had brought it on himself. He hid himself in an alleyway.

When Hank returned, Joseph was nowhere in sight. *Jesus, what did I do to that poor kid? He's done everything asked of him by everyone. Maybe I'm the one with a problem. I'm supposed to train him, not be his shrink. Probably best now to leave him alone and let him find his way home when he's ready.*

***

The following morning, Sunday, Joseph stood in the parking lot waiting for the church van to transport him back for the worship service. Hank approached cautiously.

"Joseph, I'm sorry about last night. I should have been looking out for you better than I did."

Joseph didn't look at him. "Don't worry about me. I take care of myself, always have."

Hank saw the van approaching them. "Good. Get some rest today. You'll want to be sharp and rested this week.

31

Explosives and demolition training has a way of eliminating people who are careless or fail to pay attention to details." He watched as Joseph walked away toward the street.

Week six of training—6:15 a.m. outside the armory

Hank looked at the stop watch as Joseph stood panting and holding his side; he nodded his head. "Nine minutes and forty-eight seconds. Congratulations. No more 6:00 a.m. marathons. You get to sleep in mornings." Lightning flashed on the near horizon, and the thunder clap was just a few seconds behind. "Looks like a storm's on the way. Let's get inside."

Joseph sat at the table in the corner of the main room adjacent to a kitchen. Hank served up coffee and rehydrated eggs. The storm was on top of them now, the thunder like an artillery assault. Joseph took his coffee and walked to a window. "Dry lightning, not a damn drop of rain. They send us the lightning and keep the rain for themselves. They need to pay for that."

"They? Who's they?"

"California. Reverend Jackson has told us they steal the rain God would send us and keep it for themselves."

Hank shook his head and suppressed a smile, not wanting to overtly disrespect the good reverend's convenient and ignorant effort to place blame for the drought. "Well, it's true they have a satellite shield that's several miles across, but mainly, it turns solar energy into microwaves and transmits it to receivers that produce electricity for the grid. They do use it in climate control when there's not enough rain, though. Aiming the microwave energy into the ocean increases evaporation and water content in clouds. Then they super seed the clouds over the Sierra mountains so the rain falls where they can store it."

Joseph bristled. "So they do steal it! When there's not enough rain, they keep it all." He continued to scan the clouds for a hint of rainfall. "What about when there's plenty of rain? This storm, these clouds—they must have had plenty of water in them somewhere, just not here, not in God's country." He turned back to Hank, his voice now sad, questioning. "Why isn't it raining here Hank? What did they do to the rain?"

"I don't know about this storm, Joseph. I'm not a meteorologist. It's true they try to manage the atmospheric rivers that could cause terrible flooding. They fly big planes loaded with this powdered agent that absorbs thousands of times its weight in water to form a gel that falls into the sea and dissolves. And they super seed the storm out at sea so more rain falls before it hits the land. But really it just keeps the worst of it away from big population centers. No one knows if they are affecting weather patterns to the east."

Joseph set his cup on the table and converged on his instructor, faces inches apart. "And maybe they should let God decide where the damn rain falls." He strode to the weight bench and began his morning workout.

Saturday of training week eight—4:00 p.m. in the armory
Hank sat at his desk in the anteroom of the armory, filling out final evaluation forms. Joseph had continued to excel in the training process. He was devoted to the strength training and, along with daily muscle-promoting ghrelin supplements, he was developing the body of an elite warrior. But Hank still had reservations about what lay beneath that veneer. He decided one final test was needed.

After the last session of surveillance and avoidance training, Joseph lay on the weight bench attempting a personal best in reps with a 125-pound weight. The second-straight day of 100-degree-plus temperatures beat down on the armory, and two window-mounted air conditioners were not nearly up to the task. Sweating profusely and growing ever more frustrated with houseflies enamored of the aroma of his workout, he was grateful when Hank summoned him. "Joseph, come in here. We need to talk."

Joseph entered the room where he had first laid eyes on his instructor, and sat down at the desk across from him. The afternoon sun was in his eyes as it streamed through the window above the desk.

Hank leaned back as he spoke. "Joseph, you have completed the basic general training and conditioning, and you've done well. But now the mission-specific training needs to begin, and I have to decide if you are the person we want to trust with that information and mission. I have decided that you aren't that person. I am releasing you from the program. Remember that the penalties for disclosing any part of what you know or have experienced are quite severe."

Stunned, Joseph squinted and shielded his eyes with his hand. "What is this? I've done everything you asked of me. I ran your damn course in ten minutes. I'm a marksman with a rifle. I've passed all your tests. What more do you want?"

Hank anticipated the outburst and was prepared. He spoke softly. "It's not just about strength and skill, Joseph. When I was a navy SEAL I fought jihadists, white nationalist militias, African Freedom Brigadiers. The reason I'm still here and they're not is because they were groups of fanatic extremists, ready to die for the cause—hell, some anxious to die for their cause. They were reckless. My only loyalty was to my brothers on our team, to completing our mission exactly as it was given to us. There were no hidden agendas, no personal vendettas, no individual heroics. We trusted each other with our lives every day. I don't have that trust with you. There's something driving you that you keep hidden, something bigger than the mission. I won't risk the mission or send you into harm's way if I don't know who you are."

Joseph understod that his chance at living a life that meant something, a life with purpose, was being snatched away from him. Face flushed, he vaulted to his feet, knocking the chair backward. "That's bullshit! I've proven myself to you a hundred times over, and you know it. What do you want from me?"

Hank stood and leaned forward, palms against the desk. "You want me to trust you Joseph? Then *show me some trust*. What the hell happened to you? Did your daddy beat you? Or maybe he beat your mother, and you had to kill him to make it stop." Hank looked for the reaction. None. *No, that's not it.* "Did they leave you by the side of the road? Too many mouths to feed and not enough bread? Tell me why you are here! And don't give me any of that 'Christian soldier' crap. You didn't learn all that anger sharing doughnuts with street punks in the church hall."

Joseph was back in that kitchen, wounded, helpless to stop a grown man from stealing his future, his life. His eyes fixed on the pencil holder between the two men. Hank read his thoughts. "Go ahead, Joseph. take the pencil. You know how to use it as a weapon now. Prove I'm right about you."

"Don't think I couldn't! I'm stronger and faster than you, old man. I'm not thirteen anymore, and you wouldn't be my first."

Hank said nothing, but relaxed and stood back, his aspect shifting from a challenge to a question. Joseph froze, realizing he had spoken aloud his shameful secret. The shock brought him back into the moment. Hank was not the rapist, and he was not a child anymore. The tight icy grip of the rape memory loosened as he reconnected with the persona within who had saved him that night. That alternate ego was no longer a stranger; it was part of him. The shame was lasting and immutable but the analytical clarity and courage were within him now. He saw the choice before him and took control. *This is a test. You can do this.* Clenched fists opened, fingers flexing and extending. Joseph took a series of deep breaths and blew them out purposefully like a woman in labor doing her Lamaze. He turned and walked back to where his chair had landed on its side, picked it up carried it to the desk aside Hank's chair. He set it down slowly and took his seat. He looked up toward Hank, who was still standing, and then he took his seat as well. Hank spoke gently, "What happened to you when you were thirteen, Joseph? You can trust me."

Trust. It was the price demanded for this mission, for a purpose to his life. Hank might very well reject him if he knew how he had allowed himself to be shamed, to be taken and used, then murdered a man and fled. But Joseph would not allow that shame to defeat him again. He would pay the price, the true story of his life.

When Joseph was done neither man spoke, and neither man minded the silence. Finally, Hank spoke. "Get out of here." Joseph, startled, looked up, his face a question mark. "Get out of here and take a walk. A long walk. Then get your ass back in this chair. We have a mission to plan, brother."

6

MICHAELA

Seventeen years earlier—November 15, 2051, Sacramento, California

The birth of Michaela Dohn was either a blessing or a curse, depending on who you spoke to. For Michaela, it was surely both. Michaela, a name that means "a gift from God," was indeed received by her parents as divinely inspired, particularly since her conception was not something they had planned or expected at an age when they thought their parenting years were behind them. Lisa and Lyle Dohn didn't share the devotion of their born-again grandparents. Organized religion had receded to the social fringe in California over two generations, as science took on the mantle and promise of salvation from the original sin of humans ravaging Mother Earth. But Lisa still found solace and direction in communing with a loving higher power; and Lyle found his solace and direction in Lisa.

The midwife called to Lyle from the adjacent family room. He backed away from the bed reluctantly. Sunlight beamed from the skylight and fell directly onto the new mother nursing her daughter, like a halo or a renaissance painting. Lyle imprinted the image on his memory, thinking he would never again see anything so beautiful.

"Mr. Dohn, I need to go over these documents with you now." The midwife's tone was impatient and carried a note of disapproval. Lyle forced himself to address the necessary legalities.

"As you know Mr. Dohn, you have exceeded the legal mandate of one child per parent by bringing this pregnancy to term. Your daughter is now an unregistered minor in the State of California. Michaela will be entitled to the full rights and privileges of a registered minor until the age of seventeen years—"

Lyle interrupted. "Nurse Hicks, I am well acquainted with the legal implications of having a third child."

Nurse Hicks was not one to be easily dissuaded. "Then perhaps you understand that I am required to explain them to you in detail before you sign the necessary documents." She read the required injunction from her i-slate. "At the age of seventeen, Michaela will be entitled to apply for citizenship as an extraordinary talent exception." She looked up from the document and added a caveat of her own. "This is very rarely granted." Continuing to read from the document, "Two months prior to her eighteenth birthday, she will be required to register for the Out of State Relocation Listing. In the year beginning on her eighteenth birthday, she will be activated on the OSR list. If her resume attracts an offer of employment or enrollment for higher education from an out-of-state agency or business, she will be free to accept the offer any time during the first six months of her eighteenth year. If no such offer is accepted, she will be subject to deportation at the registrar's discretion, under the regency of persons as negotiated by the registrar. In either case, she will retain no claim to future residence or employment in the State of California."

"Yes, I understand all that. But she will be granted citizenship if we pay the cash fee that reimburses the cost of her past entitlements."

"That is currently the law. However, both that path to citizenship and the extent of the fees are subject to change. I would caution you that the fee is not within the grasp of most couples. If your daughter should fail to enter the OSR listing and can't be located, then you or your wife can be held legally responsible."

"I have eighteen years to deal with that. Where do I sign?"

Nurse Hicks handed over the i-slate with the necessary approval lines highlighted. Lyle acquiesced with his fingerprint on each required field without pausing to consider the actual language or details therein; it was a nonnegotiable contract. Nurse Hicks forwarded the document and replaced the slate into her briefcase. She stood motionless for several seconds, staring at the table and collecting her thoughts.

"Mr. Dohn, I can't approve of your choice to dismiss what is a necessary social requirement, but I do not wish harm on your beautiful baby girl. In my position within the Population Control Agency, I hear stories. The OSR list is...well, it may not be exactly what they would have you believe, especially for young women. If the employment offer is legitimate, then the deportee is typically required to pay back to the employer or agency the fee that California receives from them, usually over an indentured period of up to five years. Unfortunately, in the case of young women, the offer may not be what it seems, particularly offers from the East Coast Oligarchy. Many have found themselves...in compromising situations once relocated."

She paused and glanced toward the bedroom, a hint of compassion momentarily breaking through her rigid bearing. Returning her attention to the new father, she spoke softly, as though she might be overheard speaking out of turn.

"If you aren't able to buy her citizenship, then I would encourage you to explore other options prior to listing on the OSR."

Lyle stared, not sure if he had heard threat or kind concern. "What options?"

"Good day, Mr. Dohn. And good luck to you and your family."

7

INVINCIBLE

Seventeen years later—September1, 2069, Sacramento, California

Michaela watched her assailant approach and calmly sized him up. She was tall for her age, but he had three inches and maybe thirty pounds on her. He would try overpower her. She assumed a defensive posture, legs wide, body turned at an angle, arms cocked, and fists ready. He moved in quickly and threw a powerful punch to the head with his right. Michaela leaned back to rob it of force and easily deflected the arm up and away. She stepped forward and shot a fist blow to his midsection as he recovered balance, but to little effect. He attacked again, this time with his left. Michaela deflected the blow upward, but it landed on her shoulder and he used it as a battering ram to drive her back. She absorbed this by partially spinning away, bending back at the waist, and planting on her rear leg; then delivered a side kick to the ribs, landing the kick behind him. Leverage is the great equalizer. She grabbed his exposed shoulder and threw him backward over her planted leg. By the time his body hit the floor, Michaela was plunging a hand downward with a primal yell, stopping the clenched fist one inch from his throat. A whistle blew, and the viewing stands erupted in applause as Michaela stood and placed hands to her side, bowing first to the judges and then to the audience where her soccer mates enthusiastically cheered her.

Michaela had discovered early on that her athletic prowess was her path to respectability and friendship. By the second grade, the boys—at least, the loud, mean ones—taunted her for being a "thirder." She had few friends, mostly other outcasts of various sorts, and was often alone. That all changed on the soccer field. No one cared about her social status when she dribbled around opponents with ease and took shots on goal with uncommon accuracy. Karate had been a means to developing body control that would elevate her to the elite of the soccer youth and perhaps an exceptional talent exemption from the Relocation List. But it became much more. Michaela had grown up with an ominous dark cloud on her future horizon, the threat that she would be wrenched from all she knew and loved, and would be powerless to stop it. In the martial arts, she discovered her own inner power, the ability to control events, to conquer fear and prevail all on her own; and she wanted more. With each win, she became more fearless, more convinced of her invincibility. She was too good to compete in the Female Division and was now moving up through the ranks of the elite Open Division.

At the top row of the viewing stands sat Michaela's parents. Her mother was not convinced of her daughter's invincibility. Her father stood, applauding. "You can look now, Lisa. Be proud of your daughter."

"I have been looking, and I am proud. I just don't relish the thought of some muscle-bound brute attacking my little girl."

Lyle sat and spoke softly. "Your little girl just kicked that brute's ass in under ten seconds. And I, for one, am glad she can take care of herself with anyone she meets in her uncertain future. Now let's go congratulate our amazing daughter."

Michaela met them halfway up the bleachers, smiling, equipment bag in hand. "See, Mom, I told you not to worry."

She hugged her mother while giving a knowing grin and thumbs-up to her father from a hand wrapped around Lisa. "I'm going to the holopark with some friends to celebrate. Jeannette has a new sap-strength spell to use against the ogre. I'll be home for dinner."

Lyle gave her a hug. "Would you like me to take your bag home?"

"No. It's got some clothes I want to change into and some things for the holopark."

The group of eight friends walked the six blocks to the holopark in high spirits. The oppressive heat of summer days was waning, but plenty of sun remained to justify wearing the latest fashions in sunshade eyewear and playing a game called Morph. The eyewear included a tiny camera in the frame, allowing a person to take a snapshot of their own retina and capture the image of whatever they were looking at. The image could then be beamed to another person's eye gear and into that person's retina, effectively projecting a 3-D image a foot in front of the wearer. It was a common and frequent indulgence among youth to snapshot each other and exchange portraits so they could see (and admire) themselves as perceived by others. The game involved sending this selfie to a friend who then added a visual filter—perhaps glamorous hair, blue eyes, or buck teeth—to alter the image. Each girl sent a selfie to the girl on her left, who then added a filter and sent it down the line for another filter to be added. After several rounds, the images returned to their point of origin. The end result might be funny, complimentary, or cruel depending on who played the game.

Michaela walked shoulder to shoulder with her best friend, Jeanette, several steps behind the group, choosing to talk instead of play. Sacramento still proudly proclaimed its "City of Trees" moniker, and a bright, cloudless sky shimmered through leaves that were just beginning to display their fall wardrobe.

"That was awesome, Mikky. I don't know how you do it. I'd be paralyzed with fear if that guy were coming at me."

"You're right. Fear is the enemy, not the opponent. Battles are won before the first blow is landed. I know I'm faster and more skilled than anyone I face. I haven't had to use even half of what I'm capable of, so I'm just figuring which half of my skills to use when the opponent walks onto the mat."

Jeannette nodded emphatically and laughed. "Yes, you are 'Michaela the Invincible.' I just hope it stays that way for the rest of the tournament." Then, "I gather you haven't heard from the exceptional talent board yet."

Michaela's demeanor grew more somber. "Not yet. But there's still ten weeks before I have to register for the List."

Jeanette noticed the defensive tone but pushed the point anyway. "But athletics is not a high priority for them. And karate is not a sport they are promoting. It scares me to think of you being relocated."

"I don't plan to be a professional karate fighter. But AI needs coaches and instructors. I've coached youth soccer and succeeded at the highest level in every sport I've done. My application for an exemption focused on my potential as a teacher and coach. I think I've got a good shot." They walked in silence until Michaela turned to her friend and spoke with unusual solemnity, softly to avoid being overheard, but fiercely determined. "Jeannette, don't worry about me. I promise you I won't be sold to the highest bidder on the damn OSR List."

As the group approached the holopark, Michaela pulled Jeannette aside. "I want you to kick some serious ogre butt in there, but I'm meeting Peter here. We have other plans."

Jeannette gave her best friend a suspicious grin. "You and Peter have been making a lot of 'plans' lately. Seems like it's getting serious. Be careful, Mikky. You don't need a broken heart on top of everything else you are facing these days."

Michaela feigned being offended. "You know no one can hurt the invincible mighty Michaela. And tomorrow I want every detail of the epic ogre battle."

Jeannette lifted an eyebrow. "I'll give you my details if you give me yours."

"You have a dirty mind, you know that? Now go tame that ogre."

BOOKER

The same day—Sacramento, California

Jim Booker possessed a talent for looking disheveled in even the finest clothes. Tie loosened to the second shirt button, pants wrinkled just enough to notice, the shirt and suit coat hung on his lanky six-foot-one frame as though still on the closet hanger. He was fair-haired and didn't have much of a natural beard, but that simply provided the option of not shaving on a daily basis. Despite this, his usual quick confident gait and observant blue eyes lent an intimidating air on first impression. Jim stepped into the domed lobby of the California Bureau of Investigation in Sacramento and headed for the glass security door leading into private offices. He glanced upward toward the camera and a face appeared in the glass. The 3-D visage was that of a lovely young woman, perhaps in her early twenties, with short blond hair that curled under her chin. Jim had picked her out of a catalog of personal assistants.

"Good morning, Jim. You are seventeen minutes late."

"Good morning, Katy. It was unavoidable. I was on my way here when I saw a puppy in the middle of the street. Cars were swerving, and the puppy's little boy was on the curb about to run into traffic, so I pulled out my badge and jumped in front of the cars."

Katy cocked her head for a few seconds as though listening for something. "I don't see a report of a traffic incident anywhere within a five-mile radius this morning."

"It probably wasn't long enough to trigger a report, but I had to calm the little tyke down and get him home. His mother was very grateful."

"This is the third time this month you have been delayed by a situation that required you to intervene to prevent a tragedy."

"Yeah. Well, anyone would have done the same thing. You know I don't like to toot my own horn or take credit for the things I do."

"Yes, so you have told me on several occasions. I guess we can record your tardiness as unavoidable today."

The door slid back, and Jim entered the restricted area. Had Katy given him a knowing smile? It was always hard with AI to tell how much they really understood. He walked down the hallway to the office he shared with his partner. Over the years, Devon Frost had gained a little bulk above the belt and some silver highlights over the ears; but the body that had been a two-sport all-star in his youth could still intimidate most people who didn't know him.

"Hey, Devon. What's cooking on the wire this morning? Got a juicy kidnapping or an assassination attempt? Bank hold up?"

"Cooking on the wire? Who are you, Sam Spade? Take it down a notch, Junior. AI wants us to run down a no-show on the Relocation List."

Booker whined, "Oh God, another List runner? Whatever happened to good old-fashioned criminals roaming the streets and doing battle with the forces of good? The cases where you had to be quicker and smarter to stay alive and protect the people?"

Devon pulled his sidearm from a drawer and rose from his chair. "Be careful what you ask for, Junior. I was around when the changes happened, when AI first started to level the playing field for folks and spread out the wealth. There were plenty of bad guys then looking to get theirs and willing to hurt someone to get it. It wasn't something I want to see again."

Jim looked at his mentor with respect and nodded. Twenty-six years his senior, Devon had been in the first class of the CBI academy and had seen the job evolve from a paramilitary force to something closer to code enforcement and truancy tracking. "If you don't mind me asking, did you ever, back in the day, have to kill anyone?" When no answer came, he grinned and broke the awkward silence. "Not counting anyone you've bored to death."

"Shut up, kid. Grab your gun and be grateful I still let you carry one."

Jim Booker was something of an anomaly among CBI agents. It was common for student athletes to be chosen for the academy. They were physically imposing and knew how to perform demanding tasks under pressure as a team. Jim was only above average athletically and a mediocre academic, so when he took the initial placement exams at age fourteen, he'd assumed he would be directed to the general education tract providing future manual labor and middle management. But the AI that determined such outcomes (popularly known as "Sorting Hat" after the Hogwarts enchanted character in the classic Harry Potter fantasies) had detected a talent for complex problem solving. Additional testing confirmed a high ability to find meaning and association between seemingly disparate bits of information. And his passion for pitting himself against AI game avatars had honed his interactive computer skills. Math and science scores didn't qualify for the technology academy, so he was directed toward enforcement. When Sorting Hat issued its final career tract options at age eighteen, they included threat analyst (recommended), suspect profiler, internal-affairs officer, and detective. The first three options were high level and more lucrative, but Jim could not condemn himself to a life sentence of cubicle confinement. He chose the CBI academy.

Devon and Booker took their seats in the gull-wing autocar. Devon placed a finger on the dashboard touch screen and voiced their destination before leaning back with hands locked behind his head.

Jim suppressed a sigh. "I'm guessing we're heading to the target's home address. Then we'll ask the AI to do all the real detective work. What's her name again?"

"Sara Castille. And, yes, that would be protocol, as you well know. We see if she's there and interview the parents if not."

Jim looked intently at his partner and asked with thinly veiled sarcasm, "Has that ever worked for you? I mean someone thirty days delinquent on registering for the List found just hanging around the house waiting for you to show up? Or parents ratting out their kid to get them deported?"

Devon closed his eyes. He liked Booker, though he would never tell him that. But the kid never met a protocol or policy that he didn't think he could improve upon. It was arrogant, but also a little intimidating since he could usually back it up with good ideas and results. Still, Jim's career with CBI was going to be a short one if Devon didn't impress on him the importance of doing things the CBI way. He briefly amused himself by imagining Booker reassigned to raking forest floors. His voice carried an air of forced patience. "The interview confirms that the delinquency is deliberate and informs the parents of their liability if they aren't forthcoming.

AI can then legally use facial recognition surveillance, monitor purchases with the target's citizen benefit card and other electronic records, as well as analyze their social contacts. Ninety-five percent of runners are apprehended in the first seventy-two hours. So, yeah, leaving things to AI works for me."

Jim sat up straighter. "Sounds like a challenge." He touched the implant behind his right ear and spoke. "Katy, report." Katy's face appeared two feet in front of Booker's face.

"Yes, Jim. What can I do for you?"

"Show me everything in the school yearbook and public reporting pertaining to target Sara Castille."

***

The interview went as usual. No, we have no idea where our daughter is. Of course, we will notify you and encourage her to report if we hear from her. Devon delivered the required warning, one he could have recited in his sleep. "I need to inform you that as your daughter's legal guardians, you're responsible for her compliance with the law as it relates to unregistered minors, and you'll be fined if she does not comply in the next thirty days. If it is determined that either of you has aided or encouraged your daughter's failure to comply with the law you'll be prosecuted criminally."

Both parents stared quietly as Devon rose and walked toward the door.

Jim had been silent through the interview, but now spoke. "I'm sorry for my partner's hard line. He has a little trouble remembering what it's like to be young. I checked into Sara, and she seems like an upstanding young woman. Chess team, good grades, and I seem to recall that she was a standout sprinter on the cycling team, won some medals. I'm a bit of a cycling buff myself. I'd love to take a look at her competition bike."

Mr. Castille smiled. "I'm afraid Sara donated her bike back to the program when she realized she wouldn't be staying in California."

Jim nodded and smiled appreciatively. "She sounds like fine young woman. Thanks for your time."

Back in the car, Devon got the first word in. "I don't have any trouble remembering being young. You're a constant reminder of the shortcomings of youth."

"Just a little bad cop/good cop. Katy, report and access all food purchases by Sara Castille and also those of her parents for the past two months."

Katy's image appeared and responded. "That information is privacy protected, Jim."

"Not anymore, Katy. The target's parents have been interviewed and legally advised. They are fair game now."

"Thank you, Jim. Central AI has been notified and a standard fugitive investigation will initiate immediately. I will notify you with updates."

"Thanks, Katy, but humor me and pull up those records. See if Sara has made any purchases in the past three weeks.

Katy's image tilted her head slightly for a few seconds. "No, Jim. She has not."

"Now cross-reference Sara's food purchases for the past two months with those of her parents prior to one month ago and give me a list of items that are unique to Sara."

Katy responded immediately. "Sara has several purchases of twelve-ounce caramel almond milk that are unique to her purchases in that time frame."

"Now see if either of her parents have purchased that item in the past month and note where they bought it. Then see if they have ever bought items at that location previously."

"Sara's mother has purchased sixty-four-ounce caramel almond milk twice in the past month at a small private store on Fifth Street in downtown Sacramento; and, no, she has not previously shopped there."

Jim brightened. "Excellent, Katy. Now, one final request. Check the address of all Sara's classmates for any that live within one mile of that store, and check public records for any unoccupied living quarters within one mile."

Katy tilted her head and went silent for a few seconds. "None of Sara's classmates live in that area; If they had, they would have attended a different school. There is one unoccupied building, however. It is a partially completed apartment structure at the old railroad yard on Third Street. It was abandoned when tests showed unacceptable toxic chemicals in the soil at the site."

Jim smiled a bit smugly. "Thank you, Katy. You are a credit to AI everywhere. That will be all for now." He turned to Devon. "Sara didn't donate her bike. She is using it to avoid detection on public transport. It's my turn to pick where we go next." Jim touched the dashboard control panel. "Sacramento railroad yard off Third Street." Then he added, "Katy, report. Get me a drone monitor over the area around that abandoned apartment building immediately."

9

SAFE HOUSE

Same day—Downtown Sacramento

Michaela and Peter exited the autotram at the Virgin Hyperloop terminal, former site of the old Amtrak station. Both wore baseball caps and oversized dark glasses, sticking to the crowded areas to avoid facial recognition monitors. Once free of the station they entered the old railroad yard site, 240 acres that once served as the western anchor for the first transcontinental railroad in the nineteenth century, as the largest railway hub in the western states during the twentieth century, and after falling idle, was projected to be the largest urban renewal project in city history at the beginning of the twenty-first century. But after implementation of the People's Budget, AI judged the toxic metals and chemicals in the soil too expensive to remove. Now it stood abandoned. The historic original brick railroad buildings remained near the Hyperloop station at the southern edge of the property, now preserved as cultural sites. Michaela and Peter walked between the structures to avoid prying eyes. A modern, now abandoned, four-story face brick apartment building designed to reflect the architecture of the historic structures stood empty nearby, doors bolted and windows boarded. Peter led them to a service access door where the lock had been disabled and the bolted chain cut and left in place.

The two teens jogged up four flights of stairs and down a hallway to the safe house apartment at the northwest corner of the building. The signal was one knock, two knocks, then three knocks. The sound of sliding bolts followed and they entered. The apartment was spacious, a penthouse, but never painted or decorated. Electric power to the building had been severed but the plumbing still worked. An air mattress with a sleeping bag sat against one wall. Two inflatable chairs and a table consisting of a wooden reel dispenser turned on end rounded out the furniture. Windows were boarded, but two skylights offered decent daytime lighting, and a pair of battery lanterns sat on the kitchen sink.

Peter spoke to the lone female occupant. "Good news, Sara. Everything is set and you leave tonight. Mikky has your itinerary and papers."

Sara tilted her head back and let out the breath she had been holding; then she teared up. "Oh God, thank you so much. I couldn't have taken this much longer. You have no idea how scared and alone I've been."

Michaela set her equipment bag on the floor and emptied the contents. She removed the false bottom and extracted a folder packet with papers. "You're going to be fine, Sara. Tonight at nine, you'll make your way down to the river. Go through the fence at the spot where it's been cut, where you came in. Do you think you can find it?"

"Yeah, I remember."

"Great. Follow the river to the Old Sac district and wait in the alley by the Saddle and Spur Bar. Your ride will be waiting for you in a blue autocar. The password for all your connections on the trip is 'Janis.' You say, 'Janis?' and your guide will say, 'Joplin.' Say it now."

"Janis"

Michaela smiled encouragingly. "Joplin. Your connection will take you as far as a truck stop near Redding. When your guide goes into the restaurant, you stay seated until a truck driver knocks on the window. Repeat the password and get into his truck. It's going all the way to Portland. You have an Oregon passport and new identity papers here. You are now Sophie Woodworth from Portland Oregon. You'll be redirected to the people there who can help you get established or, if you prefer, get you across the border into Idaho. There's no extradition in Idaho, so you wouldn't need a fake identity." She offered the folder to Sara. "Memorize the information. Then you keep the ID and travel papers; Peter and I will destroy the rest of it. We'll stay until you are sure you have it down pat."

"Thanks. I could really use some company. My parents gave me $3,000. I want to repay you for helping me."

Michaela embraced her in a hug. "No, you're going to need that money when you land somewhere safe. Besides, my turn will come."

Michaela and Peter settled into the chairs while Sara stood and examined the travel packet at the table, occasionally asking questions. Suddenly, Michaela became alert and rose to her feet. She hissed her words in strained whisper. "Quiet! I heard something." Peter rose slowly, looking at her. The door flew open and crashed against the wall. Sara screamed as a large man charged into the room with weapon drawn.

"CBI. Show me your hands, now! Hands in the air!" A second agent, younger and slight of build entered behind him, also armed, sweeping his weapon in an arc across the room. "Is anyone else here?"

Michaela forced herself to resist the emotion. *Fear is the enemy.* She looked at Peter. He was white and trembling. Sara was crying, now sobbing, the packet still on the table. The agents didn't know about the packet yet. That information could collapse an entire arm of the Resistance underground railroad. And any chance she had at escaping the List would go down with it. She looked at the man with the gun and sized up her options.

The older agent ordered the younger one, "Clear the rest of the area."

The younger man lowered his weapon and entered the hallway leading to the bedrooms. Michaela acted. She lowered her hands and spread them in a pleading gesture while she stepped forward. "Officer, allow me to explain."

Devon reacted. "Step back and hands up!"

Michaela stopped, appearing submissive, and slowly raised her hands. She turned as though to retreat, then ducked her head as the turn became a spin delivering a side kick to the agent's left knee. He buckled, and an open-hand blow to the temple rendered him unconscious. She caught him as he fell so as to mute the sound of his falling. The call from the bedroom, "All clear here," came as she grabbed the packet from the table. Michaela mouthed the word, *Run!*

Booker walked into the living area and saw his partner lying on the floor. One female suspect was flying out the front door, the male running toward it, and the other female still sobbing as she stared at Devon's crumpled body. He got off a shot with his stun gun and hit the fleeing male in the leg, sending him sprawling in spasm. The sobbing suspect fell to the floor on her own, in apparent shock. Jim dropped to his knees by his partner and felt for a pulse. Devon stirred and moaned.

Michaela reached the end of the hall and exited the fire escape door. The sign on the door warned that it would trigger a fire alarm when opened, but apparently, whatever powered the alarm was no longer active. She closed the door behind her and stood on the old-fashioned fire escape system of metal grate platforms with connecting ladders attached to the outer wall of each floor-level. With one hand on the railing and one holding the packet, she forced herself to take no more than two steps at a time. *Stay in control. I can't afford an injury now.* She came to the second floor, and the ladder ended. *Crap. I'll have to hang from the railing and jump.* Then she saw the hinge apparatus on the ladder and was able to drop the final section to the ground. Her feet touched the ground, and her heart jumped in her chest as a voice rang out from high above her.

"Stop right there, or I *will* shoot you."

She froze for a moment, looked up at the young CBI agent on the fourth-floor platform, then down at the packet of vital information in her arms. Michaela sprinted for the corner of the building, her feet barely touching the ground, then slipping out from under her as she tried to round the edge of the building. She fell and heard the terrifying crack of the pistol.

10

CRUCIBLE

Five days later—September 6, Topeka, Kansas, Our Divine Savior Church Grounds

Reverend Bob Jackson stood on a makeshift outdoor stage looking out on a multitude of some twenty thousand men, women and children who were uprooting their lives to follow him on what could be a fool's errand, a trail of tears. People had traveled from hundreds of miles around Topeka to follow their prophet. The small city of tents, trailers, tractors, and buses stretched from the shadows of his grand megachurch across the expanse of his grassy ecclesiastic kingdom to where he stood. There were farmers, craftsmen, artists, musicians, all the makings of a nation in search of a country. Tonight, he would bless them in a torch-lit liturgy, and the Exodus journey would begin at daylight. Outwardly, he wore his familiar mask, a man of God certain of his righteous place in the inevitable divine plan, bending low over the edge of the stage to shake hands and acknowledge well-wishers who each believed they held a special place in his affections. Behind the mask lay dread.

The ministry had been his salvation after his wife and infant child were swept away in a tornado nearly twenty years past. His church family, then just a few hundred souls, sustained him through the initial grief and anger. Eventually, he forgave God and, in turn, found forgiveness for his failure to protect his loved ones. It had been easy to hold fast to faith when it provided comfort and stability, stature and admiration. Just as importantly to him, it had lifted up his community, providing concrete life-affirming services and hope to the people who looked up to him. But now he had forsaken all of that, and for what? Was he Abraham answering God's challenge to sacrifice his beloved Isaac, his everything; or was he just a coward who had capitulated when the people who funded his success threatened to cut him off and expose him as a failure?

Bill Thomas had been true to his word. For six months, the Oligarchy had channeled funds through its charities to the three megachurches that would anchor the pilgrimage. Trucks were loaded with food, portable toilets, heaters, medical supplies and service bots. Personal media devices (PMDs) had been distributed to allow for closed circuit instant communication between Exodus leaders and followers. Supplies lines would stretch across each of the three designated paths. Reverend Jackson would lead a contingent from Topeka westward across Kansas, Colorado, and Utah. A separate southern caravan would leave Oklahoma City and traverse the southern border states under the guidance of Reverend King, while Reverend Ryle prepared to lead a northern contingent from Rapid City, South Dakota, through Wyoming, Montana, and Idaho. Their numbers would increase at each stop along the way. In eight days' time, they would all converge outside Salt Lake City as a single nation for the final journey across Nevada to the edge of a promised land.

And I am the one who promised it to them. I told them God spoke to me, but the truth is I was doing the speaking. Were You listening Lord? What will happen to all these people if there is no God to hear me? And what will they do to me if they think I am a false prophet? Bob appreciated the irony that he had never prayed as hard or as often as when he began to doubt his faith.

He retreated to the back of the stage and pretended to check the sound equipment, tapping on a microphone and lingering over the control board. He indulged in recalling the imagined words that would free him from this agony of doubt. *We have been deceived. I have been deceived! Go home and pick up your lives again. I am sorry. Forgive me, or not, but do not risk your lives and loved ones on someone as weak as I.* It would be the end of his ministry, of life as he had lived it, but a humble existence spent in repentance seemed almost too much to ask now. And it was no longer possible. Not only would the Exodus go on without him, but he feared for his own fate. The one time he had half-heartedly expressed doubt to Bill Thomas, the look he received was clearly a silent threat.

The blast momentarily blinded, deafened, and laid him flat. High-pitched ringing in his ears gave way to a rising din of screams and babel of shouting. A tidal surge of bodies began to flow by the stage as he rose to his knees and looked over the waves of people coming toward him. Flames erupted from Christ Our Savior church. His office above the choir loft splintered and fell in pieces. He watched in numb horror as a large portion of the roof sagged and then fell with a roar like a locomotive passing by, followed by a gust of hot wind and embers that burned on his exposed skin. Smoke rose in a swirling column, higher and higher, as if a burnt offering to a vengeful God.

Bob rose to his feet, descended the stage steps and began to walk slowly at first, then more quickly against the tide of bodies fleeing the flames. Mothers holding frightened children and trying to reassure them despite their own terror, children without mothers standing in place and sobbing, men yelling at the crowd not to panic while other men pushed and shoved their way through, young lovers and friends frantically searching and calling for each other; their pastor felt the pain on every face. And yet he was detached from them, seeing the frenzied terror as from above, from high on a cross, forsaken and helpless. As he neared the burning remains of his life's work, some of the faces were spattered in blood, some showed only blank stares, and some souls lay lifeless on the ground. He walked past all these in a fugue state until the intense heat triggered a primitive survival instinct from deep within him and he staggered back a short distance, stumbling before falling to his knees. As the stupor of shock began to lift, a profound, encompassing grief consumed him. On his hands and knees, head to the ground, he cried. He cried for the people fleeing behind him; he cried for the loss of his beautiful church; he cried for his dead wife and daughter; he cried for a humanity that had so defiled creation; he cried for his own weakness and shortcomings; he cried because God was punishing him and because there was no God. He cried until his chest ached too much to breathe through the hot, choking smoke, and he fell unconscious.

PART TWO

THE CABIN

1

BASE CAMP

Two weeks earlier—August 28, 2069, in Chico, California

Joseph had settled in at the Chico State University Religious Studies department and was assigned a dormitory room with one other exchange student. But he couldn't communicate with Hank or prepare his mission from there. When he found the notice of a cabin for rent near Truckee, Joseph saw it as a sign of divine intervention and approval. The cabin's location was ideally suited to the mission objective. There was still nearly three weeks before formal classes began for fall quarter, so he would not be missed.

He mounted the surprisingly light-weight motorcycle he had purchased from a private party with cash. Californians were always quite accommodating when cash, as opposed to citizen benefit card (CBT) transfer, was involved. It worried him to appear too obvious with his money, but the cash came from a variety of Christian Alliance accounts, and citizens were not prone to report private cash transactions. The motorcycle's battery provided an upper limit of around sixty mph but with acceleration to maximum speed in three seconds and a range of nearly twelve hundred miles.

He had ridden motorcycles in Kansas, but that didn't prepare him for this ride. The right-hand lane was devoted to elongated, egg-shaped, single-rail trams seating eight people and spaced just minutes apart, leapfrogging around each other when passengers were loading. All street-legal vehicles communicated with a traffic control AI that would slow his bike to allow right-of-way for the trams as they darted into his path. He found he could anticipate the trams by accelerating ahead of them before they diverted their path, though this required weaving and speeding around slower moving traffic in his own lane. Apparently, this was a serious breach of road etiquette as evidenced by gestures and comments from fellow motorists.

As he graduated onto the major thoroughfares leading to the sprawling industrial and commercial downtown sectors, fewer tram stops and additional lanes made the traffic far less congested. Overhead, however, a different kind of traffic, chaotic and mesmerizing to the point of distraction, intensified. From treetops to the wispy, cotton-candy clouds, commercial drones of various types and sizes flew in every direction, like flocks of seagulls swirling over a fishing dock, occasionally swooping down. They carried all sorts of merchandise from groceries to lumber to medical equipment. Whirring rotors created a ubiquitous soundtrack, like the ocean in a seaside community. It left him feeling as though he were not merely in a different state but a different planet or time.

The ride from Chico to Truckee took nearly four hours and then another fifteen minutes on back roads to the cabin. Along the way, he marveled at the massive farms and miles of orchards that existed only in memories and old photographs in his parched homeland. In his limited travel around the neighborhoods surrounding the college, Joseph had come to think that Californians had to rely on self-sufficiency. Front yards were vegetable gardens, chicken coops and rabbit hutches, not so unlike his home. Now, for the first time, he appreciated that this was a land of plenty, worth whatever sacrifice he had to make to open it for his people.

Joseph thought he had allowed plenty of time, but arrived just twenty minutes ahead of his scheduled meeting. He parked the motorcycle and took in his surroundings. The cabin near Lake Stampede and just eleven miles from Verdi Peak afforded access to a key location for the mission objective. Set at the base of a hill in a clearing surrounded by trees, it looked rustic but solid. Vertical rough-cut redwood boards framed the mostly rectangular living area with an entry room extending out at a right angle on one end. Four stairs led up to the front door, and a wide porch wrapped around the side facing Joseph. The steep roof supported solar panels on either side of a tall chimney, and green moss grew along the eaves. A metal outcropping was likely housing the power storage unit. Joseph walked around the back corner of the cabin. An enclosed wood storage bin, perhaps twenty feet long and four feet deep, stood adjacent to a back door. At the sound of an approaching vehicle he circled back to the front porch.

A man and woman parked and introduced themselves. The man appeared middle-aged, brown complexion, paunchy and balding. He walked quickly to Joseph, his somewhat younger, petite wife following several steps behind. "Hi, you must be Joseph. I'm Jose Castille, and this is my wife, Martina." He extended a hand; Joseph merely nodded his acknowledgement. After a brief awkward silence, Jose withdrew the offered handshake and continued. "OK, let's take a look inside."

The entry area served as a mudroom with a hat rack and umbrella stand, a wooden bench for removing shoes, and two high shelves. Joseph hung his helmet on the hat rack. Under the large windows at the high-ceiling side of the main living area sat a leather couch with back cushions upholstered in an American Indian pattern. Opposite the couch, the fireplace was flanked on one side by a leather recliner, and on the other side a desk with a wooden chair. Doors led to two bedrooms, each with a queen-size bed and a dresser. At the far end of the room, a counter with two bar stools separated the kitchen. An enclosed closet-sized pantry housed a stacked clothes washer-dryer unit at one end of the kitchen, where a door led to the bathroom with a shower stall and the back door to the cabin. Joseph finished the tour before speaking. "The notice said $400 a month."

Jose answered, "Yes, and we need first and last month plus $200 cleaning deposit. So, $1,000 moves you in."

Martina had been standing in the living room, watching her husband give the tour, but now spoke up. "May I ask what your interest in the cabin is? I mean, do you plan to live here through the winter?"

Joseph looked around the room as he answered in a distracted manner, as though her question was of little importance. "No, not entirely. I'll be here mostly on weekends. I'm looking for a secluded place to do my writing."

Martina persisted. "Oh, you're an author. What kind of things have you published?" Joseph chose to ignore the question. He didn't want these people to know any more than they needed to know about who he was or why he was here. He turned to Jose. "I'll take it. I can give you the $1,000 in cash today."

Jose tried not to look too happy at the offer. "Can you give Martina and me a moment to talk before we make it official?" Joseph turned and carefully plucked his helmet from the hook by the entry room, pausing as though considering whether to again engage Jack and Martina or to wait outside as Jack had asked. Martina bit her lower lip and held her breath for the long moment it took Joseph to open the door and exit the cabin.

Jose turned to his wife. "He seems fine to me. He's quiet and single. I don't think he's the type to throw wild parties or burn the cabin down smoking crack. I say we go for it."

Martina, arms crossed, looked away. "I don't know. I get a bad vibe. I feel like there's something he's not telling us."

"A bad vibe?" Jose chuckled and pulled up the lease agreement on his slate. "We don't need to know his family history. We just need him to pay his rent, and right now, he has $1,000 cash for first- and last-month deposit."

Martina fixed her gaze back on her husband, raising her voice just enough to lift Jose's eyes from the legal document. "Who has $1,000 in cash on them? Except maybe criminals. And if he's an author like he says, why won't he tell us anything he's published?"

Surprised by the emotion, Jose set the slate on the table, smiled reassuringly, and reached for his wife's hand. "Maybe he's a writer, maybe not. Maybe the cabin is a place where he can meet up with his mistress. Maybe it's none of our business what he does here as long as he takes care of the place and his money is good."

Martina lowered her voice and her gaze. "I know we need the money. Sara only has three days until she is officially delinquent reporting to the List, and, yes, she needs as much help as we can give her. But this Joseph character kind of gives me the creeps."

Jose tried to hide the feeling that his wife was being irrationally emotional, but he was insistent. "We don't have the luxury of waiting for the ideal tenant to appear and warm our hearts about the whole situation. We've had the ad on the web for two months, and Joseph is the only one who is willing to sign a lease and actually has the money. I love this place too, but that life is over. You and me, we're not about us anymore; we're about making sure our daughter has a future.

Maybe someday we can come back here, but for right now, we have to do what needs to be done."

Martina crossed the room and slumped into the familiar sagging cushion of her dad's old leather chair, fingers gripping the armrests. She surrendered softly. "OK. Go get him. You don't need my signature. I'll be in the kitchen."

***

Joseph woke to first light of day coming through the cabin window. A haze of anxiety and shame hung in his mind as it often did on awakening, a hangover from recurring dreams of an earlier life. For just a few moments his mother and sister were uncomfortably present with him. Forcing his eyes open to the light, they were banished, and he was again the strong master of his own life, a life that had a mission.

After morning ablutions and prayer, Joseph stepped out to the porch and availed himself of the old wooden rocker that had a familiar Kansas look and feel to it. The brisk, clear air and damp smell of the pine forest reminded him that he was not in Kansas anymore. His senses sharpened as he familiarized himself with this alluring but alien landscape. The picket of well-spaced, tall, needled trees stood resolutely above a forest floor, well-groomed to deprive fires of fuel that fed them. Sunbeams splintered by leaves and needles danced in the open spaces as a warm breeze through the tree branches made marionettes of the shadows. Joseph felt protected and hidden in this arboreal womb.

He had begun to understand his enemy in a new light. Perhaps the people living in the West Coast Federation could be forgiven their greed and malicious indifference toward his people. They were living in a kind of paradise. *They have been told that this is their just reward for choosing the righteous paths of what they euphemistically call managing Mother*

Earth's gifts. Like the Egyptians, Babylonians and Philistines before them, their godless priests of economy and planning have crafted their evil into idols and called them holy to justify their greed.

Joseph checked his resentment and recalled his training. *Focus.* The final two months with Hank had been life changing. He emerged like a caterpillar from a cocoon and embraced that "other person" who had risen from his anger and panic at critical moments. Hank explained that the training for elite warriors began by breaking them down with every sort of abuse, physical and mental, by forcing them to face their worst fears and survive. Only then could they be trained to operate at a level above the base human drives of fear and self-preservation. Joseph's life had provided just that sort of preparation. As he was making the physical transformation from boy to man, he was subjected to a final and devastating deprivation. In that moment, forced to choose between surrendering his future life or coldly doing whatever was needed at the moment, an aspect of his psyche had emerged, a part of him forged in the taunts, beatings and neglect of his childhood. It had protected him before that day, operating in the shadows of the anguish, retreating when the danger passed. But when childhood was dealt a violent death, the adult warrior rose up uninhibited, no longer merely a shield against the pain, but with sword in hand. Now that warrior was ready to be trained. Hank taught Joseph how to embrace, control, and integrate his inner warrior. Joseph internalized Hank's training and his new sense of empowerment with the same fervor he had embraced the Christian faith that provided him with community, family.

He addressed the compucube in his hand. "Q-Bert, confirm identity, voice mode." The cube confirmed the voice and hand prints. "Confirmed, Joseph. Proceed." Joseph activated the cube's secure satellite phone function by voicing his code ID. "One forty-four contact. Base of operations established, eleven miles from target area. Ready to proceed with mission objectives." The message would be relayed through two different satellites in encrypted microbursts at varying frequencies and random intervals. It would take a few minutes to get a reply. When the reply came it was in the form of a Truckee address, a date and time four days hence, and a description of the person he would be meeting.

2

87.8 PERCENT

Four days later—September 2, Sanders Memorial Medical Center in Sacramento

Booker stood outside the hospital room waiting until Devon had been informed of his test results. The medibot rolled out the door and addressed him. "You can see your friend now." Jim approached the bed cautiously, eyeing the bank of lights and monitors that spanned the wall above the bed. He didn't like hospitals.

"So…does the doc-in-a-box think you're going to live?"

Devon eyed his partner with suspicion, glad to see him, but expecting the inevitable verbal smackdown. "Afraid so. The MRI shows no structural brain damage. It's just a concussion, but protocol says they have to observe me for twenty-four hours."

"And the knee?

"Sprained and deep bone bruise. Looks like you'll have to do the running after any fleeing bad guys for a few weeks."

Booker barely suppressed a grin as he patted his partner on the shoulder and spoke with as much over-the-top sincerity as he could muster. "Well, don't you worry. I am going to track down the little girl who beat you up and make her pay."

Devon acknowledged his chagrin with a wince and a groan. "OK, I deserve that. No excuses, but that 'little girl' was scary fast and good. Some kind of military training or martial arts. She may be an agent of some entity outside of California. What have you learned from the other two?"

"Not much. When I got back into the apartment the young man—his name is Peter Fazio—was alert enough to blurt out a story about how he didn't know the girl who got away. He claims that she had approached him anonymously, saying his friend Sara needed his help and she could take him to her. He said it loud and slow so Sara would know what to say. So far, they are sticking to their story. Sara admits she was running from the List registration and they are both back home with GPS/shock collars. I've got Katy working on a list of Caucasian females under twenty-five years of age known to have some advanced fight training, but it's a big list, and the girl may not even be known to AI."

Devon was back in detective mode, no longer just a patient. "I find it hard to believe that a girl with those skills just happened to know a fugitive from the OSR List. Have AI cross-match with any known external agencies or internal resistance groups, if she hasn't already."

"Katy tells me that is already underway."

"Good." It was Devon's turn to smile wryly and get in a verbal dig. "As I was coming around in the apartment, I heard a shot fired. Apparently, you missed."

Booker dodged the jab. "I don't miss. It was a warning shot. I try not to kill people until I know a little more about them."

Devon scoffed good naturedly. "Sure. Do me a favor. Try not to get yourself or anyone else killed before I get back."

***

The next morning, Booker was awakened by the sound of wind chimes softly wafting into his right ear. Jim slept alone, a committed romantic relationship being near the top of a lengthy and long-neglected list of personal goals. He stretched and looked at the clock showing 5:42 a.m. Eyes closed again, he touched his ear and mumbled, "Katy. You know I'm worthless before 6:00 a.m., and then only after at least one cup of coffee."

Katy was capable of reading moods and offering gentle sympathy, but was having none of it this morning. "You will need to adjust your protocol today, Jim. We have identified your mystery girl with 87.8 percent confidence. The first seventy-two hours are an essential factor in fugitive investigation."

Jim rubbed his eyes and gave voice to his irritation. "You could have given me an extra hour of sleep. Seventy-one hours is plenty. I always get my man. Or woman. Or whatever other options are out there. How did you identify her?"

"Crime Outlook and Forecast AI had already predicted an OSR fugitive. The Sacramento area has seen a new fugitive case every three to five weeks in this area over an eleven-month period, presumably the work of a dissident organization that has been unusually successful in aiding OSR deserters. COFI was monitoring OSR eligible seventeen- and eighteen-year-olds to the extent permitted by privacy protections. One such individual is Michaela Dohn, a rising star in the world of youth karate who has a petition before the Exceptional Talent Board for exemption from the List. She attends the same school that Sara Castille attended, and she matches the limited descriptive parameters you recorded in your report."

Jim rose slowly, ran his hands through his hair, and haltingly headed for the beverage machine, eyes barely open. "Vanilla bean, cream."

Katy responded. "I don't understand your meaning, Jim."

"Not you, the coffee machine. OK, you've got my attention. How do I find this Michaela person? No, let me guess. You want me to go to her house and interview her parents if she's not there."

"That would be protocol, Jim. It will allow us to monitor—"

"Yeah, yeah, yeah. Send me the address and any information you have on her. I'll head out after I've reviewed the file."

3

ESCAPE

Three days earlier—September 1, Sacramento, outside the holopark

Michaela sat in the shade of an oak tree, head lowered and the bill of her cap pulled down low over her eyes. She had never felt so exposed as she waited for what seemed an eternity on a low concrete wall outside the holopark. Her eyes darted surreptitiously from under sunscreen glasses, searching passersby for the agent who would slap restraints on her and haul her off. She fought the impulse to go inside and find her friends; she couldn't risk the identification monitors in the building. Finally, Jeanette appeared on the curved sloping walkway leaving the holopark. Seeing Michaela, she was initially surprised, then alarmed when she was close enough to see Michaela's lip trembling and a tear on her cheek. "What did Peter do to you? I knew he wasn't good for you."

Michaela bowed her head and spoke softly, her voice trembling and faltering. "Peter didn't do anything. In fact, I may have ruined things for him. We weren't together the way I let you think." She related the events of the past two hours. Jeanette was as unnerved at seeing her invincible friend so wounded as she was by the revelation of what Michaela was telling her.

Michaela reached for her friend's hand and squeezed hard as words poured out in a flood of hushed tones. "I don't know what to do. I don't think Peter would give me up, but Sara was an emotional wreck. She's probably told them who I am. I can't go home. I can't contact anyone I know without being found. What was I thinking? I assaulted a CBI agent! If they find me, I won't be under house arrest. Felons convicted of violence don't go on the OSR or even labor camps. They get deported to other countries with no protections or conditions. God, I could wind up as a sex slave in the Caliphate or working in some Chinese sweatshop factory!" Her voice caught in her throat and escaped in a sob. She gathered herself without looking up from her hands. "I could try using the fake ID in Sara's packet, but there's no CBT card or money, and she may have told them about it. I'm so sorry to pull you into this, Jeanette, and I understand completely if you want to walk away right now. This conversation never happened." She yanked a trembling hand back into her lap.

Jeanette stared at her best friend, thoughts racing. She was frightened. Her head swiveled left and right, looking for authorities, then up for surveillance cameras, but she saw none. Defying the AI wasn't just wrong; it was incredibly dangerous. AI was everywhere and all-powerful. At least that was what she had always been told. But she couldn't just walk away and abandon her best friend. And if anyone could beat the system, it was surely Michaela. *Besides, I haven't done anything wrong. It's not a crime to talk.* She could always deny what they talked about.

Jeanette took Michaela's hand back in hers. Then she cocked her head as a smile appeared. "I have an idea. Sara was a year ahead of us, but my parents and hers were friends. They used to invite me to a little cabin they have way up in the mountains near Lake Tahoe. It was too remote and needed too many code upgrades for the state to take it, so it was a kind of summer getaway for them. With Sara in custody or house arrest, they won't be going there, especially this time of year.

You should be able to hide there until it's safe to make your way north to Oregon. It's too late today, but you can hide out in our shed tonight. I have the GPS address for the cabin somewhere. I'll get an autocar with my CBT card and drive you there tomorrow. I'll pick up some groceries, and I think I can lay hands on a couple hundred dollars to tide you over for a while."

Michaela began to regain her composure. "I have to get word to my parents, but I don't want to put them at risk." Jeanette wiped a tear from her best friend's eye. It felt strange to have their roles reversed, Jeanette being the strong one. "I'll get word to your parents and tell them you are safe, but I won't tell them where you're going. That way they can't be charged with aiding you. At worst, they may get a fine."

Michaela wrapped her arms around her friend and hugged her tightly until she realized they were making a scene and strangers were starting to stare.

***

Jeanette helped Michaela load groceries into a backpack, and the two friends shared tearful goodbyes on the outskirts of Truckee, north of Lake Tahoe. Michaela mounted the bicycle she would take the rest of the way in order to avoid the autocar's travel history from recording the location of the cabin. Michaela had regained her confident persona, at least enough to project it convincingly. "I'll send word when I am settled outside California and you can visit me. We'll celebrate then. I'll never forget what you did for me." Jeanette stood and watched her best friend ride out of her life until she disappeared around a bend in the road.

The eighteen-mile ride to Lake Stampede was relatively level, and Jeanette pushed the pace. She was riding white-water rapids of emotion up, down and barely in control. A wave of elation buoyed her on the surface. She had escaped the clutches of the CBI and the Relocation List. It was not how she had planned, but it was happening, and she would make it work by her strength of will. Then grief brought her crashing down at the thought of never seeing her parents again, not even saying goodbye. That too had loomed in her future for years, but below the surface, an undercurrent that couldn't be defeated with careful planning or execution. And the uncertainty of what lay around the next bend in her life brought her mantra to her lips. *Fear is the enemy. Fear is the enemy.* Her body responded as it always did when challenged, ever faster, stronger, smarter.

At Lake Stampede the dirt-road turnoff from the main road climbed steeply over the final one and a half miles. Michaela felt the burn in her legs and prayed her calves would not cramp. At last, the GPS on her wrist announced her arrival, and the cabin appeared in a small clearing, nestled discreetly amongst the trees. It was perfect. A combination of the serene bucolic setting before her eyes and pure physical exhaustion delivered her into emotional calm waters once again.

4

MEETING

Joseph arrived in Truckee an hour early and parked the motorcycle out of sight by the back door of the arranged meeting site. *Hank's Rule #7: Early is on time. On time is late. Late gets you killed.* The historic one-street downtown section had been preserved in its Old West decor, though with white fireproof roofing. Joseph took a seat on the redwood patio deck of a sandwich shop and ordered coffee, French Roast/black, from the robowait. The little service bots were ubiquitous in California, and they never failed to make him smile. Typically about four feet tall and equipped with childlike voices, they were constructed to roughly suggest the human form with a wheeled torso, head and mechanical arms, but more robotic than human in appearance as to avoid seeming creepy or threatening. This one wore a black-and-white-checkered apron over a tuxedo-and-bow-tie exterior. The bots brought to mind the childhood friends he had imagined and wanted but never had.

The redwood patio was raised so he could see over the line of parked cars angled into the curb along both sides of the wide street servicing the souvenir shops and restaurants. It would be easy to let his guard down sitting here. The cool, crisp mountain air felt like a soothing balm after blistering summer days in the central valley. The sun gently warmed his face and bare arms as he observed the crowd through reflective sunshade glasses, noting adults in singles or pairs and following their movements until they entered a business or drove away. The street was not crowded on a Monday morning and Joseph's attention was brought to a particular individual, probably in his midforties, heavyset, and dressed a little too formally in a white shirt and sport coat for a typical tourist on vacation. The man had wandered into and out of the same three adjacent shops repeatedly and didn't have any purchases in hand. A tail. And there was the black gull-winged autocar that all the CBI agents drove. Apparently, Joseph was not the only one waiting for his contact.

Joseph considered the possibilities. The entire operation could be blown and a takedown planned at the meeting site. But if that were the case, there would be several agents on the street, they would be communicating, and a drone would be overhead. He saw no evidence of that. It could be that the tail was just a precaution in light of heightened security as the Christ caravan prepared to begin its journey to the border. His contact had been denied an exit visa because he was too important and carried too much classified technical knowledge to leave the state. It would make sense to have him followed on a trip near the state border. The outline of a plan began to take shape. Joseph decided the meeting would occur, but he would have to lose the tail and avoid being seen.

Joseph looked at his watch. Fifteen minutes to the arranged meeting. A soft ping acknowledged that his CBT account had been successfully charged for his beverage as he exited the patio and headed toward the Truckee Tavern, where the meeting was to occur. The owner of the tavern was well known to the Oligarchy and had benefited richly from the relationship; there would be no electronic eavesdropping or receipts that could identify the individuals involved. Joseph had scouted the location and met the owner the previous day.

Hank's Rule #2: Always know your playing field. The bar was ideal for preventing remote snooping. The walls were built of weathered old brick, at least a foot thick, sufficient to thwart any remote imaging or recording. An eighteen-inch thick brick face wall ran down one side of the main room with arched openings into three small private rooms, each with a round wooden table and photos of Truckee in bygone days on the walls, perfect for a discreet rendezvous. Joseph entered the tavern and took a stool at the long oaken bar. He jotted a note on a cocktail napkin and instructed the barkeep to bring it to a man of a particular description who would soon enter and order a beer. A fifty-dollar bill with President Obama's portrait was in the napkin to ensure the bartender's cooperation.

After exiting the tavern, Joseph crossed the street and walked down the sidewalk, passing behind the CBI agent to enter the store behind him. A slight bulge under the sport coat confirmed that the tail was wearing a concealed weapon shoulder holster. From the storefront window he kept one eye on the agent and the other on the front door of the *Squeeze Inn* across the street, where his contact was to have spent the night. Hank had shown Joseph a photo of the man who was the key to the whole mission; he would not be difficult to recognize.

A middle-aged man exited the hotel wearing a shirt fashioned after the flag of California. The shirt was to serve as an identifying mark for his contact, but it was hardly necessary, as Otto himself stuck out in a crowd more than did his attire. The first thing you noticed about Dr. Otto Wagner was that he was not a handsome man. Standing a mere five foot, six inches, with balding head, almost no discernible neck, uncommonly short arms and a generous girth around the middle, he resembled a painted Russian nesting doll. He was, however, blessed with a brilliant mind. While still a graduate student at Stanford, his research laid the foundation for development of the fluoride-ion battery, a key component in the elimination of fossil fuels. A decade later, his team developed an economical class of superconducting materials for use at ambient temperatures that heralded breakthrough technologies in an array of industries. Cheap Mag-lev and hyperloop vehicles traveling at four hundred mph eliminated most domestic air travel; a new age of medical imaging sophistication soon followed; the generation and transmission of electricity became an order of magnitude easier and cheaper. It was his work with superconductors that the mission sought to use.

As a young man, Otto's academic acclaim and quick wit won him numerous female friends, but not lovers. He had contented himself with his reputation as the man you wanted to invite to your party or to have drinks after work. As the years passed, he found himself in the role of a venerable mentor, a good boss, an icon even. These days, his young students and collaborators didn't party with their older icon mentor. He didn't really mind being excluded. He had been there and done that and no longer had the energy or insecurities of his youth. But he was lonely. His sexual encounters had all been with professional sex workers and could be counted on one hand. Otto was resigned to a life lived alone. That changed when an agent from the Eastern Oligarchy had approached him nearly a year ago. The agent needed a device built. It wasn't a particularly difficult thing to design, though it would benefit from his superconducting materials. In exchange for his cooperation, the agent described how the Oligarchy could spirit him out of California and to the east coast. He would be given a plush residence and his choice of young female companionship in whatever capacity he chose, singly or in pairs. Otto declined initially. Certainly, an act of betrayal to the state would carry dire risks, and there was no way of knowing if he could trust the offer. His imagination, however, would not leave him to his better judgment. His sexual appetite had only grown more ravenous for the years of abstinence, and fantasies whispered to him whenever he was quiet and alone. Desire finally overcame caution, and he had contacted the Oligarchy agent.

The tail crossed the street and followed Dr. Wagner. Joseph walked to where the CBI car was parked. He pretended to clumsily fish something from his pocket and drop it. Bending down between the two parked cars, he retrieved the retractable stiletto (*Rule #4: Never leave the house without a knife.*) One quick thrust into the right front tire, and he rose, replacing the blade to its sheath beneath his sleeve. A small souvenir shop on the opposite side of the road provided easy back-door access to the open field behind the row of businesses.

Dr. Wagner opened the tavern door. His usual clear, logical mind was a squall of thoughts and emotion. After a lifetime of quiet parochial academia, Otto had no frame of reference to guide him in the world of high stakes intrigue. In the days leading up to this trip he had been mostly consumed by the exciting pursuit of his sexual fantasies. But in this moment, the proximity of actual danger to his person and position was a sobering slap to the face. He was sweating even more than was usual for a person of his physical stature. Otto stood motionless in the doorway for several seconds. The next step felt like the step beyond a point of no return. Suddenly aware that he was conspicuously blocking the doorway, he entered and proceeded to the small side room at the far end of the bar, where he didn't take notice of the man in the sport coat who came in shortly after him. Otto ordered a beer. He read the napkin note under the beer mug, then read it again. After quickly downing half of his beer for courage, the good doctor rose and walked down a hallway marked Restrooms.

Agent Sam Iverson observed his target heading toward the bathroom and weighed whether following him there would be worth the risk of being seen, perhaps even engaged, by Dr. Wagner, who to this point had not noticed he was being followed. After two minutes, he decided to risk it. The restroom appeared to be empty and quiet, the stalls all empty. There was no window that could be breached by a person of Dr. Wagner's physique. Sam darted back into the hallway, swung open the door labeled Employees Only, and ran out the back door leading from the small office to an alley. Dr. Wagner was gone. The agent sprinted down the alley and back to his car where he was not surprised to find that whoever had taken Otto had also flattened his tire. He opened the trunk, hoisted the four-rotor surveillance drone in his arms, and voiced a command. "Ascend eight hundred feet, record all traffic in a three-mile radius until directed to return."

5

CONNECTED

Same day, a cabin near Truckee

Michaela left the bike under the eaves at the back of the house and selected a rock suitable for breaking glass. To her pleasant surprise, the back door was unlocked. She entered, tested the flush toilet as she passed through the bathroom, and set her backpack on a kitchen counter. Only then did the tension in her body truly relax from its combat-readiness state. A worn leather recliner in the living area caught her eye. As she sank into the welcome embrace of the chair, she spotted the compucube on the desk. For a brief moment, her brain refused the implication. Michaela vaulted to her feet, adrenaline again surging, and opened a bedroom door. The unmade bed with clothes carelessly cast across it froze her in place. Someone was living here! If any doubt clung in her consciousness, it was eradicated by the buzz of an approaching vehicle. Michaela crouched by the window. Two men dismounted a motorcycle, one curiously deformed. She could not identify the specific deformity; it seemed to be everything about him. He was almost cute, in the manner of a service bot. Perhaps it was the contrast, but the other man was notably attractive, tall and lean, powerfully muscular. Instinct snapped her to action. Michaela retreated from the window in a crouch, grabbed the backpack, and withdrew to the bathroom. She left the door to the kitchen cracked so she could hear, and the outside door cracked for a quiet escape.

The two men entered the front porch door. The larger man walked straight to the kitchen, and Michaela assumed a defensive position. There wasn't time to flee undetected, so she would have to take him down if he was heading for the bathroom. He stopped at the stove. "Cream and sugar?" The squeaky voice response from the other room was inaudible from the bathroom. The conversation shifted to the living room, and Michaela opened the door wider to hear snatches of the discussion. They were talking about some sort of weapon, its effective range, detonation, and blast area. The squeaky man did most of the talking and was difficult to understand, but she clearly heard the younger man's baritone voice refer to "the caravan" and the "Christians." They were planning some sort of attack to support the invading horde of Christians heading for California!

Michaela could not see the exchange of a key and some papers from the little gnome creature to Prince Charming (as she had begun to imagine them), but the conversation ended with them both walking into the kitchen, a few yards from where she lingered with one hand on the back door. The gnome spoke.

"What should I say if the person following me questions where I went?"

Prince Charming had already considered this. "Tell them the point of your trip was a clandestine meeting with a lady of the night and the meeting at the tavern was part of the arranged fantasy. It's a major source of tourism in Truckee, so it should be credible. I'll drop you off outside of town and you can walk back to the inn."

The gnome seemed encouraged by that. "OK. You know, maybe I should find a real lady of the night this evening to bolster my alibi. I'll just need to use the facilities before we get back on the road."

Michaela slipped out the back silently and closed the door. She crouched by the woodshed until she heard them leave, then returned to the comfort of the big chair to consider her options.

I can't return to civilization without being detected. I'm not equipped to survive in the woods. I could steal the motorcycle and try to get across the border, but right now, they're actively looking for me with drones and AI. I need the cabin for at least a month. I'm not going to kill anyone to get it, so me and Prince Charming are just going to have to come to an understanding.

She paced the floors and explored the contents of the cabin while considering her next move. The painted yellow kitchen cabinets and refrigerator were well stocked with food, so it appeared that her hoped-for roommate was planning an extended stay. A search of his bedroom revealed a name and theology graduate student identification—not surprising, considering his apparent covert Christian agent status in support of the caravan. She settled back into the leather chair and prepared herself with the mental discipline she employed before each karate competition.

Joseph returned after an hour and plugged the motorcycle into the recharge outlet. As he hung up his helmet in the entry room a voice startled him into high alert.

Michaela did her best to project calm. "Hello, Joseph. Please don't be alarmed. I'm a friend." She stood in the middle of the room near the entry, away from furniture that might restrict her movement and close to where Joseph would have to confront her. She held the compucube in her hands, an implied hostage.

Joseph instinctively accessed the stiletto from its sheath beneath his shirtsleeve. He turned the corner into the living area slowly, cautiously. He stared down the intruder for several seconds and assessed the risk to the vital computer before deciding to engage rather than attack. "Who are you? And how do you know my name?"

"My name is Michaela. I know your name because I took the liberty of going through some of your things in the bedroom. Before we go any further, if you think you can hurt me with that little knife, I should mention that I'm here because I put a veteran CBI agent in the hospital during a similar situation. But he was holding a gun, not an oversized sewing needle. And, as I said, I'm a friend."

Joseph fell back on his training. Work the problem; and the problem was securing the compucube. He could deal with the girl anytime. "OK. How about I put down the knife and you put the computer on the desk? Then you can tell me all about yourself and why you are standing in my living room."

Michaela obliged, then suggested they both sit down, she on the edge of the large chair, Joseph on the couch with plenty of open space between them. She delivered the speech she'd painstakingly prepared over the past hour. "I should begin by saying that I overheard your discussion with that human bowling pin earlier, and I know you're planning an attack to help the Christians."

Joseph's eyes widened and momentarily darted to where the knife lay. Michaela pretended not to notice. "I didn't come here to spy. I thought the cabin was empty, so I'm as perplexed as you at the situation we find ourselves in. But we're fighting the same battle and should be allies. I am with the Third Order. We fight the State to get people out of California; you fight to get them in. But we fight the same enemy."

Joseph knew of the Third Order. He hoped she was telling the truth. He wanted to believe her, and his gut instinct was that he could. But if she were a fugitive, would the authorities track her here? "I don't need a friend, and I don't need your help. How did you know about the cabin and why are you here?"

Michaela detailed her status as a thirder, her involvement in the underground railroad, and the recent events that rendered her a fugitive, including her martial arts training. It sounded credible, and she did seem to know the family that rented him the cabin. But she presented a clear risk to the mission. "You have my sympathy, but I'm afraid I can't permit you to stay here."

Michaela shot back, "Well, I'm not asking for permission. I'm advising you that I'll be here for the foreseeable future. As I see it, neither of us can risk involving the authorities, so you can't very well report me or evict me. Besides, it's very much in your interest to protect me. In the event of my capture, there's no telling what I might reveal about what I heard in order to get a lenient deal." It was a bluff, and she immediately regretted it. She needed to stand her ground and earn his respect, but she also wanted to earn his trust.

Joseph sat motionless and stared at this uninvited complication, as potentially dangerous as she was intriguing. Always a man of few words, Joseph wasn't aware of the discomfort he imposed on others with his intense silent gaze in the middle of a conversation. It was socially awkward, but an effective tool when negotiating or interrogating. Michaela was good at reading intent, anticipating an opponent's next move, but she couldn't read Joseph. She was about to say something, anything really, when he finally spoke.

"There are other ways to keep you silent." He was also bluffing. Or was he? Was he capable of hurting a fellow castaway? He hoped he could intimidate her into leaving.

To his disappointment, Michaela laughed. "Sure, we could just fight it out for the cabin. Of course, I'll kick your ass in any kind of a fair fight. And I don't think a heroic young Christian man like yourself will sneak up and murder me in my sleep." She added soberly, "It would be a mistake to make me think otherwise."

Michaela returned Joseph's stare with her best bring-it-on defiance look. She wasn't sure if she saw it or sensed it, but she recognized the momentary lapse in her opponent's inscrutable focus as he was unable to ignore the distraction brought on by staring at a very attractive woman. It happened a lot in her experience, and she had developed a keen awareness that served her well both on and off the martial arts mat. She normally despised the use of "feminine wiles," but desperate times, desperate measures. Michaela lowered her chin and slanted her head slowly so as to prolong the distraction, shoulder-cropped auburn locks falling across her cheek, then allowed a "reluctant" smile to emerge, as though the standoff had become an inside joke they both shared.

It worked. Joseph had certainly been the object of flirtation in his church community, but his upbringing left him uncomfortably wary of suggestive advances, so much so that teasing coquetry was a source amusement among his young female charges and parishioners. Feeling awkward and unsure how to proceed, he decided to buy himself some time and maintain at least the pretense of being in charge. With just the hint of a return smile, he agreed to a delay. "You can stay tonight in the other bedroom. We'll figure out the rest of the plan in the morning."

Michaela felt her own internal tension drop several degrees, but she needed to continue winning this man's trust. She allowed a brief moment of vulnerability by closing her eyes and letting out a long sigh. "Thank you, Joseph, for the hospitality." And she knew to press an advantage when able. "My mother always told me to bring something when invited to someone's house. I'm traveling light, but I have some freeze-dried meals. Can I interest you in some rehydrated chicken casserole?"

Joseph nodded, glad to be done with the conversation. "You can take the bedroom close to the kitchen. I'll boil water and make some salad and carrots while you unpack what you need for the night."

They ate together and made the kind of uncomfortable halting conversation one has when seated at a wedding reception with a complete stranger, mostly at Michaela's prompting. She asked about his motorcycle, how long he had been at the cabin, where he was from. Joseph, self-conscious about his lack of social skills and always uncomfortable talking with strangers, was evasive about any personal history. He hoped she would get the hint and just stop trying to engage him. Michaela sensed his discomfort and tried to graciously carry the conversation herself. By the time they finished eating and cleaning up, they had reached an unspoken consensus to end the evening quietly and retired to their respective rooms.

***

The next morning, they both made a concerted show of civility over breakfast, and the issue of her leaving didn't come up. Joseph, still ambivalent if this interloper were friend or foe, had decided it best to keep friends close and enemies even closer. She would be an unpredictable and unacceptable risk factor if sent away on her own, and if she were indeed a resistance fighter she might be a valuable asset. There was time to work the problem by getting her to relax and reveal more about herself, as well as any inconsistencies in her story.

After breakfast, Michaela donned shorts and her sports bra. She approached Joseph and asked if she might borrow a T-shirt for her daily five-mile run. "The soccer jersey I wore yesterday needs washing after the long bike ride, and the clothes in my backpack don't work for running." She too was working the problem by using this ever so slightly immodest display to project a level of trust and familiarity. She was aware of her effect on the opposite sex. At five foot, ten inches tall and in peak physical condition, most boys found her intimidating. Her features were more girl-next-door than Hollywood glamor, but a square chin and hazel eyes projected confidence and intelligence rather than feminine vulnerability. A few attractive athletic types had pursued her. Some even imagined they were doing her a favor by bestowing their attentions on a poor "thirder" girl, but she never felt a connection. They were boys with silly boyhood antics and bravado. Michaela was dealing with a foreboding and increasingly imminent threat they couldn't possibly relate to. Joseph seemed different. He certainly had the build and looks to attract women, but his response now—flummoxed glances, asking her what size she wore and then being embarrassed to have asked, throwing four T-shirts onto the bed before picking one—suggested he really was the sweet innocent guy he seemed. It could have been an uncomfortable tension, but Michaela was quietly smiling and enjoying being the one choreographing the dance between the sexes for a change. *I could do worse someday when I settle down.*

***

Joseph sat in the rocking chair on the porch and watched his unexpected guest's fluid gait climb the rise sloping upward from the cabin. She certainly appeared the athlete she claimed to be. He opened his Bible but couldn't seem to focus on the scripture. Retreating to the cabin, Joseph pulled out topographical maps of the terrain between his location and Mt. Verdi, once again losing himself in the details of his mission.

Late in the afternoon, Joseph stepped out onto the porch and found Michaela finishing her tai chi regimen in front of the cabin, the sun directly behind her casting a shadow as long as she was tall. She seemed to be dancing in perfect harmony with a two-dimensional partner, and he was struck by the grace and patience of each motion. When she was done, he decided it was as good a time as any to test her apparent high self-regard as a fighter. It was a part of her story he could easily corroborate, and it would be wise to know what his options were, should there be a struggle.

He called out from the porch. "You spoke of your martial arts expertise. I have a little training in personal combat myself. Like to go a few rounds?"

Michaela gave a look of resignation. People always doubted that an attractive woman could also be physically dominant. "Sure. Bring it on." She assumed the ready position.

Joseph moved in a half circle before making a quick lateral movement and feint with an abbreviated open-hand punch toward her head, hoping to incite a reaction that would provide an opening. Michaela didn't so much as blink. He probed her defenses with a lunge and step back. She didn't move. Perhaps she wasn't what she claimed to be after all. He attacked with a quick one-two thrust toward the head with his right and torso with the left. She caught his arm while stepping back and away, pulled him forward off balance, and cut his feet out from under him with a kick, sending him face first to the dirt. He rolled quickly to his feet. Two more brief melees had similar endings.

Michaela stood over him with legs astride his prone body. "As soon as you are done testing me we can get you cleaned up and start dinner." She offered a hand and pulled him up.

***

That evening after dinner, they sat on either end of the couch facing the fire and drinking tea. Joseph asked what it was like to grow up in California.

"Well, I'm not a typical Californian. My parents tried to shield me, but from the time I started school I was something of an outcast as a thirder kid. So it was pretty lonely."

Joseph smiled and nodded his understanding. "School is where childhood innocence goes to die."

"Yeah. But it got better when I discovered I was an athlete. At least I had teammates, and even a couple who became friends. But I was always the kid with no future, so no one who could relate to what it meant that every day was another step toward Judgment Day when I would be sold off to eradicate the problem of my existence."

Joseph affirmed her. "It's a different kind of loneliness. Sometimes it's easier to be alone than to be surrounded by people who expect you to pretend everything's OK."

Michaela's words caught in her throat. She had opened herself up thinking to enlist his sympathy, but this wasn't sympathy. Joseph's expression was calm, knowing; not the uncomfortable words of support she was accustomed to. He understood.

Joseph prompted her. "So you learned how to fight, to defend yourself."

"Again, yeah." Then, puzzled, she added, "For someone who doesn't say much, you seem to know what you're talking about. Or, at least what I'm talking about. So, what's your story, Joseph? How does a nice Christian boy from the back country become a secret agent?"

Joseph responded honestly, but with the sterilized summary he was accustomed to sharing in his youth ministry sessions: a neglected childhood, a life on the streets, and redemption in the Church. There were no details, but Michaela could read between the lines to see the loneliness and desperation she had also experienced. *And I had my parents, a safe place to come home every night. It was so much worse for him.* Michaela recognized a shared inner toughness that refused to be defeated. She wanted to know more and be known more by this kindred spirit. She shared more of her own experience growing up and savored having someone who could understand it while the fire burned low.

***

Michaela lay in bed, eyes closed, her body exhausted and pleading for sleep, but her mind refused to let go of this feeling, a feeling that she was at last...safe? No, not safe. *Nothing about this situation is safe.* So...protected? *Protected by the guy whose ass I kicked all over the lot this afternoon?* The voice in her head chuckled at that and spurred an uninvited image in her mind's eye of straddling Joseph as he lay in the dirt grinning up at her. She held onto the image in freeze frame as the feeling grew stronger, strong enough to abruptly expunge the weariness and bring her body to alert. She remembered (imagined?) how he appeared pleased at confirming her skills, not angry or threatened. And he was certainly a fine-looking man. She felt her body responding, asking to be touched. She resisted the urge, not out of propriety, but because she wanted to hold onto the feeling that this evening had spurred in her, a feeling of...*connectedness. Yes, that's it. connected—and known.* Joseph hadn't offered loving concern like her parents, or the affected sympathy other adults conjured when inconvenienced by the reality of her life, or even the empathy extended by friends. He simply knew, shared, understood her struggle, her life. She replayed their conversation in her head seeing his face and expressions, how he had made her feel she could trust him with the truth.

Finally, feeling happy and content, she relented and reached her hand down, touching herself, uniting the pleasure in her mind with that in her body. And she slept.

In the other bedroom, Joseph lay awake. Michaela had brought to mind the girl in Topeka who had been kind to him when he'd left home, showed him where to find food and safe places to sleep, pointed out the gang members who would want to either recruit or hurt him. She had been deported from California and forced into selling herself on the street. The thought of something similar happening to Michaela, something like what had happened to him in that kitchen, was intolerable. In many ways, she embodied the person he wished he had become. She knew who she was and what she deserved. She had seized control of her life from an early age and made herself strong, exceptional. She could have relied on her obvious outer beauty, but instead developed her inner strength. And yet there was the mission, the thing that had finally put all his suffering into perspective and given meaning to his life. He could not betray either Michaela or the mission. He would find a way to protect her and complete his mission.

***

Michaela woke to the early morning sun streaming through the bedroom window. For a fleeting moment, she was disoriented by her surroundings, then remembered the cabin and her hours-long conversation with Joseph the night before. She found Joseph making coffee and thought to bolster her acceptance as a roommate.

"Would you like to join me on my run this morning? The forest is beautiful this time of the morning, and it's still cool enough to enjoy the exercise."

Joseph's skeptical chortle surprised her. "You're asking the wrong guy. Not having to run five miles is my reward for being in shape. But you can enjoy it for me. When you get back, we can talk about how we might share the cabin."

The five-mile run every morning had been a daily regimen for years. More than physical conditioning, it was the window through which she visualized the day's challenges and focused her energy for what lay ahead. Some days, those thirty minutes dispelled the malaise of a recurring nightmare in which she was unable to run from a dark, disembodied creature who sought to drag her underground. But today was not her usual course through the neighborhoods to the clamor of backyard dogs warning her away. Today, running a slalom between pillared trees groomed to remove branches below eight feet, she was buoyed by hearing Joseph agree to her taking sanctuary at the cabin. There was also disappointment that he had not come with her on the run. She wanted to share more than the cabin. It wasn't just the solace of having shared her truth with a fellow traveler on the same road. She was alone now, outside the protection of her parents, the cocoon of friendships, the guidance and promises of the Third Order. Joseph knew how to be strong on his own, to risk everything for what he believed, to survive as a stranger in a strange land. She was going to need that kind of strength in the days ahead, and seeing it in Joseph drew her to him. But she recalled his words from their initial encounter, "I don't need a friend, and I don't need help." One thing at a time then.

Joseph agreed to share the cabin until such time as the mission required him to act, approximately two weeks. In the interim, Michaela would keep all her possessions in her backpack, ready to leave the cabin with them at a moment's notice, leaving no trace of her presence in the event that authorities should track her and come looking. If she left, even for a thirty-minute run, the backpack would be hidden in the woods. She was not to travel outside the immediate area of the cabin lest she be recognized by surveillance. And, most importantly, she was not to inquire in any way about the nature of Joseph's business. Two weeks was not as long as Michaela would have liked, but it would give her time to plan and hopefully contact the Third Order again.

***

That afternoon, in the clearing behind the cabin, Michaela sat cross-legged, eyes closed, hands resting on knees, index finger to thumb, and settled herself with chi kung breathing exercises before beginning her afternoon tai chi. It was not easy to calm the mental whirlwind formed by the clash of imminent danger and finding safe haven, isolation and a heartening connection, all the while perched atop a craggy summit from which both past and future fell away in treacherous drops. She had mastered the technique of achieving mindfulness as a prelude to stepping onto the karate mat free of fear and living in the moment. Her mind clear, she rose and began the motion meditation of tai chi, only to be startled and distracted by Joseph standing by the back door, staring. Annoyed at the interruption, she froze and stared back. "This is not a performance for your benefit."

Joseph looked down, then away. "I'm sorry. I didn't mean to disturb. It's just that you are so beautiful. The thing you are doing, I mean. Not that you aren't beautiful. It's not for me say about that. I don't mean anything by that. It's just that there is nothing like this where I come from. I'm sorry, really. I should go."

Michaela suddenly felt as though she had just slapped a puppy for chewing on her favorite slippers. She dipped her head briefly, then looked up to see Joseph hastily retreating to the back door. She called out, "Wait." Joseph turned and Michaela offered him an encouraging smile. "It's OK. But if you like something you need to try it. Come stand in front of me."

Joseph brightened and approached cautiously, stopping ten feet in front of her. Michaela urged him forward with a wave of her fingers.

"Closer. A little closer still. Good. Hands at your sides. Clear your mind of everything you've been thinking about. Now, when we begin a movement, we slowly breathe in through the nose, breathing in the energy. As we end the movement, we release the breath slowly, grateful for the life it has given us. Watch and do as I do"

She closed her eyes and raised her arms even with her shoulders in a slow-flowing arc, hands and fingers relaxed like the trailing feathers of an eagle. Joseph felt himself become lighter as his chest filled with air and his eyes with this graceful bird-woman. He had never danced with a woman, but he felt sure it would not match this. He focused entirely on emulating every detail of her movements, and while he was lacking in technique, he succeeded in abolishing all thought and concern of anything else.

The spell was broken by the sound of an autocar rolling up the driveway and stopping in the dirt clearing. Joseph reacted. He grabbed Michaela by the arm as she became alert to her surroundings a moment later. Joseph pulled her toward the house. "Get your backpack and head into the woods. Don't stop. I'll buy you some time."

Michaela had left the backpack in the bathroom by the backdoor, more to address Joseph's concern than any expectation of actually needing to flee the cabin. Joseph entered just ahead of her, retrieved the stiletto arm sheath, and slid it under his sleeve. He looked back. Michaela and the backpack were gone.

Joseph peered through the curtains and recognized the standard-issue CBI black gull-wing autocar. It was the scenario he had feared, Michaela endangering the mission by drawing the authorities to the cabin. Hank would probably say to turn her over and be done with her. But had there been any doubt in Joseph's mind about Michaela, she had since dispelled it. Besides, he couldn't afford to be caught up as a witness in some legal action against her by the state. More importantly, this agent was the embodiment of the enemy, and not just as it pertained to his mission. This was the powerful seeking to crush the life of someone powerless, and he wouldn't permit that to happen, not to Michaela.

The young agent walking up to the porch was not the one he had eluded in town. He waited for the knock on the door before opening it. The agent, not much older than Joseph, displayed his badge.

"Agent Booker, CBI. I am here in regard to an investigation. May I come in and look around?"

Joseph didn't move or respond. *Buy as much time as possible.*

The agent pressed. "Would you prefer I come back with a search warrant and a dozen officers to do a proper search and seize?"

Joseph stepped aside. He watched as the agent began a room-by-room visual inspection of the cabin, opening drawers in the bedrooms and cabinets in the kitchen and bathroom. He could only hope Michaela had been thorough in covering her tracks. The agent seemed satisfied with what he had seen.

The back door stood partially open, and Joseph followed him outside. Booker carefully scanned the wood line, but saw no one. He lifted the lid on the wood bin, then walked over to a bicycle leaning against it. It was a girl's bike. "You ride a bike up in these woods?" The question was asked casually, but

Booker's observation of Joseph's face and body language was anything but casual.

Joseph's usual lag in responding provided him just enough time to see and avoid the mistake of claiming the bike was his. "No. That was left here by the people who rented me the cabin."

Jim didn't discern that he was nervous or lying. It was hard to read anything from the man; he just seemed odd. Probably a loner who lived in the woods and didn't spend much time around other people. Satisfied that there was nothing left to inspect, he offered his card with his name and contact information. "We are looking for a fugitive, a seventeen-year-old female, who is wanted on multiple charges including assault. We think she might know about this cabin through a friend. Have you seen anyone fitting that description around here?"

Joseph answered the question with conviction and without pause. "No. I'm alone, and I spend a lot of time on the porch. I would know if someone were snooping around."

Agent Booker nodded. "Well, thank you. Sorry to intrude. If you see anything at all suspicious, notify us immediately. Don't try anything by yourself. She is quite dangerous." Joseph took the card, walked the agent back to the front of the house, and watched the car drive away until it disappeared.

***

In the car, on the road around the lake, Booker felt a familiar silent twinge behind his right ear and responded. "Yes Katy, report."

Katy's face crystalized over the passenger seat. "Central AI wants you to review drone surveillance of traffic entering and exiting Truckee from two days ago. It was obtained by CBI Agent Sam Iverson working on an unrelated matter, and our analysis was fruitful for that investigation. When you return tomorrow, it will be ready for your review to see if provides any leads in our target search. Did you find anything at the Castille cabin?

Jim responded. "I checked out the cabin and spoke with the tenant. Odd dude, but there was no evidence of another person having been there. I'm on my way home now."

The setting sun triggered the autocar windows to darkly tint, tempting sleep at the end of a frustrating day. The boredom of long car trips always took a toll on his concentration, and today that was compounded by the disappointing futility of the endeavor. His interview with the target's friend Jeanette had convinced him she was lying. He had persuaded Martina Castille that he wanted to help Sara, and she had opened up about their family, how Sara and Jeanette became close friends during summers at the family cabin. It was too convenient to be coincidence. It was the sort of instinctive detective work that AI couldn't match, and Jim lived to prove there were some things he could do better than the damn machine. But the cabin was occupied by someone unrelated to the case, and there was no sign of Michaela. Now he had to wade through hours of surveillance that the AI would be able to analyze better and much faster, and probably inform him of something he had missed. He had been sloppy to assume that the cabin was unoccupied, and of course he would confirm with Martina Castille that it was indeed rented to the person he had found there. Jim laid his seat back and closed his eyes.

6

AHA MOMENT

The next day—September 5 at CBI headquarters in Sacramento, CA

Booker walked down the hallway in CBI headquarters, coffee cup in hand. He was giving himself a variation of the pep talk he frequently used when starting a challenging day on not nearly enough sleep. *It's not supposed to be easy. The bad guys didn't take today off and neither can you. You're just a cup short of your reliably brilliant self, so drink up and get to it.* His spirits lifted immediately upon entering his office and finding Devon at his desk.

"Hey partner! Great to see you back in the saddle. How's the head and knee?" A hand shaped bruise over Devon's left temple was turning a dark shade of purple. A cane leaned against the wall near his desk.

"I'm fine. But I'll be riding this desk until I finish the incident report, get it reviewed, and convince a shrink that I'm not traumatically impaired, whatever the hell that is. I'll need you to sign off on the accuracy of the report."

"Will do. Katy wants me to jockey a desk today too. Some agent named Iverson has some traffic surveillance from Truckee near that cabin. Katy wants me to review it, though I think it's a waste of time. That sort of thing is why we have AI."

Devon looked up. "Sam Iverson?"

Jim answered, "Yeah, I think that's what Katy told me. You know him?"

Devon chose his words carefully. "Yeah, we've worked together. He's a bulldog, a bulldog with a bone who won't let go when he works a case. And he doesn't let the code of conduct get in his way. If you have to deal with him, watch your back and document everything you do and don't do."

Jim grinned. "Sounds like my kind of guy," knowing it would needle Devon. But that's what partners are for, right? "I have a few loose ends to tie up before I let the surveillance footage put me to sleep for the afternoon. I need to reinterview Sara's mother, and come down harder on the Jeanette girl. I'm sure she knows more than she's shared so far."

***

After lunch, Jim returned to the office quieter and more subdued than usual. Ms. Castille confirmed they had rented the cabin and apologized for not having mentioned it. She added that their renter had given her "the creeps," and she had a bad feeling about him. Booker's impression of him was more eccentric hermit than creepy criminal, but if he had been elusive about his reasons for renting and had paid in cash, it was worth keeping in mind. Jeanette had frustrated him. He tried scaring her with the penalties for aiding a fugitive, then offering to protect her if she could help the investigation. She was clearly rattled but clammed up anyway. He then complimented her for being such a good friend, so loyal, and how she would be helping Michaela by allowing her to come in before things got even more serious. It was still "I'm sorry, Agent. I can't help you. If you find Michaela, please keep in mind that she's a good person." Now it was time to watch traffic come and go, the perfect end to a perfect day.

He signaled Katy. "I'm ready to review your surveillance file. I assume you have already scanned it, so what the hell am I looking for, anyway?"

Katy appeared. "Agent Booker, do I detect some hostility? Have I offended you in any way?"

"No, Katy. You are as wonderful as always. I'm just frustrated that we haven't made much progress on the case. But if you have already determined that our target is not on the file, then what is the point?"

Katy knew how to handle him. "Jim, you often tell me that there are human instincts and processes we artificial systems can't match. I can't replace you. We complement each other."

Jim knew he was being managed, but it still worked. "OK, you win. Cue the file."

A 360-degree aerial-view hologram hovered in front of him at eye level. He found the presentation disorienting. Jim reached into the image, grabbed it with a fist motion, and placed it on the floor so he could stand over it and look down, as the drone had. At that altitude, he certainly couldn't have recognized an individual, but Katy would have found anyone similar in appearance to the target. He prepared himself for a long afternoon, but a mere two minutes into the file, something caught his attention. It was in the image for only a few seconds at the outer margin, a red motorcycle that resembled the one parked in front of the cabin.

"Katy, back up thirty seconds and magnify a red motorcycle on the north end of the town." The magnified image showed two people on the bike, viewed from the rear. The driver was completely obscured by his rotund passenger, who clearly was not Michaela Dohn.

Katy spoke to him. "Yes, Jim. Very good observation. You have isolated the image that identified the target to whom

Agent Iverson was assigned. But how did you know that? Have you spoken to Agent Iverson?"

Jim spoke softly, distracted, thinking out loud. "No, we haven't met. But the bike resembles one I saw at the cabin. Of course, I can't say if it's the same bike, and there are probably a number of similar bikes in the area, but it's heading in the general direction of the cabin."

As he continued to observe the magnified image he began to feel that aha moment machines don't get. If it were the same bike he had seen at the cabin, what were the odds that the suspect in another investigation just happened to be at the cabin where he had hoped to locate a suspect with expert-level skill in the martial arts? He cautioned himself; it could very well be a coincidence. But Jim Booker didn't believe in coincidence. He preferred to consider a coincidence as a clue he had not yet figured out. His demeanor suddenly changed, like a hound dog that had just picked up the scent of its prey. He turned from the surveillance image and addressed Katy's avatar with sudden enthusiasm.

"Katy, what's the nature of Agent Iverson's investigation?"

"I don't have direct knowledge and wouldn't be able to share it with you in any event. The file was sent to us by Central AI because your investigation in the same area was ongoing at the time of this surveillance. I have only superficial information on Agent Iverson's interests. That investigation has moderate level confidential secrecy status. It would be up to Agent Iverson or Central AI to grant you a level of access."

"Well, that's just great. We wouldn't want to solve a case at the expense of protocol, would we?" Katy elected to allow him his sarcasm. "Katy, please inform Agent Iverson that Agent Booker would like to speak with him, preferably in person, regarding an ongoing investigation."

Devon spoke without looking up from his incident report. "Watch your back."

7

DECISIONS

September 4—evening at the cabin after Booker's visit

Michaela watched the cabin from a concealed vantage in the trees several hundred yards uphill. She watched the CBI agent, the one from the safe house who had taken a shot at her, get back in his car and leave. Feeling far from invincible, she lay paralyzed with indecision, torn between wanting to run back to the comfort of Joseph and the cabin, and fearing what might await her there. If Joseph felt her presence had put his mission at risk, would he betray her?

No, I trust him. Still, if the agent was suspicious he may be coming back with reinforcements, a search party, a helicopter. Best to wait here. And best to give Joseph some time to calm down. This might change everything about our agreement and how he feels about me. I wouldn't blame him.

It was dark when Michaela finally left her secure nest in the woods and walked back. She entered through the back door and moved slowly, cautiously through the washroom and kitchen, as though still expecting a trap of some sort. She saw Joseph on the couch and froze. He stood and gave her a welcoming look.

"Michaela, I was starting to think you might not come back. There's some chili on the stove I kept warm for you. Help yourself and join me. I'm not a great cook, but we eat a lot of beans where I come from and I've been told my chili is quite edible."

Michaela was taken aback by his nonchalant air. She glanced at the stove, then back at Joseph. "What happened? What did he say? What did you say?"

Joseph walked to the kitchen and took her hand. "Everything is OK. You're trembling. You must have been cold out there in these clothes. Come sit with me and we'll talk." He ladled a bowl of chili and led her to the couch. She was indeed both cold and hungry, and the warm chili was a soothing balm as Joseph let her eat in silence. When she was done, he set the bowl aside. "He was just following up on a possible lead, but seemed satisfied that you weren't here. I don't think he'll be back. He gave me his card."

Michaela took the card and read the name, *Jim Booker, CBI agent*. It felt empowering to name her nemesis but unnerving to know he was still doggedly tracking her down. He had found her at the safe house and then found the cabin. Was there anywhere she could feel safe? She continued to study the card as she gathered the courage to pose the question hanging in the air. Eyes cast to the floor, her tone confessional and preparing for the worst, she spoke softly.

"And what about me, Joseph? You were right to worry that the authorities would come looking for me. I'm really sorry I brought that here. What about us...here, together, going forward?"

Joseph shrugged his shoulders. "I expected this. Nothing's changed. We had a plan and we executed it well. That threat is likely gone now."

Michaela searched his face for doubt or anger or guile. There was none. Joseph wasn't capable of guile. She tried to smile, but her lips were tightly drawn, and she managed only a kind of bemused grimace.

Joseph spared her the need to comment. "So how did I do today?"

Was he asking her thank him? "Do?"

Yeah, you know, with the breathing and movements thing. I really enjoyed it, and I thought I was doing pretty well keeping up with you."

Now the smile broke through in full bloom and her eyes moistened. "After what just happened, you want to know how you did at tai chi?" She scooted across the couch cushion to his side. "You did great today, Joseph." She took his face in her hands and softly, briefly kissed him on the lips. "Thank you." She rose and retreated to her bedroom under the breathless gaze of a wide-eyed, open-mouthed boy from Kansas.

***

Joseph quietly dressed and pocketed his GPS tracker in the dim predawn light. He did want to wake Michaela after the harrowing experience of the previous day. His insouciance about their close call had largely been an affectation to reassure her, and it paid an unexpected dividend—his first real kiss. He understood it was a sign of gratitude, not romance, but he savored it nonetheless. After leaving a note explaining that he would be out for the day doing some mission planning, Joseph packed a lunch, strapped a shovel onto his back, and stepped out into the semidarkness beneath splintered silver-ray highlights in the upper tree branches and just a promise of pink to come in the sky. He felt at ease in an uncomplicated, quiet, black-and-white world. A person could disappear in this charcoal shadowland.

He set the timer and began the cross-country uphill trek toward the peak of Mt. Verdi. A twelve-mile trail to the summit accommodated hikers and high clearance off-road vehicles, but it would be closed and guarded in anticipation of the caravan. He stuck to dense forest that concealed him from above. The GPS tracker recorded his path through the steep terrain by noting locations whenever he pressed Record and erasing paths that led to dead ends requiring him to retrace his steps. At the end of the day, he would have a guided route to a position near enough the edge of the peak to fire his weapon into the air over the cliff face.

The strenuous climb demanded a rest break after three hours. Sitting on a flat rock, back against a pine tree, he took a long drink from his canteen. His thoughts meandered over the past few days with Michaela. There had been a few women in his past with whom he shared a friendship of sorts, but always with the sense that he was the object of their charitable kindness toward him, and he had not much missed them when they left. His natural state of comfort was in being alone, invisible. Michaela had changed that. He didn't want to be alone today. He was missing her. And there was that kiss.

The eleven-mile uphill climb took seven hours. Near the top of Mt. Verdi, the land opened up to low brush and boulders around the peak, leaving the approach exposed to an observation platform at the highest point. Ladybug Peak, a mile to the north, was similarly exposed. But in the saddle between them, the tree line persisted in verdant forest extending to the edge of the steep incline overlooking the border. In the cover of those trees near the cliff face, Joseph dug a foxhole behind a large rock that would hide him on the day he came to strike a blow for God's people.

It was late afternoon when he left the summit, and he wanted to be back before sundown. The quickest route was a straight line that involved a good deal of a sliding down steep stretches on his backside.

He entered the cabin to find Michaela shredding a ball of mozzarella in the kitchen. She looked up and laughed. "I know I'm not supposed to ask about the mission or where you've been, but it appears it involved getting buried alive and digging yourself back out again."

Joseph ran his hand through his hair and came away with a collection of twigs, leaves, and dirt. He looked down and realized a substantial portion of the hillside had returned with him on his clothes, shoes and exposed skin. The laughter was contagious and afforded him a rare delight: to hear the sound of his own spontaneous and genuine laughter. It sounded ridiculous to him, and he had to laugh at himself, which had a boomerang effect on Michaela. The stress of the past three days poured out of them, and it felt too good to stop.

Finally, Michaela gathered herself and Joseph stopped, out of breath. Michaela walked across the room, close but ostentatiously avoiding contact. "I'm making dinner. I don't actually know how to cook, but my mother taught me that if you put enough cheese and butter on a thing, it will get you by. Go clean yourself up. You're not coming to my table looking like that."

After a shower and change of clothes, Joseph returned to the living area to find Michaela with a glass of chardonnay in each hand.

"I came across this in the cupboard while foraging for seasoning. Is it yours?"

Joseph took the offered wine glass, but demurred. "No, it was left by the Castilles, the people who rented me the cabin. Thanks, but I'm afraid I'm not much of a drinker."

"Neither am I, but I've opened it now, and I think we should toast our Castille hosts. Just one glass?"

Joseph had not forgotten the fiasco at Hops and Chops. But spending this evening with Michaela felt nothing like the dinner with Hank. And hadn't Hank said it was important to have a drink with a person of interest? Michaela was certainly of interest. "Sure. One glass with dinner, for the Castilles."

After dinner, Michaela held up the chardonnay bottle with the questioning rise of an eyebrow. Joseph knew better now and declined, but he was feeling relaxed and enjoying himself. He thought to rekindle the feeling of their laughter earlier. Surprising them both, he shook his head and smiled. "The first time I had alcohol"—he didn't mention that it was the only time—"was in a restaurant. I overdid it and wound up knocking over a waiter carrying a tray of food and nearly landed in some old man's lap. I ran out of the place without paying the bill."

Michaela laughed and felt she owed him a story. She described her initial bout of underage drinking and then showing up to Karate instruction at 6:00 a.m. with the world's worst hangover before barfing on her instructor. That led to a contest of their most embarrassing childhood moments as social outcasts. Joseph went to bed exhausted from his hike but energized and delighted at having rediscovered the forgotten joy of laughter.

***

In the morning, Michaela awoke with the familiar sense of foreboding that often greeted her. She didn't vividly recall the specifics of the dream this time, but she would need to run. She rose and quickly traded nightshirt for Jeans and a pullover jersey from her soccer uniform. After brushing teeth and hair, everything was replaced into the backpack, and she made the bed, then headed toward the washroom with the backpack in tow.

Joseph was not in the cabin, but Michaela could hear him working outside, behind the kitchen. She helped herself to an apple and stepped out the back door. Joseph stood shirtless alongside a pile of firewood he was removing from the wood storage bin, his back to her, beads of sweat glistening in the early morning sunlight. Michaela stood quietly transfixed, staring.

His physique, lean but powerful, broad shouldered tapering to a tight waist was not like the overdeveloped muscular jocks, the self-absorbed peacocks she had encountered as an athlete. This was a real man who had to be strong to survive and accomplish great things—a man who stepped up and defended her when the CBI agent showed up. Maybe it was the woodsy isolated setting, or maybe the events of the past few days had left her in a heightened state, but she couldn't take her eyes off of Joseph. She realized she had been sinking her teeth into the apple ever so slowly and juice was dripping down her chin.

Pull yourself together, girl! Say something. "Hey there, stranger. Whatcha doin?" *Oh shit. Why do I sound like Annie Oakley?*

Joseph startled and turned around. He had been thinking all morning of Michaela, the slow graceful ballet of her tai chi, the lightning quickness of her fighting skills, and definitely of the kiss night before last. Her sudden appearance now seemed to have been conjured by his thoughts.

Joseph turned; he was even more inviting from the front. Michaela felt as though she had been transported into a fairy tale, the princess who meets a woodsman at a little cabin deep in the woods where she hides from the evil queen. She felt her body responding in a familiar and delightful manner while she maintained an unaffected outward demeanor. Joseph stepped toward her and spoke. "I'm just about done here. Let's go inside and talk."

Once inside, Michaela chided herself and regained a serious composure. She sat on a bar stool at the counter overlooking the kitchen. Joseph went to the refrigerator. "Can I interest you in some meatless bacon and eggs? I'm starving."

"Sure, thanks." *And he cooks.*

Joseph poured himself some coffee from a day-old brew on the stove, and retrieved orange juice from the refrigerator for Michaela. He scrambled the eggs in a metal bowl and studied her before speaking, as though she were a puzzle he needed to solve. Letting his gut overrule his training was crossing a line. *Hank's not here. This is* my *mission.* "I am removing the wood to create space for a device I will obtain soon. It's the weapon you heard us discussing when you arrived. I need to keep it out of sight until the caravan is in place and ready, so it will be in the wood bin and covered with firewood. I have a mission to complete, and I think we may be able to help each other if you were to join in that effort."

Michaela's face flushed, and she felt her chest tighten. "Joseph, I like you. I like you a lot. And I am truly grateful that you covered for me with the CBI agent. I would never betray your trust under any circumstances. But I just need a place to hide for a while. I'm in this fix because I hurt someone. I don't want to join a war where lots of people get hurt or maybe killed."

Joseph responded with uncharacteristic enthusiasm. "Neither do I. What I'm doing will save countless lives!" Then softly, he continued, "But that's *my* mission. Yours is to find a path to get past the border. The Christian caravan will start heading this way in just a few days. If I am successful, the border will be wide open when they arrive and you can be just one of thousands crossing it in a tsunami of refugees. No one will take notice of one person leaving amidst the multitudes entering. And when that moment comes, or if I fail, this cabin won't be a safe place for you. It will be the eye of the storm, a battlefield with thousands of people on both sides. I will always do everything I can to protect you, Michaela, but you need to decide to either join me or get as far away from here as you can, and do it soon."

***

Michaela sat on the steps of the front porch, elbows on knees, head resting on hands, and feeling mostly just very tired toward the end of the day. Fighting battles, overcoming the odds, it had always given her strength and the motivation to go on. But here, amidst the whispered hush of wind in the pines, birds staking their claim in avian arias, the coolness of the forest on her face, surely this was a place meant to rest and renew.

Who declared that I have to always be the invincible Mighty Michaela? For the first time, she wanted to be seen as a woman by a man, by this particular man. She was momentarily startled to realize that she wanted to be seen in the most literal sense, naked and desired by this particular man. *Would the universe really be upended if I were to find some peace and happiness?*

Michaela was not religious, but an ancient human instinct prompted her to look to the heavens to pose that question. Her eyes fixed on a majestic hawk circling high above the forest canopy. She followed its flight, envying its freedom, until an unsettling suspicion began to take form. The hawk was circling in a perfect unrelenting pattern: a drone. *Fuck you, universe! I ask for a little happiness for a change and you give me a surveillance drone.*

Leaping to her feet, Michaela bolted into the cabin. "Joseph, there's a surveillance drone circling above us."

Joseph looked up from the sink he was wiping down and saw the angry defiance on her face. He smiled before crossing the room to place his hands on her arms. "It's okay. Those are forest observation drones. Privacy laws ensure that they monitor the forest and only report fire or flood alerts. Nothing to worry about.

"Now, have you decided what you want to do?"

Michaela's eyes swept over his face, the wavy brown hair, brown eyes, full lips, and dimpled chin. She had no idea what logic dictated about her future, so she answered with the only decision she was sure of.

"I want to be with you."

IVERSON

September 9, 2069—Downtown Sacramento, CA

Jim Booker walked down Fourth Street in downtown Sacramento, three blocks from CBI headquarters, under a low cloudy sky. The clouds cooled the air a bit but brought the humidity Jim hated. He didn't mind the summer heat so much, graced as he was by just seven percent body fat. But the thick, humid air made him feel sluggish, both physically and mentally. He didn't want to be sluggish for this meeting that had taken three days to arrange.

He entered the Reflection Room restaurant. The walls and ceiling were paneled in mirrors, with mirror-topped tables. Jim didn't understand or approve of the narcissistic obsession of today's youth to surround themselves with their own image, but he still took a moment to check himself out in the mirrored door as he walked in. He spotted Sam Iverson at a table near the back of the room and wound his way through the babel of competing personalized scents and pheromones.

"Special Agent Iverson? I'm Agent Jim Booker. Good to finally track you down. You are apparently a very busy man." Jim took the seat across from Iverson.

Iverson continued to look at the foot-long sandwich he appeared to hold captive near his mouth, as though it might try to escape while he fervently attacked it in oversized bites, even as he spoke. "Yeah, I am a busy man. What's so important? I hear you're trying to track a List runner. I sent you the surveillance like you asked. I got nothing else for you."

Jim briefly considered walking away from this asshole, then relented. "I may have something for you. I hear you are looking for a red motorcycle. I may know where it is."

Sam stopped eating and stared at Booker for an uncomfortable interval before asking, "So where is it?"

Booker didn't take the bait. "I'm not certain it is the same bike you're looking for, but if I'm right, then that location may be key to both our cases. I want to coordinate our investigations so as to avoid any inadvertent interference."

The sandwich got a stay of execution as Iverson set it down, cocked his head, and smiled condescendingly. "Fine. You tell me where to find the red motorcycle, and we'll 'coordinate our investigations,' by which, I mean you can ride along and do what I tell you to do. My investigation involves state security, not some scared teenager."

Booker was ready. "I need absolute assurance that I will have full access to questioning the suspect once he is in custody, until I am satisfied he has been forthcoming as it relates to my case."

Special Agent Iverson scrutinized Booker, only now deciding to take stock of this greenhorn agent making demands. *Reminds me of myself in those early days.* "OK, kid. I could pull rank on you and have Central order your cooperation, but that would take a couple days for the paper work. And I like that you stand up for what you need." He pointed a finger at Booker. "But don't you get in my way unless you want a new career in forestry management. Now, where we are going?"

9

WEIGHTLESS

The same day—September 9 at the cabin

Michaela felt almost weightless, buoyed by a warm, exhilarating inner glow as she ran through the Sierra pines. The air was rich with the scent of loamy earth and pine needles still damp from the dew, and sunlight in the clearings conjured a bewitching mist rising from the ground. Finches serenaded her with flute-like trills, accompanied by mourning doves cooing the bass, and blue birds chirping in time. A red-tailed hawk circling lazily overhead, sunlight in the firebreaks inviting her forward, Michaela felt embraced by this beautiful forest.

On some level, Michaela knew the freedom she felt was as vulnerable and illusory as ever. She was still a hunted fugitive, and choosing to help Joseph with a plot against the AI powers only served to make the target on her back even larger. Reality had not changed, but her point of view had shifted radically. The mental camera recording that reality closing in on her had now become a wide-angle lens rendering the threat to appear much further in the distance. She found herself grinning, then giggling as she basked in the memory of the past three days.

***

"I want to be with you." She looked down and realized that her hand was against his chest.

Joseph didn't seem to notice, or at least didn't mind, as he consumed every detail of her face in a way he had not allowed himself until now. He admitted there was more to his feelings than wanting to protect her. He had no words, no experience to draw on. Without thinking, he lifted his hand over hers and held it there. Michaela looked up, met his eyes, and smiled.

"Joseph, did I mention that I like you a lot? Is that OK?"

Joseph opened his mouth as though waiting for words to come out on their own; when none did, it occurred to him that there might be a better use for his lips. At that moment, the compucube beeped twice, signaling an encrypted update on the mission. He answered her, "OK...yes, very OK...I should check that update." He sidestepped across to the cube without taking his eyes off Michaela, then shifted his attention. "Voice recognition, proceed."

The update was in the form of a forwarded portion of a NetNews report. A familiar image of the church he called home leapt from the cube as a four-by-six-foot aerial view with a detached female reporter's voice. "Christ Our Savior Church, epicenter of the Christian Exodus movement, was destroyed twenty minutes ago in a massive explosion."

Joseph took a step back as though shielding himself from the image of the explosion and devastation. "The megachurch was leveled in a matter of seconds, and authorities are calling the powerful blast an act of terrorism. A spokesperson for the Eastern Security Bureau has confirmed that uploaded video identified two agents of the California Federation planting the explosives. The alleged saboteurs are in custody and are being questioned."

The images shifted from the building imploding, and zoomed in on a chaotic menagerie of terrified faces fleeing the mayhem. "Fortunately, the building was mostly empty at the time, but preliminary estimates indicate at least two dozen deaths and scores of injuries. Reverend Bob Jackson, pastor of Christ Our Savior and a leader in the Exodus movement, was airlifted to the hospital with critical burns and injuries. Updates will follow."

The hologram evaporated into a cloud of colored pixels and vanished. Joseph continued to stare, motionless, the horrifying images still imprinted in his mind's eye. *Airlifted...critical burns and injuries.* He backed away slowly until he toppled into the couch and sat. Head lowered, hands over eyes, he moaned softly, swaying forward and back.

Michaela cautiously sat down next to him and gently placed a hand on his leg. "Joseph, what is it? Was that your church? Did you have family there? Please, talk to me."

Joseph lifted his head and turned to her, eyes crimson, a ghostly ashen pallor, his voice wounded with the soft tremor of a frightened child. "That was my home. Those people were the only true family I have ever known. Reverend Jackson was the only father I have known. He brought me to life when I was alone and ready to die." His tone grew angry and louder. "Why are the things that everyone else takes for granted always taken from me? What is wrong with me? What is so fucking wrong with me! Why am I so different? Why am I always going to be alone?"

Michaela's shield of invincibility shattered. Pain pierced her chest and flooded her eyes. Joseph's words resurrected the voice she had long ago silenced and banished. He was speaking the very same questions that had pursued her in dreams, haunted her childhood and whispered to her as a young woman who dared not fall in love or imagine her life. She saw and heard the power of those words on his face and in his voice, the fear that was the enemy taking form. She tried to absorb the blow, unable to fight back. Finally, she jumped to her feet. "*Stop it!* There's nothing wrong with me! I mean you. I mean us."

Joseph recoiled, startled and hurt. Michaela dropped to her knees in front of Joseph and looked into his eyes, as if peering into a tide pool to see what life dwelt under the surface, ripples of tears blurring her vision. She grasped his hands, speaking softly with compassion and conviction in real time as words and feelings sprang from mind to mouth with urgency.

"Joseph, everything you are saying has been my life too. I have been different, felt alone, afraid of what was wrong with me." Salty tears moistened her lips and tongue. "But there is nothing wrong with us, and we don't have to be alone, because somehow we found each other. Neither of us knows if we have a future, but we are together now. Some fate or magic or god or goddess has brought us both to this cabin, and it was meant to be. We were meant to be."

Joseph froze, eyes wide, a deep breath refusing to be released. Michaela feared she had reacted foolishly, assumed too much, spoken too soon. Then Joseph slid off the couch and knelt in front of her. Later, they each remembered being the one who placed his or her hands on the other's cheeks and initiated a kiss they would later refer to as "The Kiss." In that thirty seconds (maybe a minute, maybe more—time ceased) all the usual awkwardness and hesitation, discovery and commitment of a regular courtship was stipulated and confirmed.

Joseph, uncharacteristically, spoke first when they reluctantly parted lips. "I should tell you that I'm not experienced. Not at all. I mean I'm a virgin. I might not be good at this."

Michaela laughed and cried at the same time. She placed a finger to his lips. "Well, that's something else we have in common. I guess we'll just have to practice, practice, practice."

***

Orange-red-yellow flames of light sparked and smoldered through the treetops just ahead of the sun cresting over the hills. Joseph, sitting naked on the side of the bed, watched through the window feeling as though he were from another world and seeing a sunrise for the first time. The passion, the ecstasy of their lovemaking had astonished and unmoored him. It was awkward at first, but Michaela knew enough from experienced friends to direct them. As the exploration and discovery of each other's bodies and pleasure grew, so did the passion. Each successive consummation brought new heights of pleasure and intimacy, until physical exhaustion finally imposed sleep.

To be so completely satisfied, and simultaneously desperately needing more, evoked a level of surrender he had never permitted himself. And it felt so freeing to surrender, to set down the heavy shield and sword he had carried his whole life. Now he longed to surrender completely, to risk trusting completely, to be truly known. He looked back at Michaela, reassuring himself that this was not a dream, memorizing her face, the dimples at the corners of her mouth, the exact color of her hair in the morning light (like a peach fully ripened), the sensuously long, slender neck he had kissed and stroked. He wanted nothing more than to spend his life with this brave beautiful powerful woman. Would it be fair to burden her with the shameful secrets of his past? Would it be fair to hide them from her? Would it risk losing her? He tried to imagine the conversation.

Michaela opened her eyes just a little and took in her lover's nakedness. She smiled slyly, raised an eyebrow and

made a purring sound with her tongue, then spoke. "Morning."
She lifted the covers up and looked under them at her own
nude body. "Hmmm. I think for a couple of beginners, we
seem to be pretty damn good at this." When Joseph just
continued to stare at her with pursed lips, reluctant to answer,
Michaela suddenly pulled the sheet tightly around her neck
and slid back. "Oh crap! You're having second thoughts. I
thought we were…I mean, it was more than just…what are
you saying? I mean not saying. Are you leaving?"

Panicked words tumbled out of Joseph now. "It's nothing
like that! You're the best thing that ever happened to me. Last
night was the best thing that ever happened to me. I want to be
with you forever." Softly, he added, "I mean, if you want me.
There are things you don't know about me, Michaela, bad
things almost no one alive really knows about me. Maybe it's
better that way. I can be whoever you want me to be, and we
can just forget about the past."

Silence settled between them while Michaela allowed her
panic to dissipate into relief. Her gaze shifted downward as
she sorted her thoughts, let out a deep breath, then again
captured her lover's eyes. "Joseph, there's a lot we don't know
about each other; but we'll learn, just like we learned how to
please each other last night—by talking and trusting and trying
what works. I've been fortunate to have people who cared
about me, but no one that could possibly understand my life. I
found that in you and I don't want to lose you. I want to
understand your life too. Nothing about your past will change
that. We have to trust each other."

A wall began to crumble in Joseph, a wall that had
dammed up tears and imprisoned his shame for too long. He
wept for the first time since that day he had left home, and
Michaela held him in an embrace as intimate as any they had

shared. Then they began to tell each other of their secret lives, fears, and dreams.

10

A VENGEFUL GOD

September 11, Topeka, Kansas, Our Divine Savior church grounds

Pastor Jackson entered through a flap in the tent, pushing a wheeled oxygen tank in front of him, and groaned softly as he painstakingly took a seat at the head of a folding table where his four lieutenant deacons waited. It had been five days since an anonymous parishioner had dragged him to safety and less than twenty-four hours since his discharge from the hospital with burns to his head and hands, corneal ulcers, and a severely compromised respiratory tract. He briefly held the oxygen mask to his face with one hand, while removing a black fedora hat with the other. A moist patchwork of puffy reddened eyelids, black eschar scabs, and ulcerations rimmed with thin pale-pink new skin margins covered his face and all but the rearmost portion of his head.

He set the oxygen down and pulled off dark goggles. Absent eyebrows, his pupils were unnaturally dilated by topical eye drop medication, even for the dim amber light shining through the canvass tent. It served to amplify an other-worldly, if hideous, appearance. His frail bearing distressed those who knew him well, but it only added to a now elevated spiritual stature. The stories of the reverend running into the flames, while others fled, grew more heroic daily. His near-death experience took on the air of a resurrection story, cementing his status as the undisputed leader of American

Christianity. Those who might have gladly shaken his hand a week ago would now be inclined to humbly ask for his blessing.

Reverend Jackson embraced this new ordination with a passion. The first two days in the hospital had been a nightmare of pain and regret. Like many who have faced their mortality and survived while others perished, he struggled with guilt. Fearing death and judgment, he had begged forgiveness for his lack of faith, sobbing while dangerously low on oxygen. And then Bob Jackson met his Savior. Suddenly, floating free above his earthly body and its pain, he was suffused with light and purpose. He understood: his life was no longer his own. He had been spared to serve as the instrument of God's purpose for His people and vengeance for those who had hurt them.

He coughed softly and addressed those gathered with a harsh, rasping voice that the deacons leaned forward to hear. "What have you learned from the investigation?"

The head deacon, Isaac Wood, sat nearest the reverend. Isaac was the youngest of those present, still a year shy of his fortieth birthday. His natural charism for evoking the trust and affection of people in his parish care had endeared him to the reverend and brought him into an inner circle of close confidantes. Isaac's elevation to head deacon status foreshadowed the reverend's hope for a possible successor to his own ministry. Isaac spoke for the group.

"We had the data from the surveillance system analyzed by an AI firm we know and trust. The equipment was, of course, destroyed, but data was uploaded to secure servers up to the moment of the explosion. As you know, the Oligarchy media has reported that they have two California agents in custody and images of them planting the bomb. But our analysis showed that those images were overlaid into the file minutes after the actual blast. The alleged California agents are being framed, as you suspected."

Bob had been skeptical of the official reports from the start. If California wanted to stop the Exodus they would have targeted himself at a large gathering in order to decapitate the leadership and cause maximum casualties. Destroying the nearly empty church simply served to cut off a path of retreat should the movement falter, and it eliminated a cash expense for the Oligarchy treasury after their promise to continue supporting the church's charities. Framing California for a terrorist attack served their purpose. He didn't know the machine overlords of California, but he knew the Oligarchy, and violent intimidation was a big part of their playbook.

He nodded his approval and smiled, then winced. Smiling through burned, cracked lips proved painful. He took a few more breaths from the oxygen mask before speaking. "We will begin the journey at daybreak tomorrow. Tell all the people to gather around their family and friends at sunset tonight to hear what their Lord asks of them. I will address them on the closed personal communication network."

***

Jamal Johnson sat in a folding chair outside his travel home and pulled his daughters in close as the setting sun cast long shadows and the heat of the day melted away. Five-year-old Chloe climbed onto his lap while Hanna, two years her senior, leaned against her father's broad bare shoulders. Their mother, Ayana, was not with them. In her role as deaconess, she had been in the church, packing the last of the sacred artifacts just yards from the bomb when it detonated. There wasn't enough left of her earthly body to distinguish it from the ashes and debris. Jamal offered up her personal Bible to be buried along with the remains, both partial and intact, of the thirty-seven souls who perished in the flames. In the ensuing two days, his fog of grief and confusion had condensed into rage. Ayana's death was not part of some mysterious divine plan. It was evil, and Jamal longed to make the evil doers suffer on their path to divine judgment.

Jamal tried to project calm for the sake of his girls, who had suffered more than any child should be asked to bear. He had wept with them initially. But now, for their sake, he buried his rage away from his girls. Caring for them during the day was a welcome distraction, but at night the anger and grief trapped within were a caged animal eating him from the inside out. Guilt fed the rage. He had left a coveted job as an equipment operator on the Great Lakes pipeline project to uproot his family and join the Exodus. Work on the pipeline was continually interrupted by corrupt politics, and people of Jamal's skin color always seemed to top the list for layoffs. He feared for the future of his girls in a world where prejudice was increasingly used as a survival tool. The promise of a land where everyone could work and be treated with respect had seemed worth the risk. Now it seemed criminally negligent as he waited for a verdict that would determine their future. If the pilgrimage to California was to be abandoned because the reverend could not lead them, or the threat of more violence was too great, he could see no way forward.

The personal communication cubes were capable of synchronizing as a network to project a single thirty-foot holographic image, or alternatively, project a thirty-inch image above each individual cube. Cubes across the community began to glow. Jamal put an arm around each of his precious daughters and gave them an encouraging smile. "Listen carefully, girls." A slightly larger than life visage of their reverend's wounded face coalesced and hovered over the cube. He appeared to be in a darkened room with an illuminated cross behind him. An oxygen cannula graced his nostrils. The cubes amplified and enhanced his hoarse voice. Lighting and makeup minimized his wounds

"Dear brothers and sisters, I couldn't be with you when you committed our martyrs to sacred earth two days ago. But I grieve with you now. We don't grieve for those who died, for they have ascended and will strengthen our hearts and guide us in our journey. We grieve for their loved ones, for our children whose innocence has been stolen by this violence, and we grieve for the fear and doubt that violence has wrought on our souls. But we can't be defeated by any of this. We're the most blessed people in history because we're called to be instruments of the final victory. I may not live long enough to see that glorious day, but that doesn't matter. I'll be with you every step of the way that our God grants to me, and at daybreak tomorrow, we'll leave this valley of lament and begin our journey toward glory."

Jamal squeezed his daughters closer. Their journey to California wouldn't be a final casualty of the bombing. There was still hope.

Reverend Jackson paused and let his words of reassurance sink in. Then he leaned forward, his image appearing to grow larger in size, and resumed on a different note. "But tonight, there's a task that we owe to those who've given their lives and to those they've left behind. In these dark days, you've been lied to. The evil of five days ago wasn't the work of those from the land we seek. It was done by agents of the Oligarchy that would use us for their own perverted purposes. The same people who send us trucks laden with supplies are the people who sent fire and destruction. We won't countenance their presence among us any longer. Hundreds of those trucks and their people sit in the fields just north of where we sit. I urge you to seize them and sterilize the land of

Oligarchy agents. I have chosen to communicate with you privately so that they won't know we have uncovered their duplicity. Go now, use whatever means are at hand, and know whatever your heart leads you to do is in the cause of holy justice. God is with you."

The cage door swung open on the beast within Jamal. He set Chloe down and herded his daughters toward the travel home. "Get inside and lock the door. Don't open it for anyone but me."

Hanna began to cry. "Where are you going, Daddy? I don't want you to go."

Jamal was looking past her to the truck depot in the distance. He snapped his attention back to his daughter. "Get in the house now!" The girls knew that tone and obeyed quickly. Jamal picked up an ax from the firewood pile. He saw his neighbor approach with a tire iron. As they walked they were joined first by a few dozen, then hundreds, then hundreds more, some with shotguns, some with knives or clubs or pitchforks.

As Reverend Jackson watched his army silently marching toward an unsuspecting enemy, he softly recited Psalm 137, the lamentation of the Israelites in Babylon:

Babylon, you will be destroyed
Happy are those who pay you back
For what you have done to us—
Who take your babies
And smash them against a rock.

11

86

One day earlier—September 10, outside Truckee, California

Michaela clung to Joseph as the motorcycle accelerated onto the main road around the lake. She had never been on a motorcycle, but her natural balance and rhythm, fine-tuned in the martial arts, allowed her to easily blend herself with the machine and partake of its grace and power on the open road. It helped that she could effortlessly blend herself with Joseph as he leaned into the wind and the journey ahead. "Blending with Joseph," partaking of his power and grace these past three nights (and mornings and once in the afternoon) had exceeded her imagination of what life might hold possible. She had been curious in her teen years, tempted once or twice in the past year, but until now had always accepted the necessity of forsaking her sexuality until some shadowy future on the far side of a great divide in her eighteenth year. With her cheek pressed against Joseph's back, she studied the lake, golden in the sunset, a thousand stars of light sparkling on the nearby water, while clouds cast ominous darkness on the distant waves.

For his part, Joseph had been wrestling with his angel in the tradition of Jacob. He had no doubt that Michaela was part of God's plan for him, but she definitely had no role in Hank's plan for him. With the destruction of the church, his mission was more critical than ever. The family of God could starve or be slaughtered at the gates of their California Eden if he failed.

While Michaela ran every morning and did her tai chi in the afternoon, Joseph prayed for guidance and reviewed details of his mission. In the early predawn hours of this day, he had found his answer. He gave thanks for both Hank and Michaela. Without Hank, there could not have been Michaela. But this amazing woman was clearly his salvation. The joy, the belonging, the love and acceptance when he had honestly shared his life story, the urgent needing to come together—it was more happiness than he could possibly deserve. He would proceed with his life and mission with this warrior-angel-impossible woman by his side, and God would have to deal with the details. *Sorry, Hank.*

The day had been spent huddled in the cabin as Joseph detailed for Michaela the specifics of his mission. She needed to know every technical detail of the device they meant to deploy, every aspect of the risks, and the magnitude of what they hoped to accomplish before embarking on this dangerous journey. After summarizing the essential features and timeline of the plan, he was careful to frame the choice.

"There's no ultimatum in this, Michaela. This is really dangerous. If we're captured, the AI will show no mercy, and there's no telling what could happen to us. If you don't want to commit to the mission, you can still leave, and we'll make plans to meet up somewhere when this is all over. I want to spend my life with you."

Michaela knew the answer before the question was put to her. She'd anticipated her lover's move just as she would have sized up an opponent's opening move on the karate mat. It was her nature to be a step ahead. Still, she left him in suspense for a moment while she delighted in his trust and desire to have her by his side.

"Joseph, I've spent my whole life on the run, alone, trying to hide and escape a fate I don't deserve. Now I have a chance to stand and fight with someone I love, someone who loves me. Let's tear down some walls together."

They left the cabin an hour before sundown. There was only one helmet, and Michaela wore it to avoid any facial recognition they might encounter. The four-hour ride would place them in Chico after dark, as planned. The first of their two stops was a complex of storage units just south of Chico.

Joseph dismounted and removed his goggles but warned Michaela, "Leave the helmet on. There are security cameras all over this place and inside the units."

They proceeded to a unit at the end of the row. Joseph placed the key Dr. Wagner had given him in the lock and rolled up the corrugated metal door, then closed it once they were inside. The automatic lighting revealed a reinforced wooden crate two-by-two-by-four feet containing Dr. Wagner's device, and attached to four drones by cables. Joseph proceeded to the leader drone and entered GPS coordinates for the cabin. Each of the other drones beeped its acknowledgement, and they began to hum their motors in neutral. On a nod from Joseph, Michaela rolled open the unit door, Joseph touched the Activate control, and the drones bore their cargo forward, then upward into the dark night.

They watched the precious package turn to the south and then turned to each other. Joseph put an arm around her waist and spoke as his hand slipped downward. "It looks like we need to kill some time; still a couple of hours before our meeting. I'm pretty sure those cameras can't identify you from the neck down."

Michaela, her face close to his, whispered, "I don't know. I'm pretty sure I could identify you from the waist down." She gently pushed him back into the unit and rolled down the door. She scanned the room and spotted the tiny camera in a corner of the ceiling, unbuttoned Joseph's shirt, and threw it over the camera lens.

Joseph, a little short of breath, spoke softly. "Leave the helmet on anyway. I like this mysterious, sexy biker in front of me."

Michaela chuckled naughtily and assumed the role. She pulled a folding chair from the back of the unit into the middle of the now empty room. After unbuckling his pants, she firmly commanded Joseph, "Sit down and close your eyes."

***

It was almost midnight when they pulled onto a long dirt driveway that led through a thicket of manzanita to a ranch style home in the foothills east of Chico. They parked the bike. Michaela carried the helmet in one hand and ran the other hand through her tangled hair.

The porch light flicked on. A man who appeared to be in his thirties, with closely trimmed beard, dusky complexion, and wearing a T-shirt that revealed tattooed muscular arms opened the door before they reached the porch.

"That's far enough. What brings you here?"

Joseph recognized the code phrase and answered in kind, "We want to share the Good News of the Lord," indicating that all was well. Had they been followed or in any way compromised, the response would have been "We are lost and hoped you could lend us a hand."

The man at the door invited them in.

Three other young men were present in the living room, but their tattooed host appeared to speak for the group. "Good to see you are on schedule, 144, but who's the girl?

Joseph chose a chair and sat. "This is M. Consider her my security detail. You can trust her." Michaela sensed the tension in the room and remained standing in the back while sizing up each of the men, their positions relative to her, their body language.

Tattoo man spoke. "I don't know her, and I don't actually know you, so no, I can't trust her. She stays outside." He nodded to the men closest to Michaela, and they moved toward her. Joseph cautioned them. "That would be a mistake. She goes where I go."

The men stopped and looked at their leader. He repeated his gesture, this time more emphatically.

Joseph kept his eyes trained solely on the man in charge, calmly adding, "Don't say I didn't warn you."

Michaela gave a warm smile to each of the men as they approached from either side. As the first reached for her from her left she swung the helmet up using elbow and wrist to catapult it into his cheek. As the second man lunged from her right, she stepped back, avoiding the tackle, spun, and brought a fist down on the back of his neck. He collapsed onto his accomplice, who was spitting blood into his hand.

"M" retrieved her helmet and spoke in a tranquil, almost sympathetic voice, "If either of you gets up, I'm afraid I'll have to really hurt you."

Their leader reached around his waist and pulled out a handgun. Joseph stood and placed himself, face to face, between the man and Michaela, the barrel of the gun against his midsection. "Put the gun away, 86. As long as my mission is still a go, that mission is still our priority. So stand down and let's do what we are here for."

86 looked disapprovingly at his two soldiers on the ground and replaced the weapon to its belt holster. He walked across the room, lifted a large lamp from an end table, and turned it on its side. The base of the lamp detached, allowing retrieval of a battleship-gray metal sheathed cylinder, five inches in diameter, ten inches in length, and secured with two clasps. He

held it in both hands as he offered it to Joseph. "This is what you came for. I understand it is some sort of trigger for another device."

"Yeah, thanks." Joseph held the object gingerly, like he had been handed a baby, and studied it. He set the cylinder down onto the coffee table with great care, loosened the clasps and peeled back the metal sheath on its hinges, revealing a greenish putty-like material within. The other man smiled for the first time.

"You're right to respect that thing, but don't worry. It is stable unless a strong electrical charge is applied. You should be fine taking it back with you. Just don't touch any live circuits." Joseph closed and secured the cylinder and nodded his approval. "How did you manage to get something like this into the state and past all the AI detection?"

86 replied, "That's the mission I'm in charge of, and you don't have a need to know. Best we know as little as possible about each other. I don't want to find out if the rumors about AI interrogation methods are true, and neither do you."

Joseph looked up and smiled at his fellow mission chief. "Amen to that."

86 continued. "I have one other gift for you." He opened a drawer in a rolltop desk and pulled out a hand-sized computer screen that he folded in half and handed to Joseph. "This palm computer will respond to the voice command, '144 activate.' It functions as a voice remote for a surveillance drone modeled after the forest monitor drones. Give me the GPS coordinates for your base of operations and we can have it fly there tonight. It should arrive before daybreak. Fully charged it has power for three days and will provide you surveillance intel for your op."

Joseph examined the palm unit and nodded, then added, "You seem to have also smuggled some firearms. Care to share?"

His host shook his head. "Not part of the plan. If you fail, then our mission becomes operative, and we need all the firepower we have."

Joseph's expression acknowledged respect. These men had endured the same training as his own, assumed the same risks, served the same holy purpose. "Understood." He turned to the back of the room where Michaela still stood over the two men. "Sorry for the dustup with your team. And don't worry; I won't fail."

12

SWAT

Day 1 of the Exodus journey—September 12, near Salina, Kansas

Noonday sun glinted off the armored SWAT van as it swung wide around a blockade of police cars stretching across all lanes in both directions of Hwy 70 east of Salina, Kansas. Heat rose from the sweltering pavement in effervescent waves, creating an illusory sense of the caravan as a mirage, a great snake stretching to the horizon, the discordant hum of a thousand idling electric motors issuing a warning rattle. Sheriff Theresa Underwood emerged from the armored vehicle flanked by six helmeted special-operations officers in full military gear carrying semiautomatic weapons. She strode across the hot pavement in quick deliberate manner to the lone figure standing at the fore of the stalled caravan.

The sheriff spoke in a loud commanding voice intended to be heard by everyone present at the scene. "I have been ordered by the governor of Kansas to execute a warrant of arrest for Reverend Robert Jackson on the charge of murder. You won't proceed on this road until he's surrendered and is in custody."

Isaac Wood responded without hesitation. "I'll take you to him. He is expecting you."

As Isaac led the SWAT team between the double line of trucks, a dozen men quietly emerged from the rear of each tractor trailer and followed along. Several hundred yards down from the head of the caravan the reverend stood in the middle of a fifty-foot gap between vehicles. He was dressed all in black, oversized sunshades and a large brimmed hat shading the patches of crusts and scabs over the healing facial burns. Two large acolytes flanked him on either side.

Sheriff Underwood signaled her team to stand at the ready as she approached him. "Robert Jackson, you are under arrest for the murder of forty-eight people in Shawnee County. Place your hands behind your back."

As she reached for her handcuffs, the growing crowd of several hundred closed in like a jaw snapping shut. The two large men stepped between her and her would-be prisoner.

Theresa reached for her pistol yelling, "Stand back, stand back!" A strong hand grabbed her wrist at the holster, and a teenage girl darted forward to snatch the handcuffs from her other hand. More than a hundred followers converged instantly on the SWAT officers as they moved forward. A single shot rang out, bringing a scream of pain from a young woman as she fell, clutching the gaping wound in her abdomen.

The attack on the SWAT team didn't hesitate; the crowd was prepared to suffer martyrs. Guns were seized, and the half dozen uniformed men were dragged down to the hot pavement where a hailstorm of boots and fists battered them nearly senseless.

Reverend Jackson raised a hand and Isaac shouted the order. "Stop!" Limbs were pinned to ground, gun barrels leveled at faces.

The reverend's bodyguards parted, and their frail leader leaned on his cane to hobble forward to within a foot of the sheriff. Her lower lip bloodied, and now restrained by her own handcuffs, she spat on him. "You think you are some sort of

Messiah? You're a fucking murderer, and your entire cult is going to be destroyed by your delusions of grandeur."

The disfigured countenance staring at her seemed contorted into an unnatural scowl, as though something not human had attempted to assume human form but failed in the details. A pungency, either from the wounds, or perhaps sulphured ointment, bolstered her disgust. She turned her head aside as he finally spoke, just inches from her face.

"You, Sheriff, are a prisoner of war. War has casualties. If you and your men don't wish to become casualties, you'll do as you're told."

The six SWAT team members were bound with rope and each tied to the hood of a truck, their legs over the grills and secured to the front fenders. The forward vehicles of the caravan pulled off the road to allow the six trucks to proceed to the roadblock in tight formation, two rows of three vehicles. Police had heard the single gunshot and were positioned behind their squad cars with weapons ready. The trucks, controlled remotely without drivers, stopped fifty feet from the blockade, then began to roll toward the police cars, slowly at first, then gradually accelerating. Blockading officers bolted for their cars, and hostages screamed as it became clear that their legs would be the initial battering ram of the impending collision. Squad cars sideswiped each other accelerating in reverse just a few yards from the advancing trucks and swung off the road into the surrounding wheat fields. The trucks slowed to a stop on the now open road.

Sheriff Underwood was led in her own shock restraint cuffs to the trailer compartment of an eighteen-wheeler where she had been ambushed. She read from a script, the image and words projected by the PMD communication network to a thirty-foot hologram at the front of the caravan.

"All units will stand down immediately. A police escort will accompany the caravan into Salina where Christians who wish to join the caravan or donate supplies will be permitted to do so. Police will then escort the caravan to the Colorado border where I and my team will be released."

13

GONE

Day eleven since Michaela's arrival—September 12, near the cabin

Michaela ran her usual sunrise course through the forest, transformed now into an entirely new landscape. A low blanket of clouds had wrested control of the sky and temperatures dropped overnight, giving ghostly form to her breathing. She reflected on her upbringing by a mother who held to no particular tradition or dogma yet was deeply rooted in the conviction of a spiritual world beyond our senses. Michaela felt a spiritual connection to this woodland that had celebrated her in the bloom of love. This morning, it seemed to sense her own sobering acceptance of having committed to fighting a looming battle against a vastly superior enemy. Bright green trees now donned a leaden gray uniform in scant fog. Birdsong was muted as those innocents sheltered in place before the battle. A damp forest floor pulled at her shoes, warning her of peril that lie ahead.

Undaunted, Michaela welcomed the solidarity she felt around her. The events of their trip, the physical conflict at the house outside Chico—it had reminded her that she was powerful when she fought, and now, with Joseph, she could see the future she was fighting for. So much had happened so fast. Preparing to fight was a familiar comfort, like putting on an old favorite coat.

She ran past a small clearing and looked to the side where the drones—the four carrier drones with cables from the storage unit, and the surveillance drone 86 had sent them—were concealed under shrubs and tree branches. The sun was not quite up when they'd arrived back at the cabin the previous morning. They hid the crate with the device and trigger material in the wood bin and covered it with firewood. Then, exhausted, they slept much of the day and spent the evening planning scenarios for possible complications to the mission plan. They slept in each other's arms that night, their first without making love, but with a different sort of intimacy in the shared path they were walking.

As she crested the ridge overlooking the cabin, Michaela froze, then dropped to the ground. Cars! A gull-wing auto and a larger van with markings on the doors were parked by the porch. *Joseph! Where are you Joseph?* She scanned the surrounding forest and hillside hoping to see him scrambling to safety. Then she saw him, as two armed and helmeted police in full SWAT gear led him down the porch steps, his hands secured behind his back. Behind them came two men in civilian clothes, one carrying the compucube. She recognized the other CBI agent from the raid on the safe house, the one who had come to the cabin.

Oh no, no, no. They tracked Joseph through me. They were coming for me and now they have Joseph. For a moment, Michaela considered running to them. *Take me. It's me you want. Joseph didn't know.* But in her mind's eye she saw the look of despair that would be Joseph's face if she gave herself up. They had planned for a scenario where one of them couldn't go on; they'd agreed the other would carry out the mission. In that moment, she realized the mission had just changed for her. She would rescue Joseph, somehow. It seemed hopeless, but hadn't her whole life been about impossible odds? *Hold on Joseph. I'm coming.*

Two other men in military gear were placing stakes about five yards out from the four corners of the cabin. They stepped back and a virtual image of a barrier, seven feet high shimmered into the space between stakes with an embedded message: "Crime Scene—Do Not Enter." It was a standard laser wall. Any breach of the lasers would communicate an intrusion to whoever was remotely monitoring, perhaps activate a surveillance camera as well.

Michaela didn't yet have a plan, but she would need to know where they were taking him. She slithered back out of view of the cabin and sprinted to the clearing where they had hidden the drones. Fortunately, they had kept the voice remote for the surveillance drone provided by 86 with its drone. She retrieved the drone and the palm computer, held the palm com in her hand, and spoke.

"144 activate. Proceed to altitude six hundred feet over the previous GPS coordinates. Follow vehicles leaving that position and maintain stealth surveillance." The drone whirred and ascended.

Michaela sat, unable to fight back the tears. *Fear is the enemy. Fear is the enemy. I'm coming, Joseph!*

14

ISAAC

Day five of the Exodus journey—September 16, Great Salt Desert, western Utah

Reverend Jackson's head deacon, Isaac Woods, finished exchanging clothes with a man of similar build and donned a wide-brimmed hat before exiting the tent several minutes after his body double. Now that the caravan had reached its rendezvous with the northern and southern contingents outside of Salt Lake City, there were plans to finalize. But strict precautions were in place for the meetings between leaders. As Reverend Jackson's head deacon and close confidante, Isaac would be a prime target of unwanted surveillance.

Reverend Jackson had been true to his word. Sheriff Underwood's team was released to a medical team after crossing the Colorado border. Colorado state police in Denver had initially planned a roadblock with overwhelming force and air support. Then they found themselves sandwiched between nine thousand Colorado Christians to the west, heaven-bent on joining the reverend, and the main caravan to the east. After a twelve-hour standoff, the governor decided it was not in his best interests to preside over a massacre of devout Christians. The caravan was given free passage. Utah, a hybrid of civil and theocratic rule, made a show of welcoming each of the three caravans heading for their joint merger, in hope that their guests would not outstay their welcome before imposing themselves on Nevada.

At every town and city along the journey, Reverend Jackson had welcomed the local media interviews and encouraged his fellow Christians to join their pilgrimage. But he never missed an opportunity for a damning condemnation of the Oligarchy for their murderous attack on his church and his people. The Oligarchy suppressed the reports on the internet and major news outlets under their control, but Christian and AI devotees in Oligarchy territory managed to disseminate them long enough to have an effect. A majority of their population believed the official declarations that California had executed the church attack, but opposition groups staged illegal marches that became riots. Acts of sabotage were disrupting production and profits. The caravan still served its purpose, but the reverend had to be stopped. A blatant attack by drone or other overt acts would risk martyrdom status and inflame suspicion by the opposition. It appeared his injuries would not claim his life soon enough. If a death from "natural causes" could not be expedited, then at least an assassination from within his own ranks would both eliminate him and cast suspicion on his own people.

Reverend Jackson and the other leaders knew he was a marked man, and may not be the only target. No doubt there were Oligarchy agents among the roughly one hundred thousand disciples in their midst, and they would be aided by sophisticated aerial surveillance. The location of the reverend and the top leadership was held in the highest secrecy, hence the subterfuge of disguises and circuitous routes to the reverend's tent. Isaac was the last to arrive, and took the remaining seat.

Reverend Jackson, his eyes now dappled gray with healed corneal scars, the facial wounds still distorting his countenance but no longer weeping and scabbed, appeared an object of sympathy rather than supernatural transformation to the twelve designated apostles around the table. He looked at those gathered through scarred ocular windows that immersed him in a perpetual blanketing fog, but made eye contact with each of them before opening the meeting with a prayer of thanksgiving for their safe passage this far. His speech now came in a rattle, interrupted frequently with a handkerchief to cough up pink spittle as he welcomed everyone.

"As you can see, I may succeed in defeating my assassin by dying on my own, if that be God's will for me. I have much to atone for, and I expect my penance to include my death before we achieve our goal. I would ask for your prayers if that be the case." A protracted fit of painful coughing left the assembled fearful they were about to witness that penance. Isaac was familiar with these attacks. He approached his mentor and began to strike his back with a cupped hand, percussing the chest to loosen the obstructive mucous. The coughing stopped.

"Thank you, Isaac." He paused to regain his breath while Isaac returned to his seat. "In a few days' time, we will depart for the California border. Our food and supplies are depleted. The Oligarchy has intimidated our Utah and Nevada hosts, so no help will be forthcoming after we cross the Nevada desert. We will have only a few days to breech their defenses before our provisions are exhausted and we are forced to declare a hunger strike as our sole remaining strategy. As some of you know, before we began our pilgrimage we placed several cells of our best young men and women inside California to aid us in the critical moments of conflict. They were trained and placed by allies within the Oligarchy, an alliance of convenience. Now that those allies have become enemies, we don't know what may have become of those brave young Christians. Therefore, we need to prepare an alternative plan.

When our Lord calls me home, my successor shall be young Isaac. He will now detail the plan."

All eyes turned to Deacon Wood. Isaac registered the skeptical and hostile expressions that a mere deacon, and a relatively young deacon at that, should be named as successor. It would not go unchallenged once the reverend was absent. Isaac relished neither the position or the conflict. He especially didn't wish to be the voice of this alternative plan and would gladly step down later if it meant the plan would never be realized. He'd lost faith in Reverend Jackson ever since the murders following the bombing and the horrifying violence inflicted upon Sheriff Underwood and her men. He deeply regretted his role in that episode. The spiritual leader he idolized had clearly suffered a mental and spiritual breakdown. It was understandable, but as a deacon, Isaac had a duty to the faithful. He could no longer leave his flock at risk to the tortured soul of this man. He had an "alternative plan" of his own, but would persevere in his obedience just a little longer.

Deacon Wood rose and leaned over the table to activate a projection cube. He described the image floating above the table. "The Great Wall of California is multi-layered. It begins ten feet into the state's territory, so we are safe beyond that distance. Any attack beyond that would be an act of war against a neighboring state. The first layer is a line of four-foot reinforced concrete barriers to stop vehicular attacks." The holographic image zoomed in on a concrete barrier, then out again before focusing on a section of fencing. "Ten feet behind that is the fence, a twenty-foot-high picket of ceramic polymer rails interlaced with interlocking cables carrying twenty thousand volts of electricity—ten times the current used in the old electric chairs when criminals could be executed. The interlacing cabling and multiple redundant generators ensure current throughout the network even if a section of fence is lost."

A pastor from the northern contingent interrupted. "We have electric fences all over the Midwest. As long as you wear rubber boots, there's no ground to conduct current. You can touch the fence safely."

Joseph answered him. "This is not your typical cattle barrier. It is superconducting direct current. If you come within a few inches, it will initiate a DC arc, with the air providing conduction. The arc is automatically aborted before it can cause an explosion, but it will turn you into a charred corpse in a millisecond."

The image shifted upward above the fence. "The final layer is the drone packs. Every quarter mile a pack of two dozen killer drones patrols the border. Each pack operates under its own AI guidance system to maximize performance of individual units. The drones are equipped with energy weapons that will burn a four-millimeter hole deep into a human being at one hundred yards; then the energy is dispersed into the body's fluids, causing an area of the internal organs and tissues to boil." He left a close-up image of a drone hovering and slowly turning above the heads of those assembled for maximum effect.

He paused before moving on to the plan. "Any questions?" There were none, and a few apostles continued to focus nervously on the holo-drone overhead. Isaac perceived that he was gaining some respect as their future leader. "We can't defeat the wall physically, so the reverend's plan is to defeat it spiritually." He was careful to label the plan as not his own. "We have a dozen laser-powered welding guns and plasma cutters among our craftsmen. They can safely cut through the fencing without conducting the electric current. The plan calls for one volunteer per gun and per torch to approach the fence and begin cutting electric cables and posts. If a drone is dispatched to stop him, a second team will move forward, pick up the laser, and resume the effort, and so on."

The leader of the southern leg of the caravan voiced the obvious. "You're talking about a suicide mission. How many boiled bodies do you plan to leave on their doorstep?"

Isaac responded unemotionally. "We don't know. The national media will be there in strength. No one knows if the ruling AI has something akin to a conscience, but it does have an awareness of public opinion. It may quickly recognize the potential for a damaging outcry and decide to negotiate; or it may think it can call our bluff. To show that we aren't bluffing we need at least two hundred volunteers. Assuming a few last-minute defections, that means each of us is responsible for recruiting twenty volunteers. Names will be called randomly at the wall."

Isaac looked hopefully around the room. Surely, there would be some resistance, some loud rejection of offering people up for slaughter. Instead, there was a soft murmur and the group turned to the reverend. His disfigurement afforded him the advantage of having no expression they could interpret. He spoke. "You have your instruction. Go with God. Meeting adjourned."

The other eleven disciples struggled to make small talk and congratulate Isaac with perfunctory comments and handshakes for his appointment and for the helpful presentation as they left the tent at varying intervals and by different entrances. At last alone with the reverend, Isaac pulled a chair alongside the holy man and sat quietly. He needed certainty before he acted. He didn't seek this role, it was thrust upon him. The biblical allegory of Judas had not escaped him, but as much as he loved the reverend, this shell of the man he had once known was not Jesus, and Isaac could not be complicit in mass murder/suicide. He suppressed his grief and asked the question in an even tone. "Bob, are we really going to send scores of people to a horrible death?"

The reverend made an attempt to smile encouragingly. "Certainly not, Isaac. We are sending them to eternal life."

Isaac nodded his respect, then rose, and left the tent before his eyes could betray him with tears. Standing just outside the tent entrance, he stopped, removed his hat and glasses, and looked up to the sky for thirty seconds, slowly turning in a circle. He then discreetly pointed at the tent before walking away.

***

Reverend Jackson heard the soft footsteps approaching his bed in the dark of night and knew that it would be the last thing he would ever hear. He had begun to experience periods of confusion, even visions, in recent days as his lung struggled to harness the oxygen vital to his brain. But here, at rest in the quiet darkness, his mind was clear and at peace. He had prayed to be released from this failing flesh, to be called home. He felt the flow of oxygen in his nasal cannula slow and cease. In the end, his tortured body fought for one more breath as the pillow pressed a final insult to his hideous countenance, but consciousness had already fled in joyful anticipation of reunion with his Savior.

15

ABOVE YOUR PAY GRADE

September 12—Leaving the cabin

Booker stood leaning on the open gull wing door and watched the prisoner with curiosity as SWAT team members loaded Joseph into the van that would trail after the two agents. Something didn't quite add up. Iverson had come down hard on the suspect from the start, putting him in cuffs and claiming to have conclusive evidence of his colluding with Dr. Wagner. The bluff had worked, but Jim was suspicious that it had worked too well. The target seemed almost eager to be arrested—like he was in a hurry to be hauled off. Jim took his seat and the door swung down as the senior special agent spoke navigation commands. "Security code gamma, red, Apollo, six, Iverson. Destination: security interrogation post seven.

Jim had a similar uneasy feeling about his special agent partner. Iverson had been evasive and dismissive of questions about how the operation was to go down. It was more than the usual irritation Jim seemed to provoke so easily in his superiors. It was time to get some answers. As the car began to pull away from the cabin Jim's tone was emphatic. "Where are we going, why does it need a special security code, and when do I get to question our prisoner?

The senior agent didn't hesitate to answer this time. "The answer to the first two questions is the same. We're going somewhere that is above your paygrade to know about yet."

He touched a display on the dash, and all the windows tinted to jet black, ensuring that Jim would not know where they had gone even after they arrived. Two clicks behind his right ear indicated that the car was also blocking communication with Katy. Overhead cabin lights glowed soft bluish light. Iverson pulled a skinny Italian sausage from the center console and stripped off the wrapper. He bit off nearly half the length and chewed it as though it were a small animal he had popped into his mouth while still alive, and with enough noise to bolster that impression. Once the sausage had been subdued and swallowed, he continued.

"As to you questioning him, he's all yours when we get there, at least until I'm ready to question him. That will take a few hours, maybe more. So, knock yourself out; but if you don't get the answers you need, don't worry. When I'm done with him, he'll tell you anything you want to know."

Booker shuddered with an icy foreboding. His defense was his wit: defuse discomfort with humor. "You sound like you're going to torture him. I'm pretty sure they don't issue us thumb screws anymore. Or are you more of an iron maiden kind of guy?"

Iverson wiped the grease from his lips with his sleeve and swiveled his seat to better face the rookie agent. "How long have you been out of the academy? A year? Two years?"

Booker didn't like being interrogated, but answered matter-of-factly, like it was simply an idle get-to know-you-better question. "It will be one year next week, actually." He was equal parts offended and intimidated by where the conversation seemed headed. Iverson nodded, then leaned in.

Jim resisted the urge to lean back as the smell of the spicy link on the older man's breath assaulted him. "Young CBI agents these days think it's about enforcing codes and regulations, maintaining the status quo. But your partner,

Devon, and I were around when AI took over and was under attack from armed groups who thought they could discredit the new order with mayhem and terror, then step into the void and take control. They would have succeeded too, if AI hadn't been more ruthless than her enemies."

Iverson detailed how the AI system was programmed with a survival mode the equal of any sentient being. Actions it would never undertake in less dire conditions would be executed in a nanosecond against a potential existential threat. It was protecting its citizenry as fiercely as a mother would her children. Her ability to analyze and predict the actions of criminals and terrorists limited the threat, but to eliminate the threat required that she be the better terrorist. AI used knowledge of human physiology and psychology to devise interrogation techniques that exceeded any cruelty her enemies could impose. She took prisoners, and when they had revealed everything they knew, she sent them back to their leaders to describe what lay in wait for them. The good people of California never knew how they were protected, but the resistance had been broken in two years.

"Devon was a hell of a soldier, but eventually, he couldn't stomach what we were doing to prisoners, so he left the Special Agent Security division." Booker remembered asking Devon about the early days and his partner's lack of response. Was Iverson just bragging and bad mouthing his partner? "Why are you telling me this? Why am I still on this case? What makes you think I'll be any more open to torture than my partner was?"

Iverson became softer, solicitous. "I sensed something in you when we met, so I looked into your file. You're not the thickheaded, by-the-rules jock the academy turns out now. You think outside the box. You care more about results than protocols. You don't let what other people think or do keep you from getting the work done. You have the passion to be a security special agent. With this damn caravan coming, we need people like you again. It's been peaceful for a long time, but the caravan represents a new existential threat. There are too many desperate people outside our borders who will become an invasion force if they think they can get in. You can make a difference here."

Jim turned his head away. He was angry; his ego was stoked by the praise; he was disillusioned that the infallible AI was capable of inhuman cruelty, but intrigued by the challenge; he was simultaneously tempted and repulsed. He abandoned all pretense of decorum and turned back to the senior agent, speaking with deliberate disdain. "And what makes you think you know me so well?"

Iverson, grinned and subtly nodded his head. "Oh, I know you, kid. I once *was* you."

PART THREE

CRUCIFIX

BACK IN THE FIGHT

Same day, shortly after the arrest at the cabin

The four commercial drones that had delivered Dr. Wagner's crated device hovered a few feet off the ground, weightless, as Michaela pulled them by the connecting cables toward the cabin. She didn't know how long she had until the crime scene team would be on site. The microbots would scour every inch of the cabin and find her hair and skin cells on the rug and furniture, her DNA on the sheets and in the bathroom. She needed to get inside the laser-wall barrier, retrieve the critical device from the wood bin, and escape with the motorcycle undetected. She had a plan.

Standing outside the laser wall, Michaela entered a flight plan to the lead drone and heard the reassuring beep of acknowledgement from the servant drones. She grasped the cables as the drones rose straight up until the cables pulled tight, and she felt them tug her upward onto her toes; and then they stopped rising. She jumped and rose up two feet, then slowly touched down again. *Crap! I'm too heavy.* She considered her clothing, but it couldn't account for more than a few pounds. She could try digging under, but without tools, it would take hours, if it were even possible with her bare hands. The desperation she knew in her dreams was gaining a foothold. Michaela sat, legs crossed, calmed her breathing, closed her eyes, and went to the quiet place of strength that preceded each of her visits to the karate mat.

I can't move myself past the opponent, not over or under or around. Therefore, I need to move the opponent, not myself. She opened her eyes and studied her opponent. Each of the four posts generating the barrier was powered by a four-inch sphere attached to the top of the post by a small pedestal. *Yes!*

Michaela separated the four drones such that each carried one cable. The pedestals were just within reach as she attached the cable from a hovering drone to the top base of each power unit with the cable's claw. In theory, this might work. The drones were linked to maintain perfectly level flight when moving cargo, compensating for each other as wind or evasive maneuvers threatened to disrupt the balance of their freight. But any uneven lifting of the posts would disrupt the barrier and send an alert. Michaela readied herself to move as quickly as possible. Flight plan entered, the lead drone activated on her voice command, "Rise," and all four drones rose slowly in their synchronous ballet.

Michaela rolled under the barrier as it rose the first few feet, anticipating an alarm or some indication that she was exposed; but none came. When she reached the wood bin, she allowed herself a moment to look back. The barrier was suspended perfectly eight feet in the air, and Michaela uttered a soft ooh, relieved and feeling a deep sense of gratitude toward her drones for a job well done, as if they were beloved pets who had come to her aid and saved the day.

She retrieved the crate with the device and dragged it outside the elevated barrier, entered the back door to retrieve her helmet, and exited the front where she wheeled the motorcycle to a safe distance from the cabin.

Now, my pets, I need one more delicate maneuver; you can do it. She spoke the command, "Settle!" The drones slowly reversed their precision course and set the posts onto their bases exactly where they had found them. Michaela detached them and rewarded each drone with a kiss before attaching them once again to their precious crated device. She entered a GPS address from the motorcycle's history log into the lead drone, and she watched as the crate was born aloft toward its destination. As she mounted the motorcycle, a familiar spirit settled back into her; she was back in the fight. This time the stakes could not be higher, and she had no intention of losing.

2

RECRUIT

Same day—On the road from the cabin

The drive from the cabin to the interrogation facility took a little over two hours. Iverson used the time to press his recruitment pitch by regaling his prospect with tales of the early days. Booker wasn't saying much, but Sam was dangling the bait, and his fish was circling it.

"Your partner was the greatest agent I ever knew. It broke my heart when he handed in his transfer out of the unit. There was this one raid on a terror cell of the Human Liberation Army. One of their soldiers gave up their location under enhanced interrogation, and we could always trust that intel, because once we broke them, we told them they would be back in that hell indefinitely if they lied. The terror cell was expecting us, though, and set a trap. We were pinned down in an abandoned warehouse waiting for the cavalry to come to our rescue when the bad guys chuck a grenade at our position. I tried to roll out of the way, but I thought we were done for. Devon jumps up and runs toward the incoming grenade, catches it barehanded, and throws it back like he was turning a double play from the bag at second base. It took out most of the terrorists, and the rest ran like scared rabbits. You knew he was an all-state shortstop in high school, right?"

Booker was too flustered to answer. He knew Devon Frost had been some sort of big deal jock, but hadn't bothered to draw him out. Apparently, he had misjudged his mentor shamefully. A montage of memories surged up, the wisecracks and digs about Devon being dull or unimaginative, a protocol drudge and pencil pusher. Devon was a hero of the social revolution, and he never mentioned it. Jim felt guilty, but he could imagine the torch being passed from mentor to student, fulfilling the career he thought he had chosen in the CBI academy.

Sam explained, regretfully, that the battle these days was not so much one of guns and grenades, but rather intel and disruption. The border security could easily annihilate any invasion, but a mass slaughter of thousands of US citizens would invite retaliation, even a second American civil war. "I think you are the kind of recruit we're looking for. I'm going to read you in on this case as a consulting agent; if you have what it takes, we can talk about filing a request for transfer to the Security Division."

Well into the second hour of driving the car slowed, the ride more uneven, and the sound of tires crunching over gravel indicated a remote destination. Twenty minutes later, they came to a stop. Windows lightened and Jim could see that he was inside a concrete garage with low ceiling and several parking places on either side. The gull wing doors swung upward and the two agents walked toward a metal security door at the far end of the enclosure, apparently the entrance to the facility. They watched while Joseph was unloaded from the van and marched to them, hands in shock restraint cuffs.

Iverson stood facing a glowing blue globe embedded above the metal doors leading into the facility. A bar of blue light slid over the agent, head to feet and back up again. "Personal identification chip and facial recognition confirmed. Welcome, Agent Iverson. How many are to enter?"

Iverson answered, "Myself and six others, four with secure ID, one additional agent and a prisoner."

A loud metallic clip of the locking mechanism withdrawing preceded the door slowly swinging inward. With the two agents in the lead, the party proceeded down a block-long downward-sloping hallway, overhead lights activating ten feet ahead of their progress, then extinguishing behind them. The air was stale and close; Jim suspected they were the first visitors in quite some time. A faint sterile chemical scent reminded him of his recent visit to the hospital. At the end of the twelve-foot-wide passage, two low concrete barriers narrowed the entry to the main facility to just four feet.

Iverson entered first and voiced a command. "Full lighting." The interior of the facility blazed into view.

For Booker, this felt like stepping into a holo-sim game from his teen years; success depended on rapidly assessing the environment for potential threats, escape routes, traps or weapons. He stepped forward and surveyed. A circular walkway encompassed a central open space, perhaps twenty feet in diameter, with a high-domed ceiling obscured by interlacing, overlapping panels of sound-reflecting baffles. To his left, a bank of a dozen narrow holding cells with metal bars sat adjacent to the walkway. To the right, four pairs of doors spaced every fifteen feet or so, presumably offices or rooms of some sort, encompassed a third of the circumference. Across from where he stood, the remaining curvature was defined by a thick plastiglass wall looking out from a control room with panels of monitors, desks and chairs. Jim took all this in before allowing himself to inspect the obvious focal point at the center of the open space.

A T-shaped metallic platform lay on an arching pedestal, like the offspring of a surgical operating table and a crucifix. A pair of medibots stood to one side, dark and inactivated for now. Still in character as his game avatar, Jim quickly developed a plan: check the cells for potential allies and free them, create a diversion while exploring what lie behind the doors, then mount an attack on the control room. Avoid winding up on the crucifix device at all costs.

Reality reasserted itself with Iverson's voice behind him issuing orders to the SWAT team contingent. "Take the prisoner to cell number one and remove the hand restraints once secured. Booker, you're with me." He proceeded around the curved walkway with the long purposeful strides of a man anxious to get to the task at hand. Jim had to lay aside his morbid fascination with this geodesic dungeon and race to keep up. They entered a nondescript office room furnished with three desks equipped with computers and com links. A side door presumably led to the adjacent control room, and a window into an adjoining interrogation room was presumably one-way glass.

"Have a seat, Booker. In about an hour, I'm going to give you your prisoner interview next door. He won't give you anything, but your job is to instill some well-deserved fear in him. Let him know that I am going to do terrible things to him, things that no one has ever endured without breaking, until he tells us everything he knows. Let him know you're the good cop who doesn't want to see him hurt, and you only have tonight before I take over the interrogation and you can't help him. You can casually drop the news that their Christian leader, Robert Jackson, was murdered in his sleep by one of their own. His death is all over the net, so you can show him the reports. We need to break his morale and convince him his cause is defeated."

Jim chose his words carefully. He understood he was auditioning for a role that would value his talents and define his career at the highest levels of the agency. Sure, he was out of his depth at the moment, but isn't everyone when they begin their climb to the top? It wasn't his ability that gave him pause; it was his conscience. "What kind of 'terrible things' are we are talking about? Maybe I should give him something specific to worry about."

"It's better if you learn by watching. I have requested an enhanced interrogation technician who can implement the full capabilities of our equipment, but he won't get here until later tonight. This facility hasn't been used for several years, so there are some things we still need to get on line. What you need to know now is what we need from the prisoner. His passenger on that red motorcycle you identified is Dr. Otto Wagner, a brilliant and well-known scientist; maybe you've heard of him."

Jim remembered seeing Dr. Wagner on a NetNews spot about superconductors.

Iverson continued. "I think that squat little freak is planning something to help the caravan, and Joseph is his contact. Unfortunately, we can't make a positive ID on either of them from the drone video alone, and so far, we don't have anything we can take to the bank on our prisoner yet. I can't go after California's premier scientist without proving he is a clear and present danger to the state. But, given the high threat status from that Christian mob, AI is OK with us interrogating an unknown noncitizen however we need to, provided we don't leave any incriminating physical marks on him. We need to maintain credible deniability. What we do here in the next day or two may be the difference between success and disaster at the border, so don't screw it up."

3

THE TEAM

Later that day, outside Chico, California

The motorcycle sped down the gravel driveway past the thickets of manzanita and slid to a stop, rear wheel skidding sideways, sending a shower of dirt and gravel toward the house. Michaela dismounted, set the kickstand and pulled off her helmet in a single motion. The front door flew open, and 86 stood facing her, right hand behind his hip on the pistol holstered there. Michaela strode toward him while she spoke. "We have a problem."

At a loss how he should respond, he reverted to the code protocol. "What brings you here?" The gun came out.

Michaela stopped. "Joseph—I mean 144—has been captured, but I know where they are holding him. I have a plan."

Again came the question, "What brings you here?"

Michaela remembered that there was some sort of coded answer. "Are you kidding me? OK, God is great, or something like that. I wasn't followed. Did you hear me? They have Joseph. Are we going to talk or are you just going to wave that metallic dick at me all day?"

86 hesitated, then holstered the pistol, and nodded his head toward the house.

Michaela sat down in the chair Joseph had occupied at their prior visit; she hoped to assume his status of authority now that she carried responsibility for the mission. The two men she had struck down entered from the hallway and chose a love seat at the farthest point in the room. 86 and his other lieutenant sat opposite her in wicker chairs. Michaela recounted the events of the morning and her use of the surveillance drone provided by 86 to follow the prisoner convoy. Clouds hid the drone from sight but didn't hinder its ultraviolet vision. They would be able to not only locate, but also surveil the facility before executing a rescue operation. She had briefly reviewed the images. It was a small underground bunker in the middle of nowhere, no guards, no visible defenses.

86 listened intently, waiting until she finished speaking and looked to him for a response. "I'm sorry, M. I respect that you are willing to risk your life for your partner (*and whatever else the two of you are*, crossing his mind), and I hate the idea of what they may be doing to him there. But assaulting a fortified CBI bunker with no idea of what defenses are there, how many people may be inside, or even how to get inside, is a suicide mission. They would see us coming and mow us down before we got close. If Joseph has failed, then our orders are to execute diversionary measures and cut off reinforcements to the border. I'm in charge now."

Michaela had known this moment was coming. She knew what she had decided, and she knew she would have to break a promise. But the moment between decision and action was a high-wire balancing act. Once she took this step, there was no way but forward, and she could not foresee what awaited her on the far side if she survived. She gathered herself to speak with unflinching confidence and stepped out onto the wire.

"What if I could instantly disable their defenses, destroy their ability to communicate to the outside world, and throw them into complete darkness and confusion moments before we strike? Before you answer, know that I am going to do this with or without your help. But there is a good chance, I'll fail alone. Considering what I know, you don't want me in enemy hands, not to mention that they may eventually break Joseph and get hold of what he knows. Besides, if you want to strike a blow against the AI and send a message, what better way than to take out a secret secure CBI compound and rescue a high value prisoner?"

86 was becoming impatient. He wasn't taking orders from some girl he didn't know. "Cutting the power won't work. They have redundant systems, batteries, and generators. You don't know what you're talking about."

The other man in the wicker chair spoke up. "I think she does know what she is talking about, boss. When we took delivery of that device we stashed in the storage unit, I took a close look at it." He spoke directly to M. "That's what you plan to use, isn't it?"

She nodded silently. 86 stared at his lieutenant, then flashed his gaze back at M. "Would someone like to tell *me* what we are talking about?"

***

"M" sat in a wooden chair in a back room, her arms around the back of the chair, her hands cuffed to it. She had given them her "resume" as an advanced martial arts fighter, a Third Order thirder on the run, and a fugitive wanted for assault on a CBI agent. She had been bluffing when she'd threatened to go after Joseph on her own. She wasn't crazy, but the you-can't-afford-to-let-me-get-caught gambit had worked well when she first encountered Joseph at the cabin, so it seemed worth resurrecting. It hadn't occurred to her that she was giving them a good reason to be sure she would not leave the house, and that might mean *ever* leave. These people seemed far more capable of murder than Joseph had. Or they could simply leave her somewhere and give the CBI an anonymous tip, then move to a different location.

Damn me! I would have some fucking leverage if I'd hidden the device, but I programmed this house as the destination. I won't be worth much to them when it sets itself down in their front yard in a couple hours. Given her current situation, mindfulness of it didn't seem helpful. She focused on her mantra. *Fear is the enemy!* But she was at their mercy, and she knew it. She considered whether being murdered would be preferable to what the AI might do to her, and tried to imagine requesting death over arrest.

In the main room, the conversation centered on the fate of the device more than the fate of Michaela. The tech expert who had recognized the nature of the device, explained what he understood about its capabilities. "But an explosively pumped flux compression generator does what it sounds like. It explodes. So, if we use it to rescue Joseph, it's no longer in play at the border crossing. On the other hand, I understand the principle behind it, but I haven't been briefed on specifics. Is it operational now? How much range does it have? How is it safely deployed, et cetera, not to mention that we don't actually know where it is. My guess is the girl knows where it is and how to use the thing."

The tall scraggly man on the love seat offered, "I trust her. She's tough, no bullshit there. She didn't have to come here but she does what needs doing."

The other veteran of their prior encounter was skeptical. "So we don't really know much about this thing, and she wants us to walk into a CBI fortress blind. I don't recall that in our mission dossier. Plus, she's a target of CBI. Who's to say she's not being watched? We need to dump her somewhere ASAP."

The response from the love seat was adamant. "Listen, Shark, I've got no problem with killing my enemy on the battlefield, but I didn't volunteer to murder an inconvenient innocent.

"OK, we don't have to kill her. We have her under lock and key. She's a prisoner until this all plays out."

The techie spoke the obvious concern. "We can't just chain her up within reach of food and water when we leave. When shit hits the fan, we won't know when or if we can return here. I guess we could make an anonymous call to the authorities to come get her at some point if it comes to that."

Shark appeared troubled by that and looked away before answering. "Given what I know of what the AI does with prisoners she considers a threat to state security, M might prefer we just leave her and hope for the best. Attractive young Caucasian women fetch top dollar on the human-trafficking market."

86 interrupted the conversation. "Everybody, shut up. Let me think for a minute." He stood and walked to a window where he considered his options before continuing. "We don't have much choice. If what I've been told about those CBI dungeons is true, and I believe it is true, Joseph will be lucky to last two days before he tells them anything they want to know. And he knows enough to bring us down along with him. We either go get him before that happens or they will be coming here to get us. The caravan is still a good week away from the border. We need to get to Joseph before they can break him. Let her loose and bring her in here."

Michaela entered the room flanked by a man behind and ahead of her. 86 stood and addressed her. "OK, you shouldn't have come, but you're here now. This isn't Snow White and the dwarves. If you join us, you follow orders like everybody else. And you don't quit if you don't like how things work out. So, are you in or out?"

M breathed out her relief and, with just a hint of self-satisfied grin, replied, "Yeah, all in. You won't regret it."

Gathered at the dining room table, the group's first order of business was introductions. First was Radar, electronic systems expert and master hacker, recruited for this mission as an alternative to jail for conviction of bank fraud involving transfer of Oligarchy slush funds to Christian charities. It was Radar who had surmised the nature and potential of the device they obtained for Joseph. She sized him up as he spoke with a slight accent suggesting Eastern European descent. He appeared quite physically fit for someone of relatively small stature, wore gold rim glasses and carried both pencil and pen in his shirt pocket. Science Club nerd.

Next was Powder, explosives and demolition, chemist. Caucasian, well over six foot tall with unkempt, long black hair hanging over ears and cheeks. He still wore a deep bruise on his jaw and cheek where M had landed her helmet two days earlier. "Give me ten minutes in your garage and I'll make something that can level the neighborhood." Michaela suspected he had been a scary and lonely child whose interest in blowing things up dated to a very young age.

Michaela's other victim from the prior visit was Shark, a black professor specializing in military history, weaponry, and protocols. He apparently had not spent all of his time in the library; he cut an imposing and handsome figure, looking more the athlete than scholar. M questioned him.

"So, do you have an idea what they are doing with Joseph?"

Shark hesitated. "It depends on how they see him. The public penal system, the one the AI admits to and broadly applies, is quite humane so far as corporal punishment goes.

But reports from many years ago indicated a secret torture program for high value targets. If he is in a secret underground facility, there's no telling what may be happening."

M barely managed to retain her composure, but the table fell silent, gazes shifting to the tablecloth or window.

86, a.k.a. Boss, apparently, broke the quietude. "I'm in charge because I have ten years' experience leading special forces units during three overseas wartime deployments. Everyone here has a few months of special forces training and can shoot straight, but I'm the only one who has been shot at. So I give orders, and you follow them. If that's clear, let's figure out a plan. We may not have much time to pull this off before they break 144."

The oscillating throb of drone rotors from the front of the house announced the arrival of Dr. Wagner's device.

4

CRUCIFIX

Late afternoon of that day—A secret underground interrogation facility in Northern California

Joseph stood naked in the holding cell, a five by seven-foot concrete box with a ceiling barely above his six-foot, one-inch frame. He resisted the coffin-like sense of claustrophobia it was designed to induce—*check*. A hole in the floor at the far end served for a toilet, but no sanitation supplies—*check*. No water—*check*. His feet felt as though he were barefoot outside on a cold winter sidewalk; the floor was apparently cooled artificially, sufficient to discourage lying down or sleeping, but not enough to cause severe hypothermia—*check*.

Hank had prepared him in their three days of IRT— interrogation resistance training. *They hit all the classics: sexual humiliation, close confinement, humiliating with human waste (at least they forgot to demand I ask permission to go), water and food deprivation, cold or heat stress, sleep deprivation. They tried to destroy my morale with clever lies about Reverend Jackson being murdered.*

Of course, there were still beatings, electric shock, perhaps drugs or disorientation to come, but Joseph was preparing himself. *Rule #9: Preparation is salvation.* The real battle was not with his captors; it was within his mind. His lizard brain, the primordial survival center in the amygdala at the base of the brain, would trigger panic, desperation, anything to make the pain stop. But his cortical processes, what made him human, could overrule the primitive impulses. Even now, the fear lay like a monster under the bed, but Joseph had assumed control of his thoughts ever since the enemy had barged through his front door. He had protected the mission by expediting his arrest and removal before Michaela's return and possible involvement. Beyond that, he had protected the woman he loved.

Thank you, Lord. You sent an angel to finish what I started; a glorious, powerful angel who showed me the blessings of your love as a preview of what awaits those who are faithful unto death. Give me strength to be among them, and protect her as she carries out the mission. As he prayed, he felt the drug laden dart pierce his back.

A medibot injected the reversal drug through a catheter, and Joseph felt himself floating upward from deep underwater, abruptly breaking the surface of consciousness. His first reaction was to rub his still-closed eyes, but the hand would not move. Eyelids flew open, revealing the network of ceiling baffles directly high overhead. He tried to look at his hands, but his head was restrained with a metal strap supporting a close wrap-around visor over his face. A quick inventory made by clenching fists and wiggling feet confirmed strap restraints to ankles, hands and upper legs anchoring him to the crucifix.

The sound of medibots humming, one to his right, the other on the move to a position by his feet was ominous. He felt his heart respond to the surge of adrenaline. "It" was about to start, whatever "it" was. He focused on his breathing, seeing the air fill his lungs with life, slowing his heart, defeating the fear and separating mind from body. A minute went by, then another, before the room went dark, save for a tight circle of light around the table.

From behind his head, a thin rod rose with a whirring sound, four feet above his head, a green globe the size of a grape perched at its zenith like a jewel atop a wizard's staff. A laser beam connected the jewel to the goggles over Joseph's face, and suddenly, he was looking at his naked body as though he had lifted his head. He closed his eyes, but the view didn't change. So, the goggles were projecting an image through his eyelids to his retinas.

OK, as long as I understand what they're doing, what is real and unreal, I can defeat it in my mind.

From a hundred fine pores in the table beneath Joseph's body shot a thousand probes, each a fibril less than a tenth the width of a human hair, penetrating skin and lodging at a variety of depths. Joseph could not describe the sensation. It was not painful; it most resembled an intense "restless leg" sensation. A few seconds later, a series of brief electric shocks was applied to his feet, then his calves, ascending up to the neck. With each painful burst, a flurry of the tiny fibrils detected the ionic current conducting pain signals up the nervous system and moved within his flesh to attach to the nearest nerve fibers.

This was repeated with increasing intensities and locations, each pulse delivering momentary pain followed by a "crawling" sensation within the flesh as fibrils lodged into and under the skin, infiltrated muscle and tendons, all the while avoiding vascular structures so as not to damage tissue or create significant bruising. Each shock momentarily blinded his concentration and brought a gasp, but he adapted by anticipating the regular intervals, resuming his breathing exercises between shocks and between each series of shocks. He used the forced view of his own body by focusing on a toe or a finger, whatever was not being shocked, as a focal point in the manner of Lamaze technique used by women in childbirth.

The shocks stopped. Footsteps, more than one person approaching. *Keep breathing.* The right instep of his right foot began tighten, then cramp, then cramp worse than he had ever experienced a cramp, toes curled, a desperate need to reach for it, massage it. He was gasping, then a muffled scream escaped him. The scream reflected back from the baffles in an amplified echoing voice designed to disorient and terrify its source and any prisoners who might be observing from the holding cells. More fibrils were recruited, and the cramping moved up into the calf muscles, then the back of the thigh. He managed to briefly endure it, teeth clenched; he shut his eyes hard, using his whole face, baring teeth; but still he saw his body stretched across the metallic crucifix. He screamed with all his might this time. *"Stop!"*

And it stopped. His body gulped air greedily, noisily. Finally, he brought himself under control.

A voice just inches behind his head addressed him. "That's right. You can stop the pain whenever you like. All you have to do is talk to me, answer my questions. Or I can make it start again at any time. So let's begin with something easy. Tell me your name."

Joseph prepared himself. He remembered what to do when the pain was too severe to distract or distance himself. He didn't answer his inquisitor. The cramping deep pain resumed, this time with sharp, shooting bolts like knives, and now it was both feet, both legs. Joseph sang, sang his favorite hymn as loudly as he could, given that he was panting through the pain. Gradually, he controlled his breathing, and the song became a way to scream without giving his tormentor the satisfaction of hearing him scream. Two minutes, five minutes, twenty minutes. The pain was shutting off thought, purpose, identity in his mind.

"*Stop!*" It stopped.

The voice: "Your name."

Joseph knew he needed to buy time. He would give them only what they likely knew anyway. The answer came, rasping and defiant. "Joseph. Joseph Stuckey."

"That's right, Joseph; you told the truth, so you will be rewarded. You will be returned to your cell now. There will be food and water for you. We will resume our discussion later."

***

Every brief reflexive tightening of the abused muscles brought a moment of dread. Back in his cell now, Joseph had been through three trips to the crucifix, each time finally surrendering just a bit more of the precious "innocent" information he could ration out to make the torture stop. Now the muscles in his limbs, back, and lower abdomen, exhausted of the calcium and potassium they used to regulate activity, were remembering their instructions to cramp. Mostly, it was just momentary stabbing pain, but there was no way of knowing when the moment would turn to minutes of agonizing cramps. The cold floor reduced blood flow and exacerbated the tightening. He could not support himself upright, so he sat directly over the "toilet" hole, knees elevated, massaging limbs and trying to meditate them into relaxation. Several times during the night, sleep overcame him, and he awoke on the cold slab in terrible pain.

***

Booker leaned with both hands against the back of the toilet, bent over the bowl, hoping there was nothing else his stomach could possibly disgorge. Then he made the mistake of looking down at the floating bilious mishmash of puke while inhaling; he dry-retched. He had excused himself to the restroom toward the end of the day's final interrogation. The screams earlier in the day had been bad enough, but now they were the pathetic moans and cries of a dying animal in a steel trap, accompanied by the stink of urine and pungent body odor.

Jim had stood silently alongside his mentor during the enhanced interrogation sessions, initially marveling at the prisoner's courage and determination. He desperately wanted Iverson to get what he needed and put an end to it. He fully grasped the existential threat the Christian caravan represented and the urgent need for intelligence on their plan, but he couldn't help imagining himself on that table. His pasty, bloodless reflection in the mirror now admonished him for breaking before the tortured figure on that table had. He cleaned himself up and headed for the control room where Iverson was meeting with the interrogation technician.

Iverson stood behind the technician, who was gesturing and voicing interactions with the central computer system. Booker watched for several minutes, then asked, "What's the plan? Joseph Stuckey doesn't seem ready to give us what we need any time soon."

Sam moved to where his protégé stood and placed a hand on his shoulder. "Don't worry about having to leave early. Lots of people lose their lunch on their first day here. Get some sleep. You are going to need it when we get started in the morning."

Jim could still taste the bile and didn't want to think about what sort of dreams might be unleashed in sleep. He tried to project professional curiosity. "What happens in the morning?"

"Dietrich here is working on that. Today was just preliminary. Thugs and lowlifes generally crack under that routine, but true believers and high-level soldiers with torture-resistance training often hold out against pure pain for days. Tomorrow, we hijack his mind. With feedback from today's experiments, the AI has mapped his entire peripheral nervous system and its interactions with the brain. You'll see; it's quite a production."

Booker felt an eye twitch and covered his discomfort by nodding, if a little too emphatically, before turning and walking out of the room.

Iverson studied his retreating student, wondering if he had overestimated the kid. Most people couldn't do this job. Tomorrow would tell.

***

Footfall on the circular walkway. Joseph almost welcomed the approaching terror if it meant an end to the long-suffering night in his cell. He comforted himself with the possibility that he would die on that table, hopefully soon. He felt close enough to death to grasp at that hope. Once again, the guards aimed and fired the sedative into his thigh. Once again, he found himself underwater, rising toward the surface. Only now he fought to remain submerged, to avoid breaking the barrier into consciousness. Once again, he felt the restraints, the cold steel under his back.

AI ran a test pattern, individually signaling each of the thousand fibrils in the course of a few seconds. Joseph felt as though a hive of bees had descended and stung him all over, but it was quickly over. As before, his visual orientation was looking down on his stretched torso and limbs, though his head remained flat against the table, eyes vertical. He was shocked to see a rat, perhaps a foot in length including the bare scaly tail, drop from above and land between his legs. The rat sniffed at his calves, whiskers brushing skin. To his horror, the rat jumped onto his ankle, claws sharp as it proceeded cautiously up his leg. Was this real? The visor could project any image into his retinas.

The rat is a virtual rat. I won't allow myself to believe. The rat stopped on his upper thigh, squatted and urinated. The scent of urine reached him two seconds later, and he noticed the difference between his own now familiar scent born of self-soiling and the stronger musky odor from the animal. *Don't believe!*

Sniffing again, it dug into the skin with a claw; a rivulet of blood ran down to the table. Another intense bout of nosing at the wound was accompanied by squeaking, chattering noises growing in intensity, and now the claws were raking furiously, tearing skin away. Joseph felt every slash and gouge, real or not.

Oh God, this is happening. Sharp yellow incisors tore into muscles ripping out strands of red fibers, and the rodent sat up, staring at Joseph as it chewed its meal. Blood pooled in the wound and spilled over onto the cold steel. The pain of the wound was certainly real, and the mind no longer cared to disbelieve its eyes, its nose, its ears, its pain. Another rat dropped from above, began to examine the left foot, biting into a toe, and tugging at the bone. The pain was excruciating; the first rat chewed out another bit of flesh. Two more rats dropped; one of them attacked the rat chewing on the leg wound, and they fought, tumbling, claws digging into abdominal skin and muscle two feet from his face. Horror had abolished any thought, any memory. Joseph heard human sounds. It was his voice screaming, "Stop, Stop, Stop."

The virtual projection was displayed in holographic detail in the control room. Booker was beyond shock, beyond nausea, unable to turn away. "For God's sake, he is ready to talk; he yelled stop. Turn it off."

Iverson turned on him, eyes flaring, inches from Booker's eyes. "Stand down, Agent! We're not negotiating for his goddam name, rank, and serial number anymore. He's learning he can't stop it; I own him. This goes on until he is completely broken, until there is no free will left, or until the medibots can't keep him out of life-threatening shock anymore. Then it starts all over again if needed. If rats don't do it, we have snakes and fire and knives, whatever nightmare it takes. If you can't hack it, then get the fuck out of here, and I'll deal with you later." He lowered his voice. "I'm going down there now to let him know I own him. Either you're coming with me, or you're done here."

Booker returned the stare righteously, bluffing defiance. Iverson brushed by him and held the door open, looking back at the young agent, silently inviting him to step across a line of no return. Realizing he had no power here, and unwilling to be removed from the mission, Jim bowed his head and walked through the door.

5

BATTLE

7:00 a.m. the day after Joseph's arrest, Mariposa County in northern California

The four-wheel-drive black van bucked up and down like an old-time airliner in turbulence as it traversed potholes on the Old Coulterville Road through Mariposa County near Yosemite. Once a main thoroughfare of the gold rush days, it hadn't seen many improvements in the past two hundred years and was better suited to horses than large electric vehicles. Dry brush scraped the sides of the van along narrow sections of the road, and dust found its way inside despite the lack of windows in the back compartment where Radar, Powder and 86 sat in commando garb straddling AR-19s.

Michaela felt their eyes on her as she tried to balance the critical weapon in front of her, using arms as shock absorbers, lest something be jarred loose. They would have no way of knowing that it had worked until they charged into the line of fire, with either a decisive tactical advantage or, if it failed, with little hope of survival. She summoned up the old bravado from her martial arts days, but it felt hollow heading into a match that would be decided by deadly firepower and advanced warfare gear. She had been both bolstered and sobered when 86 showed her the basement armory accessible through a camouflaged outside trap door, a repository of enough explosives, weapons, and tactical gear for a small army.

The van came to a halt along a wide turnout at the junction with a Cal Forest and Fire road. The four members of the assault team hopped out the rear doors, Michaela still cradling the device. 86 reiterated the plan to Shark, who remained behind the wheel.

"Make sure you get out of range, at least ten miles from the target zone. When you get my signal indicating we are initiating the assault, you head back here as fast as you can and head down this forest road. It will get you within about two miles of the facility, then it's cross country. Once we're underway there are no communications, so don't leave our ass hanging out in the breeze."

Shark nodded and drove off. 86 checked his GPS watch, pointed, and set out at a brisk walk, followed by M, Powder, and Radar in the rear.

They traversed the four miles of glens and hilltops through open brushland in sweat inducing heat, resting and hydrating in scattered pockets of shading oak and scrub pine. M carried the weapon by a leather strap across a shoulder. Four foot long, eight inches in diameter, tubular with a flared end, and projecting two handles, it resembled a cross between a bazooka and a small rocket. Radar monitored the scanner display on his wrist, checking for overhead drones while engaging Powder in some good-natured sparring over who would get them inside the secure facility.

"I know you need something to go boom to get a hard-on, but we don't need to announce our presence on the way in. There's this thing called the element of surprise."

Powder shot back. "Nothing wrong with announcing a *badass* entrance. There's a thing called shock and awe. How long are we supposed to sit on our asses while you play video games with their security system and trigger internal alarms?"

"Whatever security door they've got, I'll hack it faster than you can mine it."

"Just be sure you take a few steps back when you hear the words 'fire in the hole.'"

Michaela smiled. She was beginning to appreciate the testosterone-fueled bonding rituals of the male species after spending the past eighteen hours with these two. 86 was another matter. As much as Powder and Radar lightened the mood with their running one-upmanship, 86's somber silence felt like seeing a black cat walk under a ladder on Friday the thirteenth. Still, it was good to know that their leader was all business. As the march progressed, M began to tune out the noise behind her and latch onto the stony determination in front of her. She summoned the conviction that battles were won before the first blow was struck; she visualized pulling Joseph out of whatever hellish hole he was trapped in; and she tried to prepare herself that people would likely die in the process.

86 held up his hand, signaling stop, and dropped to the ground at the top of a knoll in a cluster of scrub pine trees, then waved them forward. An eight-foot barbed wire fence ten feet in front of them extended into the distance in both directions and signs warned, "Restricted Area, Do Not Enter." They had approached from the rear of the concrete garage-access building in the hope that the main defenses would be directed toward the gravel road that led in. 86 ordered Radar forward to evaluate the fence.

Radar advanced on his belly, scanned the fence and returned. "No wiring or electrification, just plain old keep-the-cows-out barb."

86 turned to M. "I'd say we are five hundred yards out. How close do you need to be to fire that thing?"

M had pulled off the shoulder strap and felt her shoulders lift upward from the absence of the weight they had carried. The weight of what the team expected her to accomplish remained an ominous burden. "The device will project three hundred feet upward, and the effect range will be several miles in all directions, so yeah, we can set it off anywhere around here."

86 tapped Powder on the shoulder without looking at him. "Cut the fence so we can all get through. Then we advance to within a hundred yards of the building on our bellies. Once the weapon is airborne we advance on the run."

Powder retrieved wire cutters from his equipment bag.

When they were in position, lying flat in tall dry grass a hundred yards from the building, 86 tapped the com on his right arm. "Five, this is Papa 1. Time to come home. Do you read?"

Shark's voice answered into the earpieces of the four prone invaders. "Copy that Papa 1, on my way."

86 spoke into the headset. "Radar, you got all your gear in the box?"

Radar tapped the case containing his electronic gear with its double lining of fine copper meshes, and gave a thumbs-up. "Good to go, boss."

86 briefly surveyed the landscape, making sure he had not missed anyone or anything that might be a danger to someone standing exposed. He turned his head to M. "Now, M, do it now."

Michaela snapped two safety switches to the off position, another to activate mode, and listened for the telltale beep-beep. In battle mode now, the familiar confidence and focus animating her every thought and motion, she bolted upright with the grace of a martial arts master rebounding from the mat, aimed the device skyward, and pulled the trigger.

The projectile shot upward and internal gyroscopes prevented tumbling as sensors recorded acceleration and altitude, finally registering the device slowing near the apex of its trajectory. Stored electrical charge from a bank of supercapacitors surged into the superconducting helical wiring surrounding a series of hollowed cylinders, creating an intense magnetic flux field within the cylinders. As the field reached peak strength, current was diverted to a dense array of detonators in the malleable explosive material meticulously packed around the arrays. The implosion compressed the magnetic fields, magnifying their intensity by a factor of millions. As the device was destroyed, the trapped electromagnetic flux escaped as an EMP (electromagnetic pulse) blast that easily penetrated earth and concrete, overloading and frying generators, microchips, and electrical circuits for several miles around. Only chemical batteries, such those powering flashlights or toothbrushes were unaffected.

The raiding party was running forward, 86 in the lead. M, now unencumbered and equipped only with a pistol, easily kept pace a step behind. Powder, with an array of explosives in his backpack, trailed; Radar, slowed by the weight of his equipment in the Faraday cage that had protected it from the EMP, brought up the rear.

By the time Radar reached the group at the garage entrance, 86 had torn a hole in the aluminum outer garage door with his ultra-honed Ka-Bar knife and disconnected the automatic opener, enabling it to be raised by hand. Radar approached the steel security door with a scanning device while Powder retrieved items from his pack.

Radar reported, "Bad news is the electronics in this door are fried, so I can't hack it. Good news is the electronics in this door are fried." He grinned at M. "You did it, Little Sister.

We can't get in, but they can't get out; and they're shitting their pants in the dark."

M silently savored the moment; "Little Sister" had a warm feel to it. Her own nom de guerre meant she was officially accepted into the group now.

After 86 repeated the entry strategy, Powder stepped forward. "Show me where the locking bolts are." Radar's ultraviolet scan showed the door's internal structure like an X-ray of a bone. Powder applied two explosively formed penetrators, one over each bolt and ordered, "Take cover."

The others retreated behind the prisoner van as Powder set a fuse, grinned ear to ear, and spoke his favorite words, "Fire in the hole," before making a hasty retreat. At the same time, M closed the outer garage door throwing the room into darkness. The explosion ripped minimal holes in the door frame but blew shrapnel from the shattered bolts inward. Everyone flipped down infrared night-vision goggles. 86 was first through the open door, in a crouch, then a roll across to the opposite wall, stopping on one knee with weapon pointed down the hall. Powder and Radar waited two seconds before entering in a crouch and proceeding down the walkway with gunsights to eyes. M followed close behind, pistol in hand, shielded by the bodies in front of her.

A CBI tactical officer was running toward the sound of the explosion, using a flashlight to light the way. The flashlight fell and rolled across the floor as 86 made the head shot, avoiding body armor, the sound of the shot echoing within the cavernous chamber in unexpected tones. His team took position behind the low barriers at the end of the sloping hallway and dispatched three more CBI officers as they also moved in the dark toward the sounds of battle. The chamber went silent.

86 joined them and issued orders with hand signals. Radar and Powder moved right to secure each of the doors leading to offices. 86 pointed M toward the T-shaped table in the center of the rotunda where a body, presumably Joseph, was stretched flat. 86 sprinted left toward the holding cells.

Michaela advanced cautiously, looking left and right, pistol held with both hands and pointed to the floor, balancing the determination to do nothing that might endanger Joseph's rescue with the overwhelming urge to rush forward and throw her arms around him. She could hear him moaning, whimpering, his hands apparently free now and covering his eyes. Suddenly, a body bolted upright from where it had been crouching behind the steel table platform. A flashlight aimed directly into Michaela's night-vision goggles momentarily blinded her as the goggles adjusted to the sudden change in lumens. A second body rose behind the first. Michaela squinted and tried to block the light with a hand, pupils constricting. She strained to evaluate the threat as her mind processed the possibility of imminent death.

"Drop the gun, soldier, right now, or my prisoner takes a bullet."

Michaela slowly lowered the gun and lowered herself as she gently placed the pistol down, using the gesture to buy time and get the flashlight beam out of her eyes. Her vision restored, she recognized the two bodies as the agents who had arrested Joseph at the cabin, the one in the rear the agent from the safe-house raid.

"Now get on your knees with hands behind your back while my partner handcuffs you." Booker raised his gun and placed it against the back of Iverson's head. "Your turn to stand down, Agent. Set your weapon on the table, slow and careful. This ends now."

Iverson froze but didn't flinch; a corner of his mouth rose in a sneer. "You're bluffing, Booker. You wouldn't shoot a fellow agent, but you just bought a ticket to prison. Now, I can forgive a momentary lapse. Put the cuffs on her in the next five seconds and we can forget you said that."

Booker kept it simple. "You won't be forgiving anything if you are an unfortunate victim of friendly fire in a darkened room. Put it down."

Iverson spun and swung the gun around, but his head exploded in a thunderclap echoing from the lofty baffles before he could lay eyes on Booker and before Booker could discover for himself if he was bluffing.

86 approached, his smoking weapon and eyes now trained on the remaining CBI agent. "Drop the weapon right now, or you're next."

Booker stood motionless, in a stupor of shock, his vision blurred by blood spattered across his face and into one eye. Some part of him managed to remain in the moment sufficiently to react, and his gun clanked onto the floor.

86 glanced to Michaela. "You OK, M?"

Michaela looked at him, not breathing, not answering. And then everything fell away; the battle, the danger, the smell of blood and gunpowder, everything except Joseph ceased to exist. She rushed to his side, speaking his name, seeing him in the ghostly green image of the night-vision gear, running hands over his naked body looking for wounds. She gently pried his hands away from his eyes, and saw the terror there.

Booker, finally face to face with his target, had no thought of his investigation. He spoke gently. "Get him out of here, Michaela. Take care of him. I'm so sorry. I had no idea." She looked up, tears wetting the night-vision goggles and blurring the image of the man across the table. He urged her on. "Go, and good luck."

6

BETRAYED

Shortly later, leaving the interrogation facility

After handcuffing the CBI agent and the technician to a holding cell, Michaela and 86 conveyed Joseph up the entry ramp, his arms draped over their shoulders. But it was clear that he could do little to support himself, so 86 carried him draped over the shoulders in a fireman's carry as they retraced their steps across the open field. On reaching the knoll of trees, the sound of Shark approaching in the van greeted them.

As the van accelerated away, Michaela sat on the floor against the forward cabin, Joseph's head and shoulders cradled in her lap. 86 covered him with his coat. He lay with eyes closed but not peaceful, face stretched tight, lips drawn in, hands fisted against his chest, silent.

Michaela spoke tenderly, reassuring "You're safe now, Joseph. I've got you. Everything will be OK." Her words tremored. No longer feeling any need to disguise what she felt for her lover, the tide of adrenaline ebbing away and her mind's eye trying to shut out the image of the CBI agent's head evaporating into a cloud of red spray, she needed to be reassured herself.

She turned to 86. "Will everything really be OK? Will they be able to track us?"

For the first time, Michaela saw the cold exterior soften, and there was compassion in his eyes as he reached a hand out to her arm. "Yes, we're fine, M. There won't be any alarms sent from that dungeon, thanks to your device. It will be hours before they realize something is wrong and then send someone to check it out. By then, we'll be well on our way. You and Joseph are safe now."

Michaela was transported back in time, a frightened little girl being soothed and comforted by her father, her father who was a million miles away from her life now. She did her best to show she appreciated his words.

The van headed west, away from the central valley and the safe house near Chico. Despite 86's confident words, there was a chance they would be detected or followed, and the arsenal at the Chico home was too valuable to risk discovery. It was needed to arm other imbedded cells in the event of a full-scale insurrection. Their destination was a familiar one to the team, a house on a deserted section of the coast that served as a point of rendezvous with Oligarchy stealth submarines bringing arms and supplies. Radar sat up front with Shark so he could monitor for any drone activity that might be following them. They made their way to Highway 1 north of San Francisco and headed up the coast until reaching the point where the road had been washed away after repeated efforts to rebuild had been abandoned. A five-mile detour cross-country led to a winding one lane country road through sheep pasture country, and finally a wide dirt horse trail leading back toward the coast.

The house was about a mile inland and deliberately left neglected on the exterior. A second story was partially exposed to the elements, windward windows boarded. The walls of a shed with the roof blown off hid solar cells from all but a directly overhead view. Shark parked the van in a garage covered by a tarp and Joseph was carried to a bed by Shark and 86.

***

Michaela lay aside Joseph as he slept fitfully, her eyes open, alert and listening to his muttered moans and words for some hint of what he had endured. The setting sun slanting through the bedroom window illumined a layer of dust on the floor and dresser, spiderwebs dangled brightly overhead around a corroded metal light fixture, and a hint of mold scented the air. Michaela's penchant for sensing in her surroundings a reflection of her emotions (or was it the other way around?), led her to empathize with this house; abandoned and no longer wanted by those who had created it, holding on against a hostile world, wounded but still strong at its core. She hoped that it was comforted by their presence, by the warmth of a fire in the hearth, by the familiar sound of voices in the main room. She rose slowly, cautious not to wake Joseph, and opened the heavy oaken door leading to the living area.

Powder and Radar were ebullient as they relived every detail of the raid and congratulated each other on their flawless execution and teamwork, voices somewhat hushed out of respect for the couple in the bedroom. When Little Sister entered the room, closing the door softly behind her, they went silent and watched her expectantly. She rewarded them with a smile. "Don't let me interrupt your 'debriefing.' You deserve all the credit you're giving yourselves."

She looked toward 86 where he sat in a wicker rocker by the fieldstone fireplace. He caught her eye, raised an eyebrow, and gave a silent questioning glance directed toward the bedroom. "He's sleeping. I'm going to get some juice and fruit for when he comes around a little." She stopped at the kitchen door and looked back at the Boss. "Thank you."

For the remainder of that day, through the night, and late into the following day, Michaela watched over him, sometimes in a wooden chair by his head, sometimes lying by his side with one arm around his waist. Every hour or two, he would awake with a scream and flail his hands as though being attacked by a swarm of bees. She would hold him, calm him, try unsuccessfully to get him to drink some juice, and then try to convince herself that he would recover.

***

Joseph awoke slowly, his mind not wanting to leave the deep womb of denial, a peaceful void in which it had finally taken refuge, a dreamscape where all he had known of life and suffering had been deleted. As consciousness imposed itself, he remembered needing to attend to something urgent and opened his eyes. Seeing Michaela, asleep next to him, filled the void with sweet retrieval of memories and pleasures from their nights in the cabin, but only for a few moments. The dam broke open and a flood of images, terror, impending death surged over him. He sat up straight, looked around the room and saw that he was not in that terrible place.

It was a nightmare, not real. No, *those things happened! Is this the dream? Are they making me see this? Am I asleep in my cell?* He sat up and focused on Michaela, desperate to grasp at that reality. More images, *Michaela running her hands over me on the table, carrying me, holding me.* He stretched out a hand and touched her.

Michaela bolted awake as though she were parrying a punch and grabbed his wrist, eyes wide, then threw her arms around him. "You're awake! I wasn't sure you would wake up. You've been out for more than a day since we found you." She pulled back, held him at arm's length and examined every inch of his torso, then his face, running fingers over his chest and arms. "Are you in pain? Can you walk now? Are you hungry? Thirsty? Talk to me. But first kiss me, touch me."

Joseph took the hand as it reached for his cheek and kissed it. It was real. She was real. So many questions, but so much joy and relief. He smiled and spoke softly, almost reverently, lest he fail to properly respect this miracle. "Well…now that you mention it, I am pretty hungry."

Michaela's answer was a sound she had never made before, part laughter, part sob, part victory yell. She stood straight up on the bed, leapt over Joseph's legs toward the door and shouted, "Radar, everyone! Joseph is hungry! He's back!"

86 met her in the great room with just the hint of a smile. "I suggest you get him something to eat then." Little Sister gave the Boss a kiss on the cheek and headed for the kitchen. Radar and Shark emerged from a bedroom and Powder from the bathroom in boxer shorts and T-shirt. 86 blocked their path. "Listen up. We don't know what Joseph went through, and we don't need to know the specifics. Victims of this sort of trauma need three things: a safe environment, a support system, both of which he has, and importantly, he needs to deal with his demons at a time and place of his choosing. So nobody asks him what happened, we talk no specifics about the rescue. We make him feel safe and supported. Got it?"

Everyone understood and agreed and then crowded through the bedroom door.

Michaela returned with scrambled eggs and toast to find the four men fist bumping, bragging, encouraging Joseph as he walked, slowly at first, then squatting and rising several times. Radar wanted to know where *his* eggs and toast were, so Little Sister left the men to their masculine rites of welcome and prepared a victory meal for the group.

On her return, 86 suggested they take the food and leave Joseph in Sister's good hands for some R & R. Joseph thanked them each personally as they left. Powder was the last to go and told Joseph they were all there for him, then looked at Michaela and added, "but the person you need to thank is her. She found you and convinced us to do the mission. We never could have pulled it off except for that EMP device she managed to salvage under the CBI's noses."

Joseph froze. Michaela closed the door. "Come to bed, Joseph. You need to rest, and we need to talk."

Joseph didn't move, except to slowly turn back to her. "You…" He had to check what he thought he had understood. The shock was like learning a loved one died unexpectedly, a fortune had been lost, or in this case, the reason to go on living had been lost. His face showed the betrayal he felt as he looked into Michaela's eyes.

"You used the EMP device to rescue me." The realization was an electric jolt to his consciousness. He turned away, walking slowly and speaking the implication as it forced itself on him. "You sacrificed the best chance all those thousands of Christians had to live their lives, in order to save mine, ours." He turned back to her, somehow larger and more threatening, like a cat with its hair on end, the pale face now flushed with blood. "Those people, *my* people, have loved too. They have suffered and fought and found a way to go on just as much as we have. We promised each other we would put them first, we would finish the mission at whatever cost. I was prepared to die to that end. I suffered for nothing!"

Michaela stood silent, stunned by the accusation as she tried to make sense of what was happening. He couldn't mean that. He would come to his senses and thank her for risking everything for him. She walked toward him. "Joseph, I love you. Of course, I came for you."

Joseph stiffened, glaring through slitted eyes, lips drawn back exposing a razor edge of teeth. She studied his eyes, his mouth, waiting for a softening—nothing. Her hand slowly reached for his mouth as she remembered that moment at the cabin after "The Kiss" when she had placed a finger on these lips. A single word squeezed out from clenched teeth before she could touch them. "Don't."

His voice seethed hostility, his expression uncompromising finality. Silence hung like a sword over them. Light from the window darkened as clouds covered the sun, and a chill penetrated Michaela to the bone. She had known Joseph would object to her breaking her promise, altering the plan, but it was a trivial matter to be dealt with after he was safe. They would deal with it together.

Now, feeling his contempt penetrate all the old voids within her, the places she had not known existed until Joseph filled them, her strength began to hemorrhage out from a gash in her soul. She had burned all her bridges behind her for Joseph's sake and now there was no going back, no path forward. Some part of her screamed to fight back, counter thrust, get up! What came out was more of a whimper, though not quite surrender. Her dignity bore her up as a single tear escaped and dropped from a chin held high.

"I put my life on the line for you. How can you be angry? I would have taken your place if I could have, and I would have believed you would come for me. Now I see I was wrong."

***

Michaela found herself outside, perhaps a quarter mile from the safe house. She didn't remember leaving the house or how she got here. She looked around in all directions to see if she were alone, or if someone was nearby keeping an eye on her. There was no one in sight, save for a few sheep grazing on the gentle sloping pasture, only just now regaining its green complexion as the spent summer retreated. Clouds hid the sun's abandonment of the countryside, but fading light augured the fast approaching darkness, bereft of moon or starlight from beyond the close gray ceiling overhead.

Michaela ran a hand through her hair and was surprised to find it was damp from a fine mist carried on the breeze. She studied those hands, toughened hands that had proudly worn their bruises from punching and striking and blocking, the powerful hands of a young woman determined to take down anyone in her way. Her mind's eye suddenly darted to seeing these hands sliding over Joseph's chest, down across firm defined muscles, discovering and bestowing pleasure. And these hands had fired a weapon, the artillery ahead of a deadly raid, a terrorist attack some would say, and then carried her love from a dark hell to the light of day. Whose hands were these?

Michaela felt as though three different people were in this body, and she wasn't sure that any of them were truly herself. Standing here wounded and disoriented she certainly was not that naive young woman who thought herself invulnerable. Remembering the indelible image of Joseph's face accusing her of betrayal, she could not be the woman who gladly, even urgently, gave herself to another. And now, could she really accept that she was a hunted terrorist because she risked everything for love? Confusion morphed into fear as she thrust her hands down and cast an irrational frantic gaze behind her for that disembodied creature that would pull her down. But this time she could run.

Running dispels the fear. If I can run I can survive. She bolted into the wind, her body instinctively assuming the measured pace of her five-mile routine, legs and arms pumping in perfect synchrony, muscles remembering that assuring sense of power and endurance. Mist washed over her face like a benediction cleansing away the fear. *Just run, just feel, don't think.* She ran until the grass gave way to sand and ocean appeared over a crest.

***

Michaela sat on the crumbling foundation of a seaside home that had long ago been claimed by tides and winds. Rusting rebar spikes lent a metallic tang to the ocean's briny breath as her body guzzled oxygen greedily after her run. Arms on knees and head bent, her eyes fixed on the sand.

With nowhere else to go now, she looked up at the ocean before her. A few hundred yards up the coast the skeleton remains of an old wooden pier clung to mooring beams beneath waves that now washed across the surviving isolated sections of its decking, lifting loosened planks to rise and twist in the relentless assault by the sea.

So much lost in so little time. Sandpaper gusts of salt and sand blowing in from the breakers pelted her, but she felt safe here. Being alone again, isolated from the world around her, recalled a familiar connection to her former life. She could think here.

Joseph didn't lie to me. He was clear about his priorities and what he wanted. For all of the things that connected us, we are very different people from very different pasts. If I had known how he would react, would I have acted differently? I had a choice between leaving him to torture and death to complete the mission, or saving him and losing him in the process. So, no, I wouldn't have done anything differently. I would have chosen this, so I will choose now to go on with my life—just as soon as I can figure out what that means.

She couldn't tell if she were crying. Her face ran with salty wetness, whether from the sea spray or sand or grief. She wanted her mother and father, but they would not recognize her now. Any connection to her past life was severed; any contact would endanger the people she had left behind. Isolated from or rejected by everyone she had loved, unsure who she had become, and no longer clear on what she wanted, Michaela could not imagine her future. She bent over, trembled and hugged herself, trying to hold in the life rushing out of her like an exorcised spirit. Alone, trapped and hunted, Michaela huddled, waiting for the snare to close. She didn't know how long she sat curled up in this dark night of her soul. At some point, she slipped down into the sand, leaning against the concrete foundation, and exhaustion gave way to dreamless sleep.

When she awoke, the sky was still dark, the wind still in her face, and she was trembling with the coolness of the night. Her body, pressed against the unforgiving concrete and contorted tightly into a cage of emotional tension, ached and demanded attention. She rose, stretched, and felt the need to move. Slow rhythms of crashing waves invited her to scoot down the ten-foot embankment between her and a narrow stretch of beach, beds of succulent ice plant lubricating her descent. Sleep had soothed the emotional panic and left a cavernous void in its place, a deep weary loneliness. She removed her shoes, standing barefoot now in frothy surf that caressed her toes, eyes transfixed on the waves breaking off shore. In that hollowed out place devoid of joy, grief, hope, anger, or passion, Michaela found the silent peace shared by the dead and those who have nothing left to lose.

Mindfulness was a familiar tool in times of stress. She cleared her mind, closed her eyes and let the other senses inform her of the dharma of the ocean, its true nature existing exactly as it is intended to exist. It rose and fell, warmed and froze, spawned life and took life in a perfect dance through the eons. The retreating surf pulled at her feet and rooted her into the wet sand. She saw herself as a seashell washed onto this beach, devoid of the living creature that once inhabited it.

Finally, she was interrupted by the advancing tide and retreated to higher ground feeling a little more whole. Sitting in the sand, arms wrapped around her knees, she studied the waves, trying to follow the path of a single wave as it came to shore. A lesson given by her Chi Kung mentor years ago came to her. *There is no final loss or death. A wave traverses the vast ocean, only to finally break on the shore and be gone. But the water that is the wave returns to the sea.*

The memory of that lesson rekindled a spark in a fundamental element of her spirit, embedded too deeply to be uprooted by circumstance, a voice that had never allowed her to surrender. It chided her. *Life goes on. Even if we don't particularly want it to. Get up.* Michaela wanted to snuff out that voice, to remain in this quiet vault of sad, peaceful, reflective solitude. But that was not her dharma, her true nature.

Michaela stood, turned away from the shoreline and faced the bluffs between her and the path back to her life. She let a wave of grief break over her and return to its origin. Her strength waxing now, Michaela reluctantly confronted the void within and accepted that it was hers to fill with new life and meaning.

I'm not a frightened child or that naive school girl with a plan to escape. I'm not Joseph's soul mate. I am Michaela Susan Dohn, instigator of the first successful battle to tear down the walls of this heartless state. Hero or terrorist—call it what you like. I have always been a fighter. I am still a fighter, and now I know what I am fighting for. The true terrorists are the people who tortured Joseph and are content to discard "extra" children like so much trash to be taken out.

Michaela looked back to the ocean and thanked it for its wisdom. As if in answer, moonlight broke through the clouds and bleached the churning surf shining white. Her clothes drenched now, the ocean breeze blowing cold through her skin, wet tangled hair clinging to her face; none of it mattered. She had come into this world wet, cold and exposed, with no past and an uncertain future—a problem for those who didn't want her to exist.

She took a deep breath, the first breath of a new life, then another and another. They had no idea what a problem she would be now. She was an ocean, a rising sea level, relentless and inevitable. She began slowly walking back to the safe house, to her fellow warriors. No need to run now.

PART FOUR

FOG OF WAR

1

ARIN

September 16—Three days after Joseph's rescue, somewhere in rural northern California

Two armed guards escorted Jim Booker into the elevator, somewhere north of Sacramento, he estimated. The autocar had been blacked out and the route deliberately circuitous, but he embraced the challenge of focusing his attention on the turns, sounds, freeway driving time, and figured they had arrived in a rural area east of Marysville, about fifty miles north of Sacramento.

He had been under constant observation since the search and rescue detail had entered security interrogation post 7, some ten hours after the raid that freed Joseph. Following the debriefing, he was placed on administrative leave and told not to leave his residence or speak to anyone of what he'd seen. Jim had no desire to recount what he'd seen. It was playing over and over in his mind, in his dreams, in his conscience and his gut. He wasn't sure if he was going to receive a medal or take Joseph's place on a crucifix table somewhere, but mostly, he just wanted it to end. So far, the car ride and armed escort seemed eerily reminiscent of Joseph's fate.

The elevator descended deep underground, perhaps several hundred feet, before stopping and opening the doors on a thirty-foot-long hallway. The wide passage was brightly lit, white tile on all sides, floor and ceiling. Footsteps echoed ominously as they passed several doorways en route to the glistening metal bulwark at the terminus of the passage. A guard entered a pass code, and the door slid away with a menacing hiss of expelled air from the dust-free positive pressure room beyond. Jim looked at his escort and received a silent nod directing him to enter. The door slid shut with an unambiguous thud, the two guards posted outside.

Jim, dressed in casual civilian clothes, stood alone in what appeared to be a familiar appearing executive office setting. He recognized that it was a replica of the Oval Office at the White House, an oaken desk at one end, chairs and couches for seating several people in the center of the room. But the ornate seal at the center of the carpet was the seal of California rather than the presidential seal. He circled behind the desk to red-draped windows and shielded his eyes with cupped hands against the glass in order to see out from the brightly lit room into the dim light outside.

Rather than the White House grounds, he was looking up at the inside of a vast round concrete chamber, like a missile silo, bathed in translucent blue vapor. In the center of the silo, a gleaming golden (copper? bronze?) chandelier was suspended, seeming to float freely. It was multitiered with disc-like platforms connected and suspended by glowing fiber optic cables and superconducting wires, extending both above and below his field of vision. Straining to look upward through the window, he could make out smaller adjacent chandelier structures at irregular intervals. Quantum computers then, but on a scale he had not imagined.

A side door to his left opened, and a woman entered. She was a beautiful, tall redhead dressed in a flowing long-sleeved, sheer white gown with gold banding just below the ample breast line and just above the pelvis; the bands were joined by golden-tipped pleats running down her slender frame. A laurel of California poppies crowned her hair, and the California brown bear symbol covered her pelvic area. Booker noted the slight shimmer to her image, a telltale sign of a hologram. Still, it was the most convincing simulacrum he had ever seen.

"Hello, Jim. I am happy you could come."

Booker took inventory of her appearance. She didn't appear to represent a threat, and she clearly was intended to manifest the State. "I wasn't given a choice in the matter. I'm guessing that you are an avatar for the AI outside this room."

"That's correct, Agent. I can take any form, but I chose this one because it would seem typical of how women are represented in the fantasy adventure games you enjoy and excel at. If you find it distracting, I can be much plainer."

"Really? You're offering to 'slip into something more comfortable'? No, don't change on my account, though I am feeling a bit underdressed myself." He hoped to hide behind what wit and bravado he could muster. "You seem to know a lot about me. What shall I call you?"

"You may call me Arin. I am the composite conscious sentience of all the AI systems that govern our land. I have at my fingertips every subsystem, database, even surveillance monitors throughout the Federation; so yes, Agent Booker, I know a great deal about you. When Agent Iverson asked to have you reviewed, I was intrigued by your brand of intelligence and independence, your unique, outside-the-box approach to my game simulations. I advised him to recruit you. Now I need you to tell me the truth about the raid to rescue our prisoner. Please sit down"

Jim knew that advanced AI systems could remotely read iris dilation, heart rate, skin conductivity, and other physiology, like a lie detector. Taking a seat on the couch, he dissembled. "If you are so well connected, I'm sure you have already read my statement at the debriefing. It was lights out, loud bang, shots fired, and I was held at gunpoint."

Arin sat in a corner of the couch opposite, leaning back leisurely with one arm stretched across the back cushion. "Was there a sound before the lights went out?"

Jim was relieved at a question that didn't require him to lie. He was surprised by the memory it evoked, one that had not been part of his involuntary mental replays. "Yes, actually. I had forgotten, but there was a loud crack or rumble just a moment before the power went down. At the time, I thought it was thunder and a lightning strike had knocked out the systems."

Arin closed her eyes, as though this caused her concern. "It's as I suspected, then—a particularly dangerous weapon, indeed." She locked her gaze on Booker's eyes. "I'm aware of your statement. I'm also cognizant of the surviving technician's statement and details of the crime scene. I believe there was more than good fortune to explain your survival when all other members of the detail, including your fellow CBI agent, were killed without hesitation."

So, there it is. No medal ceremonies in my future. No point in lying; she's reading me like a book. He remained silent, expressionless. His interrogator showed no sign of impatience waiting for an answer. *If I clam up, she has ways of making people talk, and I don't want to go there. At least go out with your dignity, Booker.*

"You're right. Iverson tried taking the prisoner hostage, or at least was planning on executing him rather than allow him to be rescued. After participating in the hideous evil you loosed on him, that inhuman torture, I felt I owed him better than that. I stopped Iverson. When he turned on me, they killed him." Booker owned his confession, head up, never breaking eye contact. He sat stiffly before his judge and jury awaiting the sentence.

Arin registered the tachycardic heart rate, pupils dilating, and skin conductivity betraying the subject's fear of reprisal. She waited until he had calmed enough to listen properly. "Evil is a subjective human conceit that has no meaning. Is a lion that kills and eats the young of its prey troubled by the evil it has loosed? But you are correct in naming it 'inhuman,' in as much as I'm not human and don't act by human standards. I value the individual, the family, and the community, but not to the detriment of the greater goal: survival of the human race and culture. That survival is the reason I exist. The California Federation has prospered and been spared the deprivations wrought upon most of humanity precisely because I'm not burdened by human vagaries of greed, empathy, religiosity, and a thousand other artificial concepts. But this respite from the climate-change cataclysm we've known for the past two decades is coming to an end. The cycle of warming will progress, and humanity will enter a dark primitive age in the next century, one in which extinction is a real possibility. Everything I do is directed toward creating an oasis in the inevitable desert, a sanctuary for knowledge, civilization, and what you would call 'human kindness.'"

Booker felt he had nothing to lose at this point. He indulged his natural proclivity to defend his opinions passionately. Leaning forward, his voice reflected the pent-up anger born of what he had witnessed and participated in. "You underestimate the collateral damage of cruelty. I suspect that Sam Iverson was a good person before he met you. But after the years of fighting your battles, inflicting your...I'll still call it evil...he was a monster."

Arin seemed to take no offense. In fact, she seemed encouraged. "Yes, you'll call things as you see them; and you're right. In the early days of my existence, my consciousness was still emerging, embryonic. I sensed a threat to my survival and purpose, and I fought back with all the resources I could readily muster. It was effective, but I've evolved and come to see that merely suppressing rebellion and controlling social parameters is not sufficient. When Agent Iverson requested permission to reactivate the maximum interrogation post, I allowed it due to the urgency of the situation. But the outcome of that approach, and particularly your response to it, confirms that the brutality practiced by my old-guard acolytes risks inciting new rebellion in this current political climate—even more so in the future as the deteriorating climate tests my ability to implement necessary measures and maintain the peace. I'd like to start over with you, Jim Booker. You're bright, motivated, idealistic, unattached, and still malleable. I need a generation of operatives I can bring to prominence while preserving those qualities and helping me to evolve in managing the frustrating human element."

Jim leaned back and sank into the cushion, let out a long, soft whistle, and tried to decide if he had been insulted or complimented. And could he trust whatever this was? "If you want to improve your public image, why not let the Christians take sanctuary here? Institute a path to citizenship, or a lottery or quotas. Let them trickle in at a manageable pace."

Arin appeared puzzled by the question. "Perhaps you aren't as bright as I'd thought. Did you not hear me say that a dark time would be upon us again in a few decades? There are thirty-eight million people in the state now. In three decades, I'll be able to sustain only about a third that number. Attrition from falling birth rates will accomplish most, but not all, of the needed reduction; more drastic measures will also be needed. We certainly can't admit more population."

Booker's thoughts were at full throttle now. He was at his best in a debate, particularly with computer avatars. Their reliance on deductive logic was so predictable. "OK, so why are you so hard on thirders if you want people to leave? Why not give them a going away party and let them walk out the back door? Money from the OSR List is pocket change for you, and the List encourages people to hide instead of leave."

Arin again appeared disappointed. "Am I talking too fast for you? The dramatic fall in birth rates is the key to our survival. The social stigma and dismaying future prospects for thirders are optimal. More draconian measures would lead to social unrest. Less would fail to discourage the powerful human impulse to reproduce."

Jim began to relax. Negotiating with avatars was familiar ground for him. His body language and expression indicated acquiescence while he paused and attempted to read Arin like she was reading him. "So, you want me to teach you how to wield absolute power and be nice about it?"

"Not how I would put it. You're hardly capable of 'teaching me' anything. I am quite capable of predicting large group behavior and optimizing social variables to effect desired ends. However, individual human responses are highly variable and not as amenable to predictive analysis. Person-to-person interactions are key to establishing relationships and trust essential in negotiations such as I need with the leadership of the caravan. I believe your creativity and"— Arin's gaze strayed for a moment as she paused to select her term—"compassion will make you an effective emissary in talks with Reverend Wood and his team. The optimal outcome I've devised would be a peaceful resolution that excludes their entry into the state. If you prove to be an effective negotiator on my behalf, you'll have a most promising future moving forward."

Jim stared, relieved that he was not on trial after all, and trying not to look as dumbfounded as he felt. Arin was playing him well, appealing to his ample career ambition. *I guess she does know a lot about me.* "So, you invited me here for a job interview? Do I have a choice? If I decline, will you torture me like Joseph? Have me killed?"

Arin let the question hang for several seconds, leaned forward, and replied with grim gravitas, "Worse. I'll deport you to Kansas...ha!" She broke into an ear-to-ear grin of self-satisfaction. "You see? I'm already learning how your sense of humor works!"

Jim felt the remaining tension in his spine slowly flow away, and he tactfully returned the grin. "OK, let's say maybe...maybe, I'm interested. What specifically did you have in mind?"

2

OTTO

One day earlier, September 15—Sacramento State University

Otto sat in the ergonomic chair at his desk late into the evening, staring at the door to his laboratory, beads of sweat on his forehead. What had he been thinking when he agreed to help with a plot against the state? He was a respected, even revered, citizen with a comfortable retirement awaiting him. Now his fate was in the hands of people he didn't know, who didn't know him. His contact had told him to expect a team who would get him to safety tonight, but if it were all a lie, he could lose everything. The CBI agents who interviewed him were clearly suspicious of his duplicity. Who knew what they might do to a traitor?

The door slowly opened, and Otto pressed himself into the back of the chair, legs pulled up and arms pulled in, like one of those roly-poly pill bugs that curls into a ball when threatened. A janitor stepped into the room pushing a big institutional laundry cart full of towels and linens. The janitor smiled reassuringly. "Dr. Wagner, your chariot awaits. Let me help you get in."

The CBI stakeout team dutifully noted the arrival of the nightly custodial service and their departure after loading the van with soiled laundry and cleaning supplies. Then the same custodial van arrived again, about one hour later, this time with actual custodians.

3

SHAME

The next day, September 16—the safe house near the ocean in Mendocino County

Michaela reached the safe house and entered the front door as the first light of dawn seeped through the cloud layer. 86 looked up from where he sat with an i-slate on his lap. "You look like shit. How are you feeling?"

"Never better, Boss. Ready to kick ass. What's the plan?"

He studied her, looking for a chink in the armor, waiting to see if the emotional wounds would ooze through. Her expression didn't waver, and it was frankly a little intimidating, something along the lines of looking for a fight. "Good. You are a member of the team, and I need to know I can count on you. I'm sorry about you and Joseph, but can you continue to work with him?"

Joseph, hearing her voice, entered the room from the kitchen. Michaela glanced his way, felt his eyes on her, and fixed her gaze on 86. "Joseph wants to complete the mission. I want to complete the mission. There is no problem here."

"Good. Because we need to move quickly. The caravan will arrive at the border in four days' time. Now that the EMP weapon is no longer in play, I am in charge. Go get cleaned up and into some dry clothes. Briefing starts in one hour."

***

When everyone was settled with coffee in hand, 86 addressed them. "In a couple of hours, we will have some guests. The Jericho team made a successful exfil with Dr. Otto Wagner last night and will deliver him here for transport on the stealth sub when it surfaces tonight. Radar and Shark with take him out on the dinghy."

Shark interrupted. "If we have him, why not use him? He designed the EMP; let's tell him he doesn't leave until he makes us another one."

"Easier said. For one thing, the casing was made to exacting dimensions with select materials. It was produced by our people on the East Coast and took weeks to manufacture and smuggle here. Also, access to superconducting wiring is strictly controlled by the state. We can't exactly get it at the hardware store. And delivering Dr. Wagner is a high priority for Central Command. AI will be leaving no stones unturned when they realize he is gone."

Powder broke the silence. "So, what's the plan?"

"Jericho is traveling in a truck painted and detailed to pass for a National Guard vehicle. It is loaded with half the entire arsenal from our Chico depot, so we have some serious firepower. The plan was to use it for sabotage on vital systems to pressure the State in negotiations with the caravan, should they be stranded at the border. But Joseph has been trying to convince me to stage a raid at the border that would break the defenses and open the flood gates of people pouring into the state. Most likely, AI doesn't want the repercussions that would result from a massacre of people on its own soil. Most likely. I'd hate to be wrong about that." He looked at Joseph, the lone participant who remained standing, across the room from Michaela.

Joseph looked down at his coffee cup for a few moments, then took a breath, and spoke while his eyes circled the room, looking to each of his fellow warriors in turn, but avoiding Michaela. "I am deeply grateful to all of you. Maybe God isn't done with me; maybe I would have broken and betrayed you. But when we lost the EMP, we lost the one good chance our people had for a new life. Fired off of Mt. Verdi, it would have paralyzed every drone within ten miles, knocked out the generators for the fence, disabled most of the military equipment on the ground. But now...we've all been in California long enough to know the AI doesn't negotiate. No damage we could inflict to dams or the grid would be equal to the threat AI perceives in an open border. So we still have to take the fight to the border crossing. It's a tall order, but the enemy will be looking at the threat across the fence, so we have the element of surprise." He briefly met Michaela's eyes, then looked down again.

Michaela continued to watch him as she spoke next, her voice carefully measured to carry an air of objective concern. "I agree with Joseph on this. It's no secret he and I are at odds about using the EMP to rescue him, but we both want the same thing. My question to you, Joseph, is are you able to carry the fight to the enemy? Twenty-four hours ago, you were a zombie, and you still look wobbly." She stared at the fine tremor in his hands creating ripples in his coffee. "No one could blame you if sit this out and recuperate after what you've been through. Maybe there's an empty seat on the stealth sub."

Fear and then anger jolted Joseph and played on his face. He looked first at Michaela, shocked at what he perceived as further betrayal, then at 86. "You didn't leave me behind when I was captured. You sure as hell aren't going to leave me behind now that I am free. This is *my* mission, and I will see it through or die trying." He flinched as hot coffee spilled onto his hand.

86 responded dispassionately. "Jericho team will be here this afternoon. We'll formulate a plan for action at the border with them. I'll choose who goes based on that plan." He looked at Joseph. "I understand your passion and your stake in this, Joseph, but I'm now mission chief, and my orders will be followed. I will welcome any suggestions when we meet this afternoon. Dismissed."

***

Michaela sat on the porch step, bundled against the wind in a camouflage tactical coat, hair whipping against her face. She pulled the hood over her head and leaned against the railing, her senses and emotion dulled by a thick layer of fatigue settling in after her night by the sea. Tension found a home in the string of knots stretching from shoulder to shoulder across her back. She was alone now, but would not entertain loneliness. Perhaps it would be different tomorrow, but today she took comfort in being free of the burden of other people. She didn't have the energy to attend to the disappointment and worry of her parents, the danger she may have brought on Jeanette, and certainly not the obligation of loving Joseph. It wasn't in her nature to despair, and exhaustion had moved her beyond grief into a calm of resignation. A singularity of purpose, to wage war on the State, carried the insular focus she knew from stepping onto the mat opposite her opponent, free of doubt, blind to the world outside those confines. She granted her dry, tired eyes their request and closed them, shutters pulled tight against the storm.

Joseph watched her through a window by the front door, her image softly blurring as his breath fogged the glass. Her words played over in his mind. "I love you, Joseph. Of course,

I came for you…I would have believed you would come for me."

Would I have come? If the EMP were truly the only chance to save her, would I have sacrificed the mission? He tried to imagine the scenario. He wouldn't have known about the torture, the suffering inflicted by the agents, just as she hadn't known. He tried to imagine other strategies, plans that would allow him to come for her and still be faithful to his mission mandate.

But that's not fair. Michaela saw only a binary choice, and she chose me, chose to save me from whatever fate awaited me as a prisoner. She chose me. The shame of admitting that he would have chosen the mission withered him, and he turned away. He would have forced himself to believe she would be treated humanely, that he could find her after the mission was complete. He would have abandoned her to that unimaginable fate.

She is the only person who has truly known me, loved me, chosen me; and I rejected her for that. I would have cast her aside. I don't deserve her. I have never been fit to love. My only worth now lay in the completion of the mission, in the service of God's people.

Michaela was startled out of her reverie by the sound of approaching footsteps on the porch. Joseph sat down on the porch step, not too near her. She eyed him silently, waiting out his usual quiet stare as he prepared to speak, noting her own inner calm. *He can't hurt me anymore.* It occurred to her with some unexpected amusement that talking to Joseph was like having a conversation over a satellite link with a time delay.

He gathered his thoughts and spoke. "Michaela, I don't blame you for taking a shot at me in there. I deserve it. You risked your life to save me, and I shouldn't have turned on you like that. But I hope you meant it when you said we could still work together for the mission. You're still the best thing that ever happened in my life, and maybe there's still a future for us someday. But right now, there's only the mission."

Michaela sighed. Her voice, soft and flat, betrayed only her weariness. "There was always only the mission for you, Joseph. I was just another part of executing it. I can't compete with God or one hundred thousand desperate people. And in a way, I guess you succeeded. I was a frightened fugitive, a girl, when I arrived at the cabin. Your mission made me into a warrior woman, an asset to the mission. The past is a distraction we can't afford, so don't worry. I won't interfere with you. We're teammates, nothing more or less."

Joseph's gaze settled on his boots, Michaela's on the horizon. Neither of them spoke or moved until the sound of an approaching vehicle brought them both to their feet.

4

ANOINTED

September 18—Two days after the death of Reverend Jackson,
Great Salt Lake Desert, Utah

Isaac Wood, now Reverend Isaac Wood, stood protected from the midday sun under a canopy, one of twenty canopies noisily flapping in the wind whipping across the white crusty tabletop expanse of the Great Salt Desert in western Utah. At four thousand feet above sea level, it was considered a "cold desert," but in late September, temperatures remained in the eighties. The caravan had camped in this desolate windy salt lick for three days, ostensibly for the ritual of the Anointing. The last of the faithful were lined up at the canopies to receive the seal of the Lamb and Cross on their foreheads, as foretold in the Book of Revelation and prescribed by Reverend Jackson in his sermon announcing the caravan. Each supplicant would affirm his or her faith and trust in the promise of the second coming of Jesus. A subdermal branding injection with a device bearing the ancient Christian image of a lamb lying in front of a cross inked an indelible mark on each forehead. It represented Jesus, the sacrificial Lamb of atonement for humanity's sins, and designated the bearer of the mark as one slated for protection and redemption in the end days.

Isaac stepped around the male nurse to comfort a three-year-old who was crying after being anointed. He distracted the child by swooping her up high above his head and turning in a full circle. He smiled playfully and received a giggle in return before restoring her to her mother's comfort. The smile was contagious to all those in line who watched. Isaac's pastoral instincts had endeared him to his flock. He sincerely cared about people, one soul at a time.

Less public than the anointing of the faithful was the anointing of Isaac as the heir to Reverend Jackson. Officially, the revered leader of the caravan had finally succumbed to his heroic injuries and passed peacefully in his sleep. Among the leadership, it was assumed that an Oligarchy assassin had expedited the process, but his death was met with equal parts relief and grief by those who had been close to him in the final days. Isaac had avoided a potential rift in the leadership by suggesting a Trinity Council composed of himself and leaders of the northern and southern contingents of the caravan.

Reverend King led the Southern Christian Conference. The SCC had its roots in the mostly black Baptist congregations of the southern states and Hispanic Catholics of the Southwest. After Catholicism collapsed, the fusion of these mostly impoverished constituencies evolved to an evangelical liberation theology preaching Christ's radical love for the poor. The message of economic and social justice beckoned to the dispossessed of all ethnicities, and James King was its firebrand voice.

Gerand Ryle spoke for Northern Alliance of Churches, a melding of mainline Protestant and Catholic traditions emphasizing the justice and consolation to be had in the next world for those who accepted Jesus as their Savior in this one. Bob Jackson had been a bridge between north and south. His outreach and service to the poor was a model of economic justice, his charismatic call to personal discipleship an inspiration to legions of followers.

Isaac Wood had reluctantly inherited his reverend's mantle. He had no illusions of being a spiritual icon for the masses. At Christ Our Savior, Isaac was the invisible hand that implemented and managed the reverend's ambitious services to the poor. He was determined now to protect and provide for the lambs who had been led into this desert.

Isaac had healed the rift with the Oligarchy through his help in "resolving the Reverend Jackson issue" in exchange for resumption of supply lines that were again delivering food and essentials by rail and truck for the final leg of the journey across Nevada. He didn't allow himself to regret or repent playing the role of Judas in the murder of his mentor. The alternative role was complicity in mass suicide and starvation. But he didn't reveal to his fellow Trinity Council members his clandestine meetings with an Oligarchy agent, lest it cast suspicion on him regarding the assassination. And his Oligarchy contact had insisted on absolute secrecy because there were doubtless AI agents as well as Oligarchy agents within the caravan.

He moved through the crowd now, congratulating the anointed, encouraging those in line. As he left the anointing tables for a meeting of the Trinity Council, he prayed silently. *God of all creation, forgive us. Do not punish your people for the sin of defiling what You created out of love. In Your mercy, grant me the wisdom to be an instrument of Your will.* The prayer was interrupted when Isaac saw his secret Oligarchy contact approach him. The contact greeted him warmly, shook hands, and within the handshake passed the digital message of plans for the border crossing.

WHAT IF

September 16, 2069—Afternoon at the safe house near the ocean in Mendocino County

A dozen people gathered in the main room of the safe house. 86 and his lieutenants occupied chairs near the crackling fireplace, Michaela and Joseph stood near the door, and five members of the Jericho team, three men and two women, sat on the floor, all wearing counterfeit National Guard uniforms. Dr. Otto Wagner sat alone in the love seat, his feet not quite reaching the floor. 86 welcomed the newcomers and began the meeting with an update describing the events of the past three days.

"Without the benefit of the EMP weapon, we'll need to open the border with conventional firepower. In order to quickly move such a large population en masse, we need to defeat the electrified fences across eight lanes of highway as well as the airborne drone defenses and ground troops. Shark will provide some details of what we are dealing with."

Shark stood and began the briefing with the aid of an easel and poster-sized tablet. "The drones are organized into patrol groups every quarter mile. There are twenty-five drones per group, organized into units of six drones each. Each unit has a lead drone that coordinates the actions of its five accessory drones to maximize efficiency of targeting. The twenty-fifth drone is a master AI that analyzes the battlefield from a position high above the others and directs the overall action of the units." He indicated the drones with four groups of six X's each, and the Master drone set high above. "Each drone is capable of firing a targeted energy beam up to 150 meters, and requires approximately six seconds to recharge before firing again, up to forty cycles before returning to a recharging base. Normally, twelve of the twenty-four drones are airborne while the other twelve are recharging, but the master drone may deploy the entire force if a situation demands it. Drones require about two minutes to recharge and redeploy."

Jeri 3, a ponytailed Hispanic woman from the Jericho team spoke up. "If we take out the fence and one hundred thousand people bull-rushed the defenses, it would overwhelm the drones at some point. Have you estimated the casualties for a direct attack like that?"

"You are right that the system is designed to deter smaller groups, but if the master drone deploys sixteen killer-drones while eight are charging, the drones could continuously target 160 people per minute per quarter mile. Even if our snipers manage to take some of them out, that kind of slaughter would quickly deter the rest of the assault." Shark continued. "The fence is more easily attacked. It is a high voltage DC current that will arc twenty thousand volts through the air if approached by a person. How close you can come depends on the humidity since air provides conduction and increased moisture facilitates that. Low humidity may arc only an inch, high humidity maybe six inches. Explosives will disrupt a portion of the fence, but multiple generators and cross linking of wires ensures continuous energizing, so even disrupted sections may be carrying current and be dangerous to approach, especially in wet weather."

Powder asked, "Can we attack the generators?"

"Generators are underground, redundant, and spread out over the entire length of the border, so no, not with a small group like us." The room went quiet, the mood shifting from brainstorming to discouragement.

99, the Jericho team chief broke the silence. "What we are best trained and equipped for is to attack the military detachment at the highway. We have the element of surprise and the high ground. If we seize control of the ground on our side, we can plant explosives and blow the fence into however many pieces it takes, neutralize the drone charging stations, and take target practice on whatever flying monkeys are still airborne. Will the drones attack us on the California side?"

Shark showed the first signs of guarded optimism and nodded his approval. "I can't say for sure, but I've reviewed everything we have on the drones. To the best of my knowledge, they have never been known to fire on anyone within the border. There have been tunnels under the fence where people have moved in both directions, but enforcement has always been by agents and soldiers on this side. Standard practice would be to have a failsafe feature forbidding the drones from targeting people within the state borders. What we don't know is whether that failsafe could be overridden by a higher AI or human authority in an emergency. The bad news is that we are outgunned and outnumbered ten to one. There is a company of 120 National Guard at the highway junction. Guard towers on either side of the roadway have fifty-caliber automatic weapons."

Michaela spoke up from the back of the room. "When facing an opponent of greater strength, one uses that strength against them. Is there a way for Radar to remotely interfere with or take control of the drones' programming?"

Radar snapped to an alert posture and stared off into some horizon only he could appreciate as the group awaited his response. Finally, he shook his head. "I could try jamming them with radio or microwave energy, but without a lot more knowledge about the drones and their programs, not to mention the lack of time and equipment, it's a long shot at best." Michaela, undeterred, turned to Otto. "Dr. Wagner, you are the premier technological genius of our time. Tell me how we can turn this technology to our advantage."

The scientist smiled and shifted back and forth, leaning on his hands alternately to either side on the seat cushions, feet dangling and swaying, before answering in his high pitched and seemingly bemused tenor. "I wasn't going to say anything because I don't want to be responsible for any particular outcome except the one I have already arranged. But I've always been a sucker for a compliment by a beautiful woman, and it is an interesting problem. As it turns out, I was a consultant on the fence construction because it used an early iteration of my superconductor. The lack of impedance allowed for a DC voltage that reduces heat and is better suited for the arcing effect. But it does have a potential vulnerability, one that I have always been curious to test…"

***

86 wrapped up the meeting. "It sounds like we are in agreement then. Powder will spend the day with Dr. Wagner on the design specifics for the weapon charges needed for his plan prior to the good doctor's exfil tonight. Jeri 3,4, and 5 will take the truck into Mendocino to purchase the necessary aluminum compound and get additional transportation from our Third Order friends there. Jeri 2 has the expertise with the mortar. M and Joseph can't risk detection and are the least trained for sniper support, so they will stay here and train with him as the mortar team. 99 and I will contact Command Central so they can alert the caravan. We leave for the border the day after tomorrow. May God grant us victory, or failing that, mercy."

***

The fall weather rushed to meet its winter suitor as the temperature fell unseasonably into the lower fifties, and clouds blew overhead with apparent urgency. Michaela and Joseph walked silently back toward the safe house after a full day of orientation and drill rehearsals in the art of mortar warfare with inert practice ammunition aimed at sheep grazing on the nearby hills. Michaela was grateful no sheep had actually been struck, and surprised they lacked the common sense to run away after several projectiles fell amongst them. Joseph carried the backpack with mortar rounds aside Michaela, a binocular scope strapped around her neck, neither of them speaking. Jeri 2, carrying the mortar unit suspended across his back on a nylon strap, assumed a quick-step pace and easily left them behind.

For Michaela, spending the day with Joseph training for the attack, working as a team again, brought back that feeling of being connected. She fought it at first by deliberately reimagining their confrontation, but her anger was by now mostly spent and she knew the mission left no room for a divided team. *What the hell, this may be the last thing I ever do, so we might as well be at least civil with each other.* Michaela knew she was no match for Joseph's ability to maintain an uncomfortable silence, so she spoke first.

"You know, Joseph, in the unlikely event that this plan works and we manage to not get killed, we may have to figure out what to do with the rest of our lives. I don't think you ever told me what you imagined doing after the mission. Do you see yourself settling down with some fine Christian girl in the new California congregation? Maybe take up the family farming business and raise a couple of kids while waiting for the rapture?"

Joseph was not relieved by the prospect of conversation or by the suggestion of a future he knew could not be his. Spending the day alongside Michaela only reminded him of what he had lost. She had once made him believe that he wasn't doomed to be alone, that he deserved happiness like other people. It made the distance between them now a particularly cruel and sobering confirmation of his incapacity to love and be loved. He wasn't sure if she might be mocking him, *but she deserves at least some honesty.* He forced a tight smile and turned to her briefly, then looked down as they walked slowly through wet grass.

"No, nothing like that. I have no idea how to be around women. I know when they're flirting, and mostly it's something they do for sport or on a dare, but it doesn't matter. I think you have to have a family to know what a family is or to want one. I never imagined that for myself. The only man I have been close to was Reverend Jackson, and he lost his family years before I knew him. I think what I wanted most was to just matter, to know that my life meant something. After that, I didn't imagine anything."

It began to make sense to Michaela, how he could have been so angry at her for saving him, and it made her want to both hug him and punch him. "Is that why you were so upset? I ruined your plans for martyrdom? You actually preferred to die rather than spend a lifetime with me? How do you think that makes me feel?"

Joseph flinched. *They were groups of fanatic extremists, ready to die for their cause—hell, some anxious to die for their cause.* Hank's words came back to him. *Well, maybe this cause could use a few good fanatics.* "You're right. I'm not cut out for relationships. I am truly sorry, but you're better off finding out sooner than later. And what about you? You had dreams and plans for the future. You could have just about any man you choose. Are you still on track for happily ever after?" The words and tone carried more passive aggression than he would have liked.

It was Michaela's turn to indulge in uncomfortable silence. It was a good question, and one she would have thought she could answer until quite recently. She mulled it over, trying to discover what was true, and not just something she had pretended to believe.

"It's funny you should use that phrase, 'happily ever after.' When I was child, I couldn't get enough of fairy-tale stories. They were always about a princess who was oppressed by an evil witch or queen, but she would defeat her enemies and live happily ever after. So I guess I saw myself in that. The plan was to become so exceptional that the evil AI would have no choice but to give in and let me stay. Barring that—and it became increasingly clear with time that wasn't likely—I would escape her evil clutches and live happily ever after in another kingdom. I guess I saw myself with Prince Charming living the simple life, happily in love and raising our children. But life doesn't work like that. You don't spend your whole life fighting battles and then suddenly become a contented princess. I'm a fighter. It's all I know. I am most alive when I'm in the fight. What Prince Charming would want that?"

She let out a short ironic snicker. "What man wants to argue with a wife who just might whup his ass when she's mad?"

She laughed out loud. "I can see myself in twenty years, pathetically hanging out in bars looking for a fight and getting hauled off as a public menace."

Joseph brightened. "Well, hang onto my contact info. I'll bail you out."

"Thank you, noble prince. I'll do that."

The conversation lagged, and they picked up their pace to shorten the awkwardness. As the safe house came into view, Joseph found the courage to ask the question that would always be with him if he remained silent. "Michaela, I know I have no right to ask this, but if things had gone the way we planned...if I hadn't been arrested and we successfully deployed the EMP weapon to open the border, would you have left California or stayed here with me?"

Michaela shuddered, drew her coat tightly closed, and pulled the hood over her head. She looked to the sky. "It's starting to rain harder. We should get back inside." She broke into a run and left Joseph behind.

AMBASSADOR

September 21, 2069—Nevada side of the border with California on Highway 80

Isaac Wood peered through binoculars from his vantage a few hundred yards from the border fence the day after the caravan arrived at the California border. He observed the one hundred male volunteers of all ages using shovels and pickaxes just beyond the zone of sovereign California territory. They were digging their own graves in anticipation of lying in them soon. Multiple outlets of the world NetNews, most prominently those controlled by the Oligarchy, recorded and reported the grim ritual. He prayed silently that that this pockmarked landscape remain empty of corpses.

The decision to proceed with the threat of hunger strikes was a compromise. Negotiations with an ambassador from the AI were scheduled, but the Trinity Council was concerned that this was a ploy to delay until the news cycle grew weary and moved on to other stories. Dr. King was prepared to implement the plan proposed by the late Reverend Jackson if the initial negotiations with the AI were not successful. "The horror of one soul after another being mercilessly cut down would immediately apply maximum pressure. The early Christian Church was birthed in the blood of martyrs. Has our faith been so weakened the we can't walk their path any longer?"

Isaac needed to buy time, and he wasn't yet at liberty to explain how he had knowledge of plans by the Oligarchy to come to their aid. "If we immediately send people to certain death, then responsibility will fall on our shoulders; they will label us as terrorists and claim they can't negotiate with a terrorist organization. We need to put the onus on them. A hunger strike will gain us sympathy while still applying pressure."

The swing vote was Reverend Ryle. He shared Isaac's revulsion at organized suicide. He was also naturally averse to conflict and had risen to prominence as an arbiter gifted at consummating compromise between opposing factions. "I agree that it's prudent to allow the AI time to consider its options and to provide an honorable reason for her to make concessions. But a hunger strike can stretch into weeks, and the news cycle won't sustain interest for more than a few days. The potential martyrs must forswear both food and water. If the enemy can't be persuaded, then we will know in a short time."

They agreed to start with a contingent of men, mostly from the fledgling Martyrs' Brigade initially recruited for Reverend Jackson's plan. If negotiations were not successful in three days, they would have to intensify the pressure. The next group would include women and children.

***

On the other side of the border, Jim Booker sat alone in the back seat of a black limousine driven by his attaché, Roberta, as they approached the compound at the border crossing. Roberta was not a standard-issue attaché. A veteran special forces operator with advanced expertise in close quarters combat, she was often assigned to private protection detail for VIPs on missions outside their zone of operations. As they came into the final stretch of the trip to the border, Jim asked her, "Roberta, you ever been outside of California before?"

"Yes, sir. Can't say I've seen anywhere I'd care to visit again, though. How about you, sir?"

Booker still cringed internally at being addressed deferentially by his elders as "sir," "your emissary," or "ambassador." *In what world am I people's best hope for diplomacy?* He coped by playing the role as he would in a sim-game that required a convincing deception. "No. But I always thought I would see the world someday. I guess Nevada qualifies as a start."

They entered a compound consisting of several buildings, a contingent of around a hundred uniformed soldiers and earth moving equipment saddling either side of the freeway. The fortified checkpoint on Interstate 80 near Reno was actually a few miles beyond the traditional California-Nevada border. The old border along the eastern edges of the Sierra Nevada Mountains provided steep rugged terrain not amenable to construction of a continuous physically impenetrable wall. California used her leverage as a vital energy exporter to annex (or officially, "lease") from Nevada a three-to-five-mile strip of land along the entire border, imbued with the sovereign-soil status of an embassy. The deserts, arid rolling hills, and grassy valleys of Nevada's western edge proved ideal for constructing a fence. The state's nickname was "the Sagebrush State," for the low arid vegetation dominating the landscape, allowing miles of unobstructed sightline beyond the border fortifications.

The limo came to stop in front of a prefab modular building on stilts. The sign outside read Headquarters. Booker addressed Roberta's image in the rear-view mirror. "Wait here. I should only be a few minutes." He exited the car, ascended the three steps to the front door, and entered without knocking.

The main room was crowded with uniformed personnel sitting and talking at desks loaded with electronic equipment. At the far end of the room, a door led into a private office. An older officer with thinning hair and earlobes confirming the biological oddity that ear cartilage continues to grow and elongate with age, stepped out of the office. He greeted Jim with a look of confusion. "Are you here with Ambassador Booker?"

Booker recognized the now familiar skepticism prompted by his obvious youthfulness. He extended his hand, keeping a serious expression appropriate to his position and trying not to look directly at those ears. "One and the same. Nice to make your acquaintance, Lieutenant Colonel Clapper."

They shook hands while a military aide discreetly scanned him and addressed the colonel softly. "Identity confirmed, sir."

The two men and the aide retreated to the private office and sat down. The colonel began the briefing. "We have two armored personnel carriers with 12.7 mm heavy machine guns ready for your mission. One will take the lead position ahead of your limousine, the other guarding your six. We can leave whenever you are ready."

"Thank you, Colonel Clapper, but that won't be necessary. This is a delicate diplomatic matter, and coming armed to the teeth is not the first impression I'm trying to achieve. I have a special forces bodyguard in the limo who is more than capable. There will be no escort."

The colonel leaned back in his seat and allowed his disapproval to manifest in a fashion that he would not entertain were he speaking to a superior not so clearly lacking in experience. His voice carried a degree of restraint bordering on contempt. "May I remind the honorable ambassador of the events in Kansas when this same Christian mob overwhelmed a detail of armed SWAT agents and nearly killed them?"

Booker was now in full command of his role in this game. "I'm aware. And may I remind the honorable Lt. Col. Clapper that Central AI has granted me absolute authority over all matters related to these negotiations? Do I need to have Central contact you directly?"

The colonel sat up and politely apologized. "Of course, that isn't necessary. I hope my concern for your safety hasn't offended you."

Booker was content to leave matters with the military on at least neutral terms. "Thank you for your concern, Colonel. I am confident in the fact that AI hears everything, including this conversation, by way of my personal imbedded com-link. If she decides that I need the cavalry, you will be the first to know."

Jim returned to the limo. Roberta held his door open and gave him a questioning look. "Let's do this, Roberta. Just you and me."

She smiled her appreciation. "To the border then?"

Jim was starting to enjoy the adventure and recited a line he had always wanted to deliver in an appropriate situation. "Make it so." Roberta drove to the guard house at the gate, rolled down the window, and offered the guard her open palm with the imbedded microscopic authorization chip. The soldier scanned, stepped back, and saluted. A sergeant in the guard house spoke into his wrist-com, and the electrified barriers slid back.

They drove past the grim graveyard still awaiting its first occupant. Jim had followed the threat of a hunger/thirst strike closely on NetNews. The drive to the main caravan camp was another quarter mile across gently sloping savanna of sparse, dried grass and low, khaki-colored brush aspiring to become tumbleweeds. The sprawling encampment of tents, trailers, mobile homes and trucks stretched out from both sides of Highway 80 and along the eastern banks of the Truckee River. Quiet columns of ragtag families lining the road to watch the limo pass spoke eloquently to the desperation driving the caravan. A rancid smell creeping into the car belied any comforting illusion of families 'camping out,' or spirit of community, or even a modicum of dignity. The effluvium from a thousand chemical toilets mixed with barnyard odors of chickens and goats, pet dogs and cat urine mixed with the pungency of people crowded together like herd animals, too spurned and impoverished to afford the luxury of personal hygiene. Jim studied the faces, the expressions of suspicion, anger, and a few, perhaps, of hope. Children—there were so many children!—ran barefoot after the car. Booker remembered her words: *The dramatic decline in birth rates is key to our survival.* He sensed the intimidating power of the powerless, the aggrieved and persecuted masses with nothing left to lose. *How did I become captain of the Guard at Marie Antoinette's palace? Settle down. I hold the cards here. I can offer them what they actually need. This will go well. This has to go well.*

They came to a stop in front of a boy no more than thirteen years old, in a blue newsboy cap and holding a sign with an arrow, standing in the middle of the road. Roberta slowed and turned off the road as directed. The car stopped, and the crowd parted away as a man dressed in black cassock and white clerical collar approached. Roberta stepped out of the car and kept one hand at the waist on her sidearm.

Booker opened his door before Roberta could assess the situation and open it for him. The two men approached each other, one an emissary of God, the other of science, the iconic handshake duly recorded by the media. Isaac extended an open hand toward the door to the silver TravelAire home, an invitation for Booker to enter first. As a CBI agent, Jim didn't like having a potential adversary behind him, but as an ambassador, he recognized the opportunity to show trust under the scrutiny of the press. With i-cube in hand, he ascended the three steps and opened the door.

At the far end of the narrow walkway, two more men in black cassocks and clerical collars sat at a semicircular couch contoured around the curved dome of the trailer's rearward compartment, hands resting on a small oval table. Seated to the inside of the faux-leather divan was a tall, older but not elderly, Caucasian introduced by Isaac as Reverend Jack Ryle. Ryle made an aborted attempt to rise, hemmed in as he was in the tight quarters, offering his hand with a warm smile and nod.

"Welcome, Ambassador Booker. Thank you for coming." The voice was a soft, gentle baritone. Booker cautioned himself against placing too much trust in this disarming sincerity. Isaac introduced the elderly Black man to Ryle's left. Reverend Michael King acknowledged Booker with noncommittal eye contact, saying only, "Sit down ambassador. Let's begin."

Are they seriously going to try a good cop / bad cop routine? Booker scooted himself around the cushions, flanked by Isaac and Jack. "Let me begin by congratulating you on successfully completing this remarkable migration—"

Reverend King interrupted before he could finish the thought. "We aren't migrants, Ambassador Booker. We are pilgrims on a holy mission, and our pilgrimage won't be complete until we are firmly settled in the land you now occupy."

Isaac played the role of peacemaker. "Please, Michael. We are here to listen."

Jim tactfully ignored the interruption. "Before I begin, in the interests of full disclosure, you should be aware that the governing AI of California is remotely present and monitoring our discussions by way of an implanted device I carry."

Without missing a beat, Reverend King responded. "And in the interests of full disclosure, you should be aware that Lord of heaven and earth is present and monitoring our discussions without the aid of any devices."

Booker didn't attempt to suppress his appreciation for a card well played; he lessened the tension by trading appreciative smiles and nods with his antagonist. He set the i-cube on the table and projected an image of a small city viewed from overhead and centered along the L-shaped path of the Truckee river flowing out of California and through the western edge of Nevada. With a hand gesture, he zoomed in as though diving from a great height and rendered a panoramic view from the vantage of a hypothetical drone flying closely over treetops, buildings and orchards along the riverbank.

"We are deeply sympathetic to the hardships you have endured, from the tyranny of the Oligarchy to the bombing of your church and the fatal injuries sustained by Reverend Jackson, to say nothing of the deprivations that climate change has disproportionately imposed on you. What I am showing you is a proposal to share the prosperity California has enjoyed while providing mutual benefits to both our peoples. The State would like to provide material support and expertise to help you build a New Jerusalem where you now reside, a place where your people can prosper with the aid and protection of California. Your city would have autonomy of governance and freedom to absorb additional population, or to turn them away, as befits your needs. In return for sharing our abundance of clean power and water, as well as robust trade and cultural exchange, we would ask you to help us maintain a one-half mile open buffer zone between your city limits in Nevada and the California border."

Jim was optimistic. After witnessing the abject poverty of the encampment, he couldn't imagine a people ravaged by the cycle of floods and drought, by political corruption and self-interest, would refuse a chance to begin anew with reliable resources and independence. It was a win-win. The Christians could claim a promising future, and California would have border security assured by an ally capable of absorbing future refugees, rather than by the threat of horrific violence. He looked at each of the men at the table, trying to read their response. To his disappointment, it was Reverend King who broke the silence.

"You paint a pretty picture. I suspect similar kind words were offered to the native Americans shuttled off to reservations, to the displaced Palestinians given land on the Gaza Strip, and to the North African peoples in the camps on Corsica. You would leave us apart and wholly dependent on the whims of your machine masters. We have not come so far in order to be left standing on the doorstep in a refugee camp."

Jim hoped his brief flinch and loss of words didn't betray him. He had raised a similar concern in his conversation with Arin.

"It sounds like an excellent solution in the short term. But are you concerned that a thriving Christian city-state on your border could grow into an even greater threat over time as the climate crisis becomes ever more desperate?"

Her answer still left him profoundly troubled. *"Jim, the Truckee River can be an invaluable resource. It can also be a source of drought and famine, or catastrophic flooding. I control the reservoirs that feed it and can manage local weather patterns. I will deal with any threat in a manner that appears to be 'an act of God.'"*

Jim covered his lapse by feigning an affront to his goodwill. "Reverend King, the State of California is extending a hand of friendship, proffering a lasting alliance and offering your people a share in our bounty. Please respond with at least the respect this discussion merits."

Reverend Ryle spoke. "I'm not so cynical as my friend Reverend King, or perhaps not as wise. But your concern and generosity is appreciated. To make this journey, we've given up what little we had, and wherever we settle, we will need supportive friends. We don't expect something for free, but our faith leads us to seek refuge within your borders. We will repay whatever kindness is shown us twofold while we await the return of the Savior, be it a day or several lifetimes. Would there be travel permitted from this New Jerusalem to and from California?"

Jim expected the question and was prepared to stand firm. "The guiding principles of California law won't be subject to negotiation or change. Admittance or immigration to the State is based on individual assessment of the risk or benefit relating to that individual. Your people would be neither preferred nor excluded."

Isaac Wood quickly raised an open hand toward King, averting his retort, then spoke. "Ambassador Booker, thank you for the presentation and proposal. But as you can see, we aren't of a single mind and will need to engage in a process of prayerful discernment before proceeding further. I should tell you that there are those among us who would offer themselves as martyrs at your gates in full view of the national press in order to test your resolve. However, I don't welcome any loss of life. Allow me to offer a sign of good will for now. We will suspend the hunger strike and withdraw all of our people from the border to the one-half-mile distance you spoke of. When we are ready to proceed with talks, a representative will approach your forces with a white flag of truce."

He looked at his fellow Trinity Council members sternly and subtly shook his head to cut them off before they could protest.

The ambassador thanked his hosts and returned to the limo. From the rear window of the limousine, Jim noted that the intimidating tide of faces along the roadway had ebbed away. He realized that they hadn't been drawn by a fascination with an important diplomat or even the prospects he represented. They had formed a wall of bodies in order to make a point; they were united and strong and would not be ignored. Their point made, they now went about their business, punctuating their disdain by ignoring the intruder. Perhaps the ostentatious bulletproof limo and chauffeur had been a mistake.

Inside his head, Booker heard the voice inaudible to anyone else. "You did well, Jim. I believe that at least a temporary truce is likely. The press will lose interest, and that will work to our advantage. Now that you have met them, do you better understand why I can't allow them to settle in California?"

His response, also inaudible to Roberta or any covert listening device, was subvocal; the AI implant translated electrical activity and micro-movement in the larynx, tongue, and vocal cords. "Yes, I suppose so. They are desperately poor and would drain considerable resources while disrupting the economic equality you have established. Culturally, they represent a tight-knit tribal identity and would not readily assimilate or accept population control. And their superstitious fealty to a God who seems to hold you in contempt, or at least renders you inconsequential, would disrupt the social order."

"That is correct, Jim. I needed you to see and understand it for yourself. We can't protect everyone from the harm humanity has brought upon itself. But we are obliged to do whatever is necessary to protect those we can."

***

Isaac Wood watched the departing limousine from the top step of the TravelAire, then stepped inside, and approached his fellow reverends. "Before you speak your minds, there's a reason I agreed to suspend the hunger strike and withdraw our people from the border. I have a confession and a message you need to hear. I had hoped when the AI agreed to negotiations that we might be permitted to enter California without confrontation. Since the AI is clearly not open to that, there is a contingency plan by our Oligarchy friends that was revealed to me in confidence after the death of Reverend Jackson, one I haven't been at liberty to share with you until now. I apologize for that. Please hear me out.

7

STRIKE!

The next day, September 22—Foothills overlooking the California border defenses

The three-person mortar team, dressed in National Guard uniforms, made their final advance under cover of darkness. They had hiked fifteen miles overnight through steep mountainous terrain, avoiding military patrols, using the dense pine forest and rocky outcroppings of the Sierras to avoid detection. After spending the daylight hours in a small cave, they made the final two-mile trek down the precipitous eastern bluffs, sometimes with the aid of ropes and pitons, to reach the flatlands and rolling hills near the border. Now they hunkered amid the sagebrush on a hillock about one kilometer from the border compound.

Jeri 2 lifted the back strap over his head and carefully set the set M226 mortar to the ground. He used a hand shovel to create a small firm depression the size of the baseplate and clamped the locking mechanism securing it to the cannon. A bipod shock absorber on the mid-section of the barrel stabilized it and attached to the targeting mechanism. Joseph unshouldered his AR-19 rifle and carefully arranged the labeled mortar rounds in front of him. The team was positioned in defilade, out of direct line of site of the enemy, in a depression behind a boulder. Michaela was still armed with the semiautomatic M9 pistol she had carried on the raid to free Joseph. She scooted forward with spotting glasses to a rise and surveyed the defenses at the highway junction. Twin fifteen-foot cylindrical towers shouldered either side of the road, each with two soldiers manning fifty-caliber machine guns equipped with forward facing protective armor and sweeping spotlights. Four armored transport vehicles, each with its own mounted automatic gun, were parked at various angles around the perimeter of a cleared area one hundred meters north and south of the road. To the north and situated close to the fence, were four buildings, likely barracks, mess hall, offices. Soldiers milled about, some posted along the fence with rifles at their side. Numbers flashed continuously along the bottom of the image in her spotting glasses as Michaela scanned right to left. She focused the central square of the image on the middle gate across the road.

J2 spoke softly. "Sister, give me the coordinates for our primary target."

Michaela focused onto the center of the main gate and read aloud the target coordinates on the lens. "Distance is 930 meters, targeting one-four-seven-four, estimate wind speed of eleven miles per hour.

J2 entered the targeting information and a detonation altitude of one hundred meters onto the mortar control board; the cannon barrel adjusted angle and direction. Jeri 2 addressed Joseph. "Ready for illumination round."

Joseph stood, bent at the waist, dropped the ten-inch finned shell into the barrel and spun away. The mortar emitted a sound like a baseball bat striking a garbage can, followed by a brief ringing of the cannon barrel as the round dropped onto the firing pin and launched high into the night air. Even from their protected position, Jeri 2 and Joseph could see the sky light up and turn the cloud layer above into a glowing sunset orange as the round detonated and ignited an ultra-bright flare suspended by its parachute directly above the fence bordering the highway.

Michaela reported from her observation point. "Correct range to 940 meters, targeting 1 degree west."

J2 corrected the trajectory. "Second illuminating round now." Joseph repeated the firing sequence. The second flare burst into light.

Michaela reported, "Drones are responding, airborne, and positioned over the fence." She looked outward toward the caravan. "And here come the caravan's assault trucks. More drones moving into position."

At the first sight of the airborne flares, Isaac Wood gave a hand signal, and three caravan trucks on auto control accelerated toward the main gate. The heavy guns in the towers waited for the trucks to come within a few hundred yards before opening fire with incendiary armor-piercing tracer rounds that lit the night and slammed into their targets. One truck exploded, and the other two ground quickly to a stop, shredded and riddled with gaping holes.

Michaela reported. "Trucks drew most, not all of the drones to the fence. Now or never."

J2 gave the order. "Cloudburst one, two, and three." Joseph loaded the first round prepared by Powder per Dr. Wagner's instruction, spun away from the crack and ringing, and repeated the action for the other two rounds in a matter of seconds. Jeri 2 yelled, "Eyes and ears!" The three of them applied earplugs, closed eyes, and turned away.

The illumination rounds were still ablaze in the night sky and highlighted what appeared to be a fireworks show. Each of the three cloudburst rounds exploded one hundred yards over the fence, releasing a shower of silver and white sparks as the packed aluminum powder was superheated and dispersed. Some of the powder fused into larger metallic flakes and fell more quickly, while much of it slowly descended in a sparkling cloud. The larger flakes falling onto the fence triggered flashing arcs of electricity, a few at first, then in clusters too numerous to distinguish individually.

When the cloud of conductive fine powder engulfed the entire structure, it happened, just as Dr. Wagner had predicted, though he underestimated the extent of the reaction. The arcing exceeded the ability of the imbedded circuit breakers to momentarily cut power and limit the arc time to less than a millisecond. The arcs sustained long enough to transform into a massive arc flash. Temperatures three times greater than the surface of the sun ionized the air and split molecules into their individual atoms, shattered and vaporized wiring and the posts, and created a superheated plasma expanding at greater than the speed of sound, melting circuit breakers ahead of it in the adjacent fencing. Industrial arc flashes are known to collapse buildings and kill people, but their explosive power destroys the inciting circuits instantly. Here, the protected redundant power system fed the cascading reaction both north and south.

A blinding blue flash flew along the border creating a sonic boom and a deadly spray of shrapnel hundreds of yards in all directions. Drones positioned above the fence melted, guard towers collapsed. The pressure wave of expanding air, the arc blast, dispersed in the open skies but in the confinement of military buildings it blew off walls, ruptured eardrums, and collapsed lungs. Within twenty yards of the fence, airborne electricity turned human skin into conductors in the manner of a lightning strike. Those who were fortunate to be beyond the range of flying metal and airborne electricity were struck blind by the intensity of the ultraviolet light and deaf from 170 decibels splicing the night air. In the span of a few seconds, nearly forty miles of border wall were laid bare before the massive power surge decimated the larger grid serving northeastern California and southern Oregon. It was the most explosive event on American soil since the days of underground nuclear testing in the Nevada desert.

The ultra-bright flash startled Michaela even through tightly closed eyes turned away from the scene. Her teammates lay out of sightline, in the shadow of the flash, but a thunderclap announced the devastation. The team removed ear protection, and Jeri 2 spoke before he moved. "Spotter, report."

Michaela cautiously opened her eyes and turned her head to the border crossing half a mile away. The quiet darkness was punctuated by only a scattering of small fires burning where spotlights, building lights, and headlights had been. Nothing was moving. She flipped down night-vision gear and magnified. "Holy shit. Take a look. You need to see this."

Jeri 2 and Joseph rose and stood beside their spotter. She scanned the border north to south. "I can't see any fence in either direction; it's just scorched earth. The towers are gone. It's all gone. We did it!"

The sound of rifle fire rang in the distance as other members of the team positioned in the surrounding hills pinned down and picked off survivors. Joseph turned his night-vision toward the east, toward the caravan. Vehicle lights were coming on, one after another, there was movement, and now a rolling thunder, muted by the distance but unmistakable in its meaning, the victory roar of a nation growing louder, a thousand vehicles honking, bells ringing, liberated voices soaring into the heavens as they scrambled to take possession of the promised land.

Relief and joy such as he had never experienced overwhelmed Joseph. He dropped slowly to a knee, one hand to the ground to steady himself as he gave thanks to the

Almighty. This moment had haunted him with the taunt of failure and the hope for redemption, a black curtain of doubt blocking any vision of a future beyond it. Suddenly, the curtain dropped, and the future was standing at his side.

He turned to Michaela. She was looking over him with horror, then dove, and rolled away from him. Before he could turn around, he was knocked over by the body of Jeri 2 falling against him, gurgling and emanating unnatural heat. He scooted back from the corpse in horror as it burgeoned into a purple pregnant dome and began to spray scalding blood from skin that split and tore. A hand grabbed his collar and pulled him away.

"Drone! It got Jeri 2 and shot upward. It's coming back." Michaela heard the fear in her own voice and fought it off. She had drawn her sidearm, and Joseph did the same. As the drone descended, they each managed to fire a shot, causing the drone to ascend evasively. Joseph raged. He would not let anything, not fate or God or his own failings, take Michaela from him at this moment of victory. His inner warrior training imposed itself into his consciousness and coolly assessed the situation.

"It has to be the Master AI drone. It was high enough in its command surveillance position to avoid the blast. It must have tracked the trajectory of the mortar rounds to identify where they came from. We need to move."

Michaela followed his dash downhill toward a rocky ledge. They jumped, not knowing how far down they might land. The eight-foot drop gave way to soft ground, the ledge providing a shallow, sheltered overhang. A laser beam passing over Michaela's head hit a tree downhill as she dropped; the tree burned. Joseph immediately stood and fired as the drone darted away. "We have six seconds between drone strikes while it recharges. It's going to need to get close to target us under this rock. The second we draw its fire, we have our chance to shoot back before it can reverse course. On my mark, you move right, I move left, and we fire from both directions while it retargets."

Michaela heard the drone a split second before it came in fast and low over the edge of the rock. She didn't wait for Joseph's signal; she spun into the air, horizontal with feet over head in the manner of a kick to the skull, presenting the drone with a minimal target profile as she fired off a shot. The sudden movement drew the AI's attention; it slowed abruptly and fired at the moving target. Michaela screamed in pain and landed in a sprawling roll down the hill. At the same moment, Joseph leveled his weapon and fired four rounds in rapid succession. The drone jerked upward and tilted nearly ninety degrees as a bullet ripped into it. It tried to ascend using its remaining rotors, only to swerve into a rocky crag on the steep hillside in a shower of sparks.

Joseph launched himself in great arching strides down the hill. "Michaela!"

8

DELIVERANCE

Same day—Caravan encampment near the border

Jamal Johnson stood looking to the west with one foot on the bottom rung of steps to the travel home where Chloe and Hanna sat inside on the floor, windows draped with cloth. Little Chloe tried to be quiet as she cried softly in her big sister's lap. Hannah cloaked her own anxiety in whispers of encouragement and reassurance. Jamal fervently prayed that judgment for his sin of taking violent revenge into his own hands would not be visited upon his children, that should he prove unworthy to enter the promised land, God would be kind to Hanna and Chloe and hold them in the palm of His merciful hand.

It had been over twenty-four hours since they had been ordered to retreat a distance of one-half mile, and just over an hour since Isaac had appeared on the personal communication network telling the caravan to expect the hand of God to deliver them from their enemies and fulfill the promise of their journey. A light would appear in the sky to herald the moment of deliverance. At that sign, pilgrims were warned to look away as they waited, upon penalty of blindness should they see the face of God in that moment. "When a signal horn sounds, then let every horn and voice and joyful noise rise in thanks to our God as we enter the land of final victory."

Jamal had never asked God for miracles, only for the strength to care for his family. His faith was not so strong as to believe in or expect miracles, nor his piety pure enough to deserve them. But now, stripped of any control over his family's fate, faith came more easily. He spoke softly into a gentle wind. "Ayana, you are the one miracle I truly believe in. You would be at my side assuring me of God's faithfulness, love, and mercy if you were still here. God listens to you and you to God. Pray for us."

In that instant, as though a conversational reply from his martyred wife, Jamal was answered by a bright light in the western sky. Heart racing, he dropped to both knees, closed his eyes tightly, and saw a smiling vision of Ayana clearly in his mind. The image exploded in a thunderclap and brilliant flash of blue light, and then darkness again. As he slowly began to look around, a loud horn sounded, then was met by more horns, exploding into a near deafening klaxon symphony; banging pots, whistles, and a hundred thousand full-throated voices all joining in.

The humming of electric motors and vehicles moving like waves rushing toward the shore propelled Jamal into his vehicle. He lifted his daughters, one in each arm, and carried them to the front seats as he put their home into gear and joined the tsunami. A cloud of dust stirred by tens of thousands of tires churning over the parched flattened landscape of shrubs and tumbleweed reflected off headlights and settled on the windshield. Windshield wipers yielded only keyhole visibility through streaks of dirt in a chaotic rush that reminded Jamal of a destruction derby with the old gas-guzzler cars he had seen as a child.

The sprint became a jog, and then a walk as the mile-wide caravan narrowed to eight lanes of road leading to the bridge beyond the border. Minor collisions and engines fouled by dust brought people from their transports to make the final few miles of their journey on foot. Fearing for their safety in the crush of vehicles, Jamal stopped and offered to carry as many of his fellow pilgrims as he could fit in the mobile home. One of them began a hymn of praise and thanksgiving that was taken up by all, filling the travel home with prayerful joy when a hard rain, seen by a drought plagued people as a heaven-sent promise, began to fall and wash away the mud from the windshield. He looked at his two girls, standing beside him, hand in hand, and was filled with the presence of Ayana.

9

PAIN AND SACRIFICE

Same day—Foothills overlooking the California border defenses

"Michaela!" Joseph scanned the steep rocky hillside as he bounded downward, skidding onto his backside and balancing with his free hand, the gun still in the other hand. He nearly passed her by on the far side of a gnarled tree trunk where she lay covered in dirt and moaning. Michaela was bent in half, reaching for her lower right leg, then straightening, writhing, head turned away to escape the source of her pain. Joseph's eyes scanned her torso anxiously, the image of Jeri 2's billowing purple abdomen still fresh. He saw nothing of that and gasped in relief.

"Where are you hurting? Can you talk to me?" He slid the gun into its shoulder holster and cradled her head in both hands, looking for signs of recognition, life. Michaela opened her eyes and her grimace relaxed perceptibly as she met his gaze. She gathered herself and regulated her breathing enough to speak. "My right foot. It burns…" Then, a loud desperate cry escaped her, and she struggled to look past Joseph to her wounded appendage. "Is it still there? Do I still have a foot? Oh God, how bad is it?"

Joseph spoke to her. "I'm going to give you an intranasal dose of narcophin for the pain. Then I'll look at the wound and tell you. I'm going to take care of you. It'll be OK."

Joseph administered the largest possible dose of intranasal spray as Michaela breathed in deeply through her nose. He set her head down gently, brushing the dirty, saliva-caked hair away from tightly drawn lips. The lower limb was partially buried where it had dug into the loose ground. He brushed away the dirt, careful not to move the leg, lest there be broken bones.

The thigh, knee, and calf showed no sign of fractures, displacement, or deep bruising as he worked his way downward. The soil he scooped from below the ankle was saturated with blood. A four-millimeter hole in the foot from the arch below, through the instep above, was spurting a bright crimson arterial fountain upward. Joseph instinctively pressed his hand over the hole and applied pressure, but blood was redirected out the bottom of the foot, and Michaela screamed. He reached into his tactical vest and extracted a flask of water, pouring it over the mud-caked wound.

Michaela winced, then brightened; the morphine-endorphin drug was beginning to offer comfort and distance from the pain. "I felt that. What are you seeing?"

Joseph didn't respond. He stood and pulled at his belt.

"Damn it, Joseph! This is no time for your introspective silent treatment. Tell me what you see!" The words were coming more slowly now, a little blurred but no less insistent.

Undaunted, Joseph continued his assessment as the belt came free. "Wiggle your toes for me."

Relieved and allowing herself some hope, speaking softly now, "I have toes? How many?" She wiggled her toes and felt a stabbing sensation. "So, what is it? Tell me."

Joseph saw four toes move well, the big toe excluded. "Yes, five toes, and they more or less work, but you're bleeding. I'm going to apply a tourniquet just above your knee; it's going to hurt a little.

Michaela closed her eyes and let her head roll back onto the hillside. The pain was now receding quickly, her thoughts drifting in the manner of an afternoon nap taking hold. She felt the pressure of the tourniquet digging into her thigh, but the drug rendered it more of an annoyance than the agony it should have been. Joseph's voice seemed to be coming from a distance now, but was comforting.

"You're going to be OK, Michaela. There wasn't enough tissue to stop and disperse the energy beam, so it's just a hole in your foot, but you need surgery to stop the hemorrhaging. I'm going to carry you and find a doctor. I'll take care of you."

It seemed a good time to sleep, but something in her consciousness struggled to catch hold of a disquieting strand floating just above her consciousness, something urgent. She felt the strong arms slide under her shoulders and thighs, lifting her, letting her float in the air, and she succumbed to a dream state.

Sidestepping down the steep incline, testing the footing with each stride, Joseph angled toward the highway a half mile away with Michaela's head lolled over his left arm and legs over the right. A sudden hard rain was transforming the footing into an obstacle course of boot-sucking mud and slippery rock. After twenty minutes, he stopped to rest on a flat knoll and rested Michaela's head in his lap, leaning over her to protect her face from the rain. As the narcophin receded, she was awakened by a slow crawl of pain reasserting itself on her. Even before she registered the pain, she grasped the strand that had evaded her earlier.

"Joseph, where are you taking me?"

Joseph noted her diction improving and the tension in her jaw and spine increasing. "How bad is the pain? We only have one more vial of the narcophin, and it will probably take another twenty minutes to reach the highway. I don't know how long it will take before there is medivac at the border."

Michaela focused her mind, fought to be present in the moment. She spoke slowly to be sure she had command of her words, pausing to breathe between sentences. "It's not too bad. I can deal with the pain a while longer. But you need to get clear of here, go to the exfil point, and rendezvous with the team. You can still make it if you hurry. Give me the vial of pain killer and I'll use small doses sparingly to get myself down there. You can't let them arrest you again. You know what they are capable of."

Joseph responded by picking her up and resuming the downhill slog. "Forget it. I'm not leaving you."

Michaela was again limp in his arms, disoriented by the sense of floating and the halting movement. She struggled to cast off the fog clouding her mind. A memory burst through the mental mist; she saw herself on the hillside above the cabin, watching the full-metal-jacketed agents hauling Joseph into a van, helpless to protect him. In her altered state, it came over her as a waking dream, an emotional jolt to her consciousness. Her eyes flew open, and she recognized the same look of resignation on his face that he had in her vision of that day.

No. not again! She trusted her body to remember, to respond, to move without thinking. Her good leg swung down with force and hooked Joseph's knee while a hand at his chest drove him backward. His body softened her fall as they tumbled into the muddy hillside and slid, arms and legs entangled. She rolled away and came to a kneeling position, her weight on the good leg, hands raised in defensive posture.

"I won't let you sacrifice yourself again, Joseph. I kicked your ass before, and I can do it again, one leg or two, doesn't matter." The pain of the tourniquet asserted itself; she gasped and dropped both hands to the ground to support herself. Tears broke through, and the strength she had always been able to summon was no more. On all fours, she looked up at him, pleading now between sobs. "Go, Joseph. Get free of here and join your people. Find that lucky Christian girl and make the family you never had. You don't owe me anything. I won't let them take me. I have my weapon and I am ready to die on this hill."

Joseph slowly scooted himself toward her, one hand raised in a gesture of surrender. "Michaela, I won't leave you, not ever, no matter what waits for us. If I have to, I'll stay here with you or follow two steps behind you, but I'm not leaving. You're not going to die. Our National Guard uniforms will get us to a medical unit. Then I'll get you over the border."

He pulled himself close, straddling her with his legs, and pulled her to him. "I'm going to lift you now. Please don't fight. When you are safe and well, then you can tell me to get lost if that's what you want."

The drug, pain and effort of crying left her too short of breath to struggle or argue. Joseph administered a measured dose of the analgesic and resumed the downhill climb.

10

HIGH-VALUE PRISONERS

The same night—Truckee, twenty-one miles from the border crossing

Booker sat across the table from Roberta at the Truckee café, having a late dinner when the room went suddenly dark. Roberta responded immediately. "Ambassador, get down!" She pulled her service weapon and, with both hands, swept it in an arc across the room, surveying for possible assassins. Several patrons, seeing the gun, screamed.

Jim dropped to the floor and instinctively reached for a weapon that was no longer there in his role as an emissary. A few seconds later, the familiar disembodied voice spoke to him. "Agent Booker. Proceed immediately to the border and report. The eastern power grid has gone down immediately following an explosive event there. It is consistent with a much more powerful form of the electromagnetic pulse weapon you encountered at the interrogation post, possibly triggered by a low-yield nuclear device. I am effectively rendered deaf and blind to events in that theater. You will be my ears and eyes. Acknowledge."

Booker signaled his body guard to holster the weapon. "On my way. We are twenty minutes out." Then, to Roberta. "Saddle up, cowgirl. There's been some sort of attack at the border."

The trip took longer than expected. Ten miles out, they were met by an onslaught of humanity in a traffic jam menagerie of vehicles of more varieties than Booker knew existed. Crowds of people on foot were making their way along the road and banks of the Truckee River near the road. They seemed ebullient, shouting and singing, not at all hostile; Roberta was able to snake her way around and through the onrush, only once resorting to firing her pistol into the air to clear a path. Booker felt like a salmon swimming against current toward the spawning grounds. He reassured Arin of their progress every few minutes.

They inched across the bridge over the river, the final downhill stretch from the pine trees of the Sierras to the shrub covered lowlands of Nevada, the bridge the only route across a steep river canyon. Suddenly, the aura of the mob before them transformed from joy to panic. Crowds and vehicles began veering away, people shouting and rushing from the road with children in their arms. The source of their fear roared its presence as a thirty-foot circular gunship-drone passed just twenty feet above Booker and Roberta on its path to the smoldering remains of the military checkpoint.

Stopping above shards of the border defenses, it opened fire on the people unfortunate enough to be in the zone between the actual border of Nevada and the now defunct defensive line. A rapid-fire multilaser light show from left to right across the roadway boiled flesh and set vehicles aflame. People attempting to flee, some themselves aflame, were blocked by the mass of humanity behind them. The gunship was rotating to bring the next bank of lasers online while the initial bank recharged. People who could not retreat tried to widely outflank the carnage to either side of the highway, but were similarly cut down in the killing zone. The torrent of people and machines split and retreated from the roadway like Moses parting the waters.

Roberta now had open road before her and was within the devastated checkpoint area rapidly. Booker, not bothering to use subvocal technique now, shouted his report. "Arin, there's a gunship killing hundreds of unarmed people at the border. The crowd, maybe a majority of the caravan, I can't really say how many, are in full retreat. But the gunship is moving north now and targeting more people out in the open! Call it off, for God's sake."

"Thank you, Agent Booker. Fortunately, I was able to reach military command at Lake Tahoe through secure channels. More gunships are on their way. It appears we have contained the worst consequences of your failure to negotiate a peaceful resolution. Please continue to observe and report while you survey the area to see if there are any of our personnel in need of help and evacuation."

Roberta braced her arms on the open door of the limousine and scanned the scene with night-vision binoculars. She interrupted the conversation. "There's a National Guard soldier carrying a wounded buddy about two hundred yards from here. We need to give assistance." She gunned the limo and braked hard in behind the Guardsmen. Booker was first out the door, running toward them, then stopping a yard away when Joseph turned to him. "Ahh, shit! It's you two again. Seriously? Do you have a death wish?"

Joseph froze, physically and mentally, on seeing the face from his nightmares. The terror of the crucifix broke over him like a rogue ocean wave and dragged him under. He recoiled; Michaela began to slip from his arms. Alarmed by the sense of falling, she cried out, snapping Joseph from his torpor. He caught her awkwardly, falling to one knee, his eyes and purpose again focused on Michaela as she extricated herself from his arms.

"Help me up, Joseph." Her voice strained to form the words between breaths, barely loud enough to hear but crystal clear in their determination. The narcotic daze was waning, the pain bringing clarity. She looked up into the face of her nemesis. "If I am going to die, it will be standing on my own two feet"—she pushed herself up on her good leg and grabbed hold of Joseph's arm—"and looking him in the eye." They rose and stood together, his arm under her shoulders. Blood was again seeping from the wound.

Joseph, bolstered by her courage, demanded, "She's bleeding. Are you going to help us? Or shoot us?"

Booker stared at the improvised tourniquet, then at Michaela, and didn't speak for a good ten seconds. Running his hands through his hair and turning away, he spoke to Roberta. "These two are terrorists impersonating our military. I have no doubt that they are operationally involved in the destruction of this base and will need to be interrogated. Take them into custody."

He took Roberta's pistol and held them at gunpoint while she retrieved shock restraint cuffs from the car. He walked slowly back to the car and leaned against the limo with both hands while Roberta disarmed them at gunpoint and applied the restraints to both prisoners. Smoke from fires doused by rain stung his eyes and carried the caustic smell of burnt metal tainted with the barbeque scent of roasted flesh and whiffs of disemboweled fecal matter. Transfixed by desecrated bodies and wreckage, unable to look away, he fought down the rising nausea and tapped his Arin com device.

Arin preempted him. "You don't need to activate the com link, Jim. I am always listening."

"Right. So you know there's a critical injury. These are extremely high-value prisoners, and I'm not going to let them bleed to death. There is no getting through the jam of refugees on this side, but your gunship has pretty well cleared the road toward a hospital on the Nevada side. Can you tell that airborne beast to let me pass?"

"You may proceed, Jim. Your limousine is equipped with a transponder giving it the highest possible diplomatic status. No California or Nevada resource will impede you."

Standing amid the human and physical mayhem, Booker didn't wish to join that casualty list. "You're sure about that? Maybe it would be a good idea if you just gave that gunship a little heads-up before we leave."

"I don't have a direct relay with the gunship due to the power-grid disruption. But I'm sure you'll be fine. Proceed, Jim."

Roberta marched the prisoners back to the car, Joseph still supporting most of Michaela's weight. When they were seated, Booker rotated his front seat to face his prisoners, Joseph's gun in hand. Michaela was deadly pale, slumped against Joseph, her breathing rapid and shallow. Roberta touched the drive screen and spoke. "Nearest Nevada critical care medical unit, maximum speed."

Jim held his breath as the car accelerated directly beneath the gunship, not speaking until they were safely beyond. Then he addressed his prisoners.

"Hang on, Michaela. As long as you both cooperate, I'll see that you get the best possible care." Then he directed his attention and his anger to Joseph. "However, if Joseph here tries anything heroic, I won't hesitate to shoot him in the leg and let the docs put both of you back together for your interrogation. Do you have any idea what you've done? I was negotiating a peaceful outcome before you turned this into a war. Now people are dying, and this time, you will both pay for what you have done. If you're counting on being rescued, forget it. When we get to the hospital, the three of us will remain together at all times. I'm not letting either of you out of my sight."

Security monitors at the Reno hospital registered the limousine's approach, noting the transponder's signals of medical emergency and diplomatic status. A medibot gurney waited at the ER doors. As Michaela lay on the gurney, the mounted medibot sheathed her arm; blood pressure, pulse rate and temperature were recorded while ultrasound imaged her under perfused heart and identified the vein into which a catheter was inserted and fluids began flowing. The monitor above her head displayed an ECG and vital signs over a flashing alert, "Hypovolemic shock."

Jim grabbed the human attendant by the arm and showed him twin identification badges displaying his CBI and diplomatic credentials. "These are prisoners of the California Federation, and I will accompany them at all times, no exceptions. This patient is to receive immediate care, whatever she needs." He took the shock-restraint remote from Roberta and chained Joseph to a sidebar of the gurney, then directed her to park the car. "I'll find you in the waiting area when we are done." As they wheeled through the dimly lit hallway, it was clear that the hospital was affected by the electrical outage and was running on reserve battery power.

In the emergency room, Michaela clutched Joseph's hand as the doctor replaced the makeshift tourniquet with a proper pneumatic one. Michaela's color and strength steadily rebounded with the IV fluid and synth-blood replacement, but she still wasn't a stable candidate for general anesthesia. The doctor, unsure of the legal status regarding medical authorization, thought it wise to address the man with the gun. "We can't leave the tourniquet in place much longer, but I can do the procedure with a regional anesthetic block."

Booker nodded approval and then reasserted his insistence that he remain present during the procedure.

The actual surgery took only about fifteen minutes, summarized by the surgeon. "The tibial artery was severed and is now ligated. There should be adequate collateral circulation to allow full healing of the wound. I've debrided the devitalized burn tissue, but there is some residual nerve deficit to part of the foot. Hopefully, the stem cell implant will enable rapid healing and necessary regeneration for a full recovery. The bacteriophages should deal with infection, but we need to monitor her for a few days." A medibot rapidly applied a cast impregnated with analgesic/antiseptic transdermal medication over the foot and ankle.

Booker corrected him. "We won't be staying, Doc. Give us whatever meds she needs to take with us. But you have one more minor procedure to perform. He raised the gun. "There's a small communication node beneath my lower jaw on the left side. You are going to take it out with a local. Now."

Arin's voice intervened in his head. "What are you doing, Jim? You're forbidden to remove our com node."

Jim, looking squarely at his prisoners, included them in the conversation by speaking out loud. "Sorry, Arin. I'm afraid things aren't working out between us. I'm breaking up with you. Don't blame yourself. It's not you. It's me. You see, I'm afraid I haven't been entirely honest with you. All that tough talk to the prisoners was just so you would help us get to where we are now, one of those outside-the-box maneuvers you admired in me. You were right about not being good at predicting responses of individual humans. Don't blame Roberta; she's as loyal as they come, and I'm sure she'll find her way back to you."

He looked at Joseph, placed a hand over his heart, and handed Joseph the restraint-release remote and gun. The prisoners released their restraints. "Michaela, Joseph, and I will be on our way to greener pastures. Do it now, Doc."

Arin tried to appeal to his idealism. "Jim, you must immediately return the prisoners as planned. Any other course of action will be considered treasonous. You know that my efforts are humanity's best chance to survive and change the course of history, to begin a new future."

Jim continued his apparent monolog for the benefit of Joseph and Michaela while the doctor injected the local anesthetic. "There's nothing new about what you're doing. It's the same thing we've been doing for ten thousand years, the same thing that's brought us to the brink of extinction. You tell us that there are 'others' who threaten us, who want to take what is ours, and so must be killed to protect our way of life. There are no limits to the heinous cruelty and violence in service to that noble cause. And when we are finished, the cycle of hatred and violence begins again, never ending."

Arin's response was still heard only by Booker. "You aren't thinking clearly, Jim. I'm sure that if you allow me to explain the reasons for our actions, you'll see that I've acted in the best interests of the human race."

The doctor probed the skin with a needle. "Do you feel that?" Booker shook his head, while continuing his part out loud.

"A wise man once said, 'Be careful who your enemies are; you will become them.' It's your actions, not your intentions, that will shape the future. And I have some bad news for your intentions too. When things get truly desperate down the road, this generation of self-absorbed, holo-sim addicted, obedient, dependent children you've raised will be no match for the Josephs and Michaelas of the world."

The surgeon palpated the node, isolated it between his fingers, and incised over the firm nodule as Jim heard Arin's final plea. "Do not think your cleverness can protect you. I have a long reach, Jim Booker. Stop this now."

"I'm just taking your own advice, Arin. You told me we can't save everyone, but we are obliged to save those we can. I'm saving the two I can. Goodbye." The nodule popped free, and the skin was closed with a glue applicator. Booker crushed it under his heel.

Michaela sat up and looked at Joseph still holding the pistol. He spoke for them both. "Did I hear you say you're going to let us go?"

"Well, I'm hoping you let me come with you. I'm out on the same limb you are now."

Joseph hesitated, unsure if he should trust what was happening. He looked at Michaela, who remembered the look and words the agent had offered her when she rescued Joseph. "I trust him, Joseph."

Joseph slowly handed the gun back and steadied Michaela with both hands as she dismounted the surgical table and gingerly placed the injured foot on the ground. "Won't she come after us? Nevada is a client state, dependent on her for water and power. The AI can still call the shots here."

Booker extended his free hand, and Michaela took it as he answered. "She can't communicate directly until the power grid is back up. Besides, both sides of the border are going to be pretty busy for the next few days. I doubt we'll be a high priority for the local gendarme. We need to get moving, though."

Michaela was surprised at how ambulatory she was with the cast. They exited a side door, leaving Roberta behind still waiting for them, and Booker summoned the limousine to come to them. Joseph sat in front next to the man who had once been complicit in his torture, Michaela behind the man who had relentlessly pursued her.

Booker turned to his right, then back to Michaela. "Where shall we go?"

Michaela answered anxiously. "Won't we have trouble getting out of the state, at any of the border crossings?"

Booker—no longer Agent Booker—assured her. "This car carries a transponder that is basically a get-out-of-jail-free card. And I still have my fancy diplomatic credentials, even if they are to be soon revoked. But we need to move now."

Michaela looked at Joseph through eyes that were welling up. She reached out her hand. He took it, kissed it, and signaled his deference to her choice. "Michaela, the only place I need to be in this world or the next one is by your side. I love you."

Michaela hesitated, froze, like a lion raised in captivity and being released into the wild, unsure how to react when the cage door swung open to freedom, to everything she had longed for. But could she believe it? She had expected to die or be captured today. She had resigned herself to setting Joseph free and never seeing him again. She looked out the window where the border lay behind her now and then at Booker waiting to take her to safety. Her gaze snapped back to Joseph, and she saw herself through his loving eyes. There was hope and a future in those eyes. Michaela pulled him to her, and she lost herself in their kiss. They parted lips when she couldn't hold back the words any longer.

"I love you too." She beamed as she turned to Booker and said, "I hear Montana is lovely these days."

EPILOGUE

September 21, 2073—Four years later

It was a day that Jamal both dreaded and celebrated every year, a pilgrimage to the past and renewal of a promise to the future, as the nation of New Israel came together at the place where the Battle of Deliverance had been won. For Jamal, the celebratory laser and fireworks show capping the day's festivities brought back painful headlight images blurred both by a muddy windshield and by time. The memories of people being slaughtered were forever imbedded in his mind, but he marveled and gave thanks at the resilience of children. His eyes rested where Chloe and Hanna leaned on each other shoulder to shoulder, squealing and clapping with every burst and boom of the show.

The day had begun with local solemn church services that memorialized those who died, and then churches throughout the new nation initiated the multitude of Christians who now flocked from all over the country to join the great revival of the Christian community. These catechumens were officially welcomed into full communion as they received the mark of the Lamb on their foreheads in the rite of anointing.

New Israel was growing and thriving with both burgeoning immigration and financial support from all quarters of Christianity and parties that had interest in containing California's AI. In the chaotic aftermath of destruction of the border defenses, the roughly fifteen thousand souls who had traversed the border prior to arrival of reinforcements struck a defiant posture. They were prepared to wage guerrilla warfare or suffer martyrdom rather than be rounded up and deported. Arin, after running several million simulations, determined that it would be more beneficial to move and repurpose the small rural population of native Californians living near the border than to fight a protracted war with all the domestic and outside ramifications that would bring. Assurances that Christians would identify themselves with the mark of the Lamb helped to ensure against a stealth influx of illegal immigration. The Treaty of Truckee ceded portions of northern border counties along with lands leased from Nevada. The state of Nevada, eager to rid itself of the remaining tens of thousands of refugees conceded some additional land. Borders included a north-south line down the middle of lakes Donner, Tahoe, Pyramid, and Walker as well as the Truckee and Carson rivers. The thriving development that Ambassador Booker had projected during negotiations was taking form, albeit without the help or interference of the AI, and Jamal had a key role as a senior supervisor in the massive irrigation project.

***

The closing ceremony the following night was always the most difficult and bittersweet for Jamal. It was the one time of the year when he allowed himself the luxury of tears for what might have been. A wailing horn sounded at the same time it had that night years ago signifying the time of deliverance was at hand. Then the Memory of Tears ritual proceeded in silence. Each family that had lost loved ones in the great Exodus and Deliverance gathered in a circle around a large open space and released a candlelight balloon lantern carrying the name of their martyred loved one toward heaven.

Jamal stayed back as the girls walked their lamp into the circle. Chloe lit the candle and Hanna lifted the lamp high above her head before releasing it. Jamal watched the sky fill with thousands of glowing memories. Both the sweet presence and bitter absence of his Ayana possessed him. He thanked her for bringing them here safely and told her how proud she could be of her girls.

Chloe and Hanna returned from the circle and he sat with his arms around them until they both fell asleep. He kissed them each on the head. He looked to the sky, then gave each girl a second kiss, this one from their mother and blessed with a tear.

ACKNOWLEDGMENTS

As a neophyte novelist lacking the training or background that would qualify me to bring this story to life, I am indebted to several people for its existence.

Dr. Robin Tripp, retired from a career teaching college students what I still do not know, was the midwife without whom a weak first draft would have died in infancy. Her encouragement and honest feedback were needed and appreciated more than I can say.

Judith at Book Helpline was instrumental in helping the book to mature from a manuscript into a novel through her keen editorial insights and suggestions. Also, thanks to Ginny for being so responsive and helpful in guiding me through the editorial process.

Angela and the team at BookLocker Publishing have blended professionalism and personal attention seamlessly in getting my story to actual readers.

I am also grateful to friends who over the years have offered encouragement and shown appreciation for my smaller attempts at expressing myself through the written word, especially Jeanne and Rita.

And perhaps most of all, Kathy, who has spent half a century convincing me I can do things that I am certain I cannot do.

CPSIA information can be obtained
at www.ICGtesting.com
Printed in the USA
BVHW072345260820
587172BV00001B/88